THE DOCTOR AND THE KID

Also Available by Mike Resnick

Ivory: A Legend of Past and Future

New Dreams for Old

Stalking the Dragon
Stalking the Unicorn
Stalking the Vampire

Starship: Mutiny
Book One
Starship: Pirate
Book Two
Starship: Mercenary
Book Three
Starship: Rebel
Book Four
Starship: Flagship
Book Five

The Buntline Special—A Weird West Tale

MIKE RESNICK

THE DOCTOR AND THE KID

A WEIRD WEST TALE

an imprint of Prometheus Books
Amherst, NY

Published 2011 by Pyr®, an imprint of Prometheus Books

Inquiries should be addressed to
Pyr
59 John Glenn Drive
Amherst, New York 14228–2119
VOICE: 716–691–0133
FAX: 716–691–0137
WWW.PYRSF.COM

15 14 13 12 5 4 3 2

Library of Congress Cataloging-in-Publication Data

Resnick, Michael D.
The doctor and the kid : a weird west tale / by Mike Resnick.
p. cm.
"An imprint of Prometheus Books"
ISBN 978–1–61614–537–8 (pbk.)
ISBN 978–1–61614–538–5 (ebook)
1. Holliday, John Henry, 1851–1887—Fiction. 2. Geronimo, 1829–1909—Fiction. 3. Edison, Thomas A. (Thomas Alva), 1847–1931—Fiction. 4. West (U.S.)—Fiction. 5. Steampunk fiction. I. Title.

PS3568.E698D63 2011
813'.54—dc22

2011032792

Printed in the United States of America on acid-free paper

To Carol, as always,

And to Ralph Roberts,
Writer
Editor
Publisher
Producer
Entrepreneur
Computer Guru
Friend of three decades

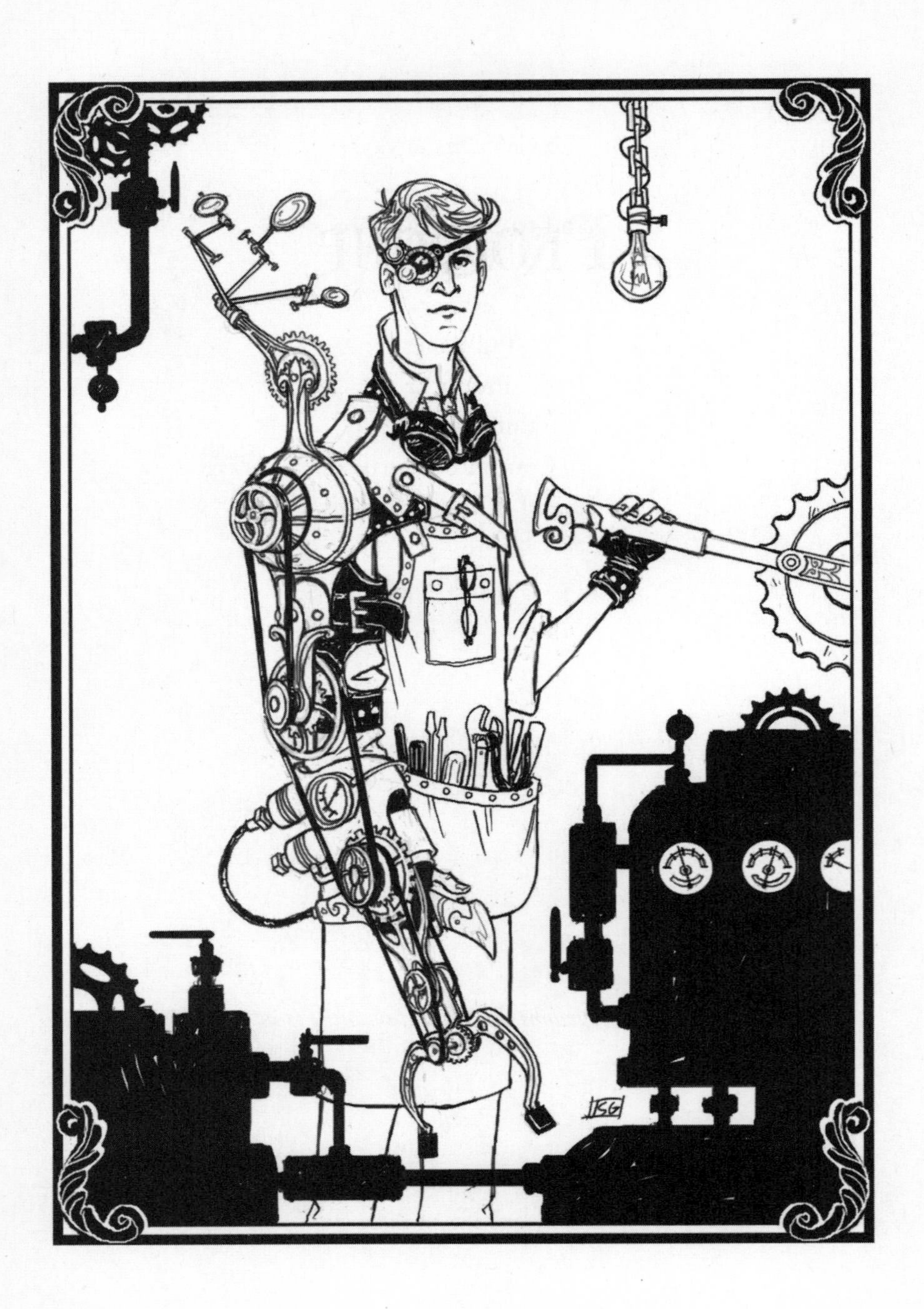

Prologue

From the pages of the March 25, 1882, issue of the Leadville Bullet*:*

The Remarkable Miss Anthony

Susan B. Anthony, the famed suffragette, will be spending the coming week in Leadville, where she will be giving a number of speeches. Her reputation has reached beyond our shores, and she will be touring Europe, speaking all over the continent, next year.

She will be signing autographs this Saturday at the Baptist Church bake sale.

New Arrivals

Dr. John H. Holliday and his companion, Kathryn Elder, have arrived from Arizona and have announced their intentions to settle here. Dr. Holliday has rented a studio where he plans to set up his dentistry business, and is also said to have invested in the Monarch Saloon and Casino.

Holliday was a participant in the famous altercation in Tombstone, Arizona, last autumn, which has come to be known as the Gunfight at the O.K. Corral. Both he and Wyatt Earp have been absolved of any guilt or complicity in the incident by the local Tombstone court.

R. I. P.

Leadville resident Abner Fuller was shot and killed while visiting family members in New Mexico. Two eyewitnesses claim the murderer was the famed desperado Henry McCarty, alias William Bonney, alias Billy the Kid. A warrant has been issued for his arrest, joining numerous other warrants. If anyone has any information concerning his whereabouts, please report it to the Bullet *and we will telegraph the information to the New Mexican authorities.*

Mr. Fuller's body had been shipped to Leadville and will arrive on Tuesday. Funeral services and burial are expected to be Wednesday afternoon.

Another Distinguished Visitor

Famed British writer Oscar Wilde filled the Tabor Opera House to capacity with his humorous lecture last night, and will speak again this Friday before heading back East to conclude his American tour. He was seen dining with Susan B. Anthony last night at the new Captain Waldo's restaurant, which replaced the original that was lost in a fire last spring.

Famous Gunfighter Acquitted

"Texas Jack" Vermillion, a former associate of the Earp Brothers in Arizona, and a participant in the questionable police action now known as Wyatt Earp's Vendetta Ride, was found innocent of the killing of Wilbur McCoy in the alley between Shale's General Store and the Buntline Manufacturing Plant, just off Front Street, on March 14. Dr. John H. Holliday and two other bystanders testified that Vermillion shot McCoy in self-defense. The jury deliberated for less than ten minutes before reaching its verdict.

Brass Mole Finds New Vein

The remarkable Brass Mole, the electric machine designed by Mr. Thomas Edison and built by Mr. Ned Buntline, uncovered a new silver vein in the Montrassor Mine at the previously unattainable depth of 1,637 feet. According to the Cornwall Assay Office, this is as rich a sample as any yet brought in.

New Game Debuts Saturday

The sport of baseball, so popular in the United States, will debut here on Saturday afternoon, when the Gunnison Prairie Dogs take on the Twin Lakes Six-Shooters. Tickets are ten cents apiece until sold out. Come see what all the excitement is about!

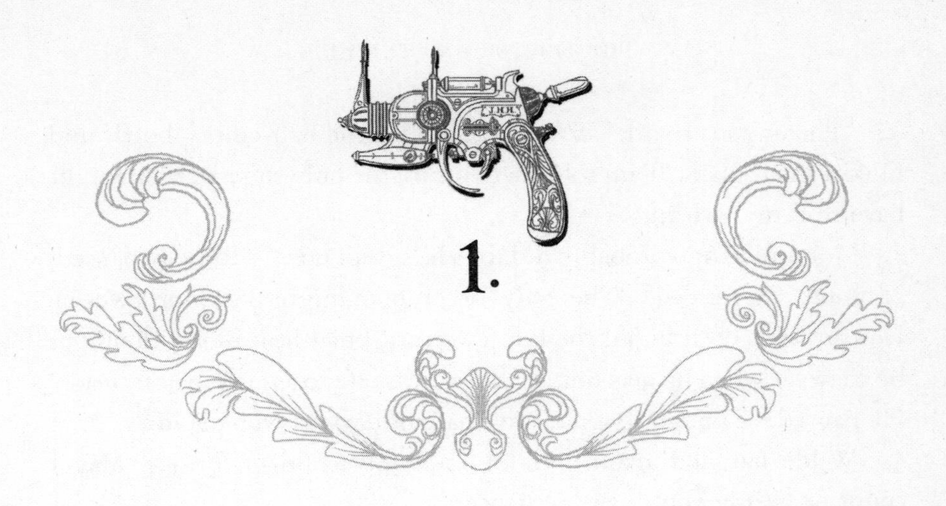

1.

HOLLIDAY WAS CUTTING INTO HIS STEAK at the Sacred Cow when the large shadow fell over his table. He looked up to see an elegantly dressed pudgy man standing next to him.

"Are you the notorious Doc Holliday?" asked the man.

Holliday checked to make sure the man was unarmed. "I am," he replied.

The man extended a hand. "I am the notorious Oscar Wilde. I wonder if I might join you?"

Holliday shrugged. "Suit yourself."

Wilde sat down opposite him. "I didn't see you at my lecture last night."

"Good."

"Good?" repeated Wilde, arching an eyebrow.

"It means you're not hallucinating."

Wilde threw back his head and laughed. "I *knew* I'd like you!"

"I'm flattered," said Holliday. "Not many people do." He gestured to the bottle on the table. "Pour yourself a drink."

"Thank you. I will." Wilde reached for the half-empty bottle and filled a small glass. "I am told that you are the only shootist who might have read my writings."

"Johnny Ringo probably did, but he's dead now." Holliday paused. "I hope," he added. "The only other one might be John Wesley Hardin. He's been in jail the last few years, but I hear he's studying to be a lawyer when he gets out, so at least it's safe to assume he can read." He paused. "Though I've met my share of lawyers who couldn't."

Wilde laughed again. "I'll be speaking again on Friday. May I count on seeing you in the audience?"

Holliday shook his head. "No, I'll be playing cards at the Monarch, over at 320 Harrison Street."

"Surely you can stop gambling for an hour or two to come hear me speak."

"Do I ask you to skip speaking and come on over to watch me gamble?"

"Speaking's part of my livelihood," protested Wilde.

"Gambling's part of mine."

"Touché."

"Whatever that means," said Holliday.

The waiter came by and asked Wilde for his order.

"I'll have what my friend is having," replied Wilde.

"Including a bottle of whiskey?"

Wilde smiled. "No, I'll just borrow his."

"Within the limits of propriety," said Holliday. Wilde looked for a smile, but couldn't find one.

Wilde shifted his weight, trying to arrange his bulk comfortably on the plain wooden chair. "So what is the notorious Doc Holliday doing in Leadville?"

"Trying to be less notorious," replied Holliday.

"Seriously," said Wilde. "Is there some gunfight brewing?"

"I hope not."

"Surely you jest."

"Look at me," said Holliday irritably. "I'm a dying man, wracked with consumption. I can't weigh a hundred and thirty pounds. I'm a dentist by trade, but I've pretty much given it up, because you can't keep your clientele when you keep coughing blood in their faces." He stared at Wilde. "There's a very good sanitarium in Leadville. I'll move into it when I can't function on my own any more." A brief pause. "I came up here to die, Mr. Wilde."

"Excuse me," said Wilde. "I didn't know."

"You're damned near the only one."

"I haven't heard anything about a sanitarium here in Leadville," admitted Wilde.

Holliday coughed into a handkerchief. "There are other good ones, I'm told. I came here because everyone told me the air was pure and clean at ten thousand feet, and it is." He grimaced. "What they didn't tell me was that it's so damned thin that the birds prefer walking."

Wilde nodded his head and smiled. "I may borrow that line from you someday."

"There's no charge. You're welcome to the consumption, too."

"You fascinate me," said Wilde, pulling a thin cigar out of his pocket and lighting it up. "I may have to write a play about you."

"For a British audience?" said Holliday. "If you insist on wasting your time and money, come on over and do it at the Monarch."

"You own it?" asked Wilde.

"Part of it."

"Then why not call it Doc Holliday's, and put a huge sign out front?"

"Because there's fifty or sixty men that would like to see me dead," answered Holliday. "Why make it easier for them?"

Wilde leaned forward. "Did you really kill all those men you've been credited with?"

"Probably not."

Wilde studied his face. "I can't tell if you're kidding or not."

"I'm supposed to have killed two men who were five states apart on the very same day." Holliday smiled. "They must have thought I was riding Aristides."

"Aristides?" repeated Wilde.

"He won the very first Kentucky Derby, which my friend Bat Masterson assures me is on the road to becoming a very important race."

"Bat Masterson? What does a gunman know about horse-racing?"

"We're not all one-dimensional shootists, Mr. Wilde," said Holliday. "I'm a dentist. Masterson is a sports journalist. And it looks like Hardin is going to be a lawyer." Holliday snorted in amusement. "I'll bet it won't stop him from killing people. It just means he'll have a defense lawyer he can trust."

"What about this Billy the Kid that everyone's talking about?" asked Wilde.

"I'm not talking about him."

"I mean, what else does *he* do?"

Holliday shrugged. "I hear he's barely twenty years old. I don't imagine he's had much time to find a profession yet."

"Besides killing people, you mean," said Wilde.

"That's only a profession if someone pays you to do it," answered Holliday. "I've never been paid a penny. Neither have most of us. And if you do it for free, no matter how reluctantly, then it's not a profession, it's an art form."

"Or a hobby," suggested Wilde. "How reluctant *are* you about killing people?"

"You make it sound like it's all I do, Mr. Wilde," said Holliday, and Wilde couldn't tell if he was being sardonic, angry, or merely conversational. "Occasionally I eat and sleep, and even pull a tooth or two." A brief pause. "But I will say that I never killed a man who didn't deserve killing."

"If you're looking for men who deserve killing, you might spend some time with Miss Anthony," observed Wilde. "I had dinner with her last night, and I gather she's had enough death threats to fill a small book."

"Believe it or not, Mr. Wilde," said Holliday, "I have spent most of my adult life trying to avoid confrontations, not seeking them out." He paused. "But I think you may overestimate the dangers to Miss Anthony."

"The threats are real," insisted Wilde. "She showed me some of the letters. Semi-literate, most of them, but dangerous."

"If anyone harms her, or even attempts to harm her, we're likely to have a replay of Lysistrata," said Holliday with a smile.

"You know the story of Lysistrata?" said Wilde, surprised.

"I have had a classical education, Mr. Wilde," replied Holliday. "Why, I've even read *The Nihilists*."

"You have?" exclaimed Wilde. His chest puffed up with pride. "What did you think of it?"

"I thought it showed promise."

Wilde's face dropped. "Only promise?"

"You're a young man with your whole career ahead of you," said Holliday. "I'm a dying man who is difficult to impress."

"It's a shame you won't live long enough to see the United States spread all the way to the Pacific Coast."

"No one currently alive may be around for that," answered Holliday. "It all depends on Tom Edison."

"Thomas *Alva* Edison?" said Wilde. "The inventor?" Holliday nodded. "What does he have to do with it?"

"Didn't you notice the electric street lights when you came to town?" asked Holliday. "And if you arrived by stagecoach the likelihood is that you rode the Bunt Line, one of those bullet-proof brass coaches that's powered by one of Edison's motors and requires no horses."

"I came by train," answered Wilde. "And I knew about the lights. I knew Edison had set up an office—or would it be a laboratory?—here in Leadville. But what does that have to do with expanding to the Pacific Coast?"

"The United States ends at the Mississippi River," said Holliday. "It would like to extend to the Pacific, but so far the magic of the Indian medicine men, especially a pair known as Hook Nose and Geronimo, have stopped them. Oh, we have some towns and ranches here and there, but we're here under sufferance. And since Edison is currently our greatest mind, the government has paid him to come out West and see what he can learn about the magic and how to counteract it."

"He was in Tombstone last year, wasn't he?" asked Wilde.

"Yes. He still spends some time there."

"And now he's in Leadville?"

Holliday nodded. "That's right. The silver mines in Tombstone are just about played out, so he came up here with an invention that can extract silver faster than any ten-man crew you ever saw."

"*You* were in Tombstone last year." Holliday nodded again. "And now you're in Leadville too." Wilde frowned and stared at him. "It can't be a coincidence." He suddenly smiled. "Can it?"

"I don't mine silver. He doesn't gamble."

"You didn't answer the question."

"You noticed." Holliday, his dinner finished, stood up and left a silver dollar on the table. "Tell the waiter that includes his tip."

"I think I'll visit the Monarch later," said Wilde. "I'd like to see you in non-violent action. I might even risk a dollar or two at the faro table."

"Suit yourself."

Holliday walked to the door, buttoned his coat, and stepped out into the chilly Colorado night air. The Sacred Cow was on Third Street, three blocks from the Monarch Saloon, and he decided to take a short cut, saving half a block by cutting down an alley. Suddenly he was aware of a large snake, some ten feet long. Its head rose up until it was looking directly into his eyes. Holliday knew what was coming, and waited patiently. A moment later the snake vanished, to be replaced by an Apache brave in buckskins.

"Goyathlay sends you greetings, White Eyes."

"My eyes are bloodshot," answered Holliday. "What does Geronimo want?"

"He wants to remind you that the two of you had an agreement once, in Tombstone."

"We made a deal," agreed Holliday. "But it's over and done with, and I assume we're at hazard again. What now?"

"Nothing."

"All I'm supposed to do is remember we had a deal for a few days in Tombstone?"

But he found that he was speaking to empty air.

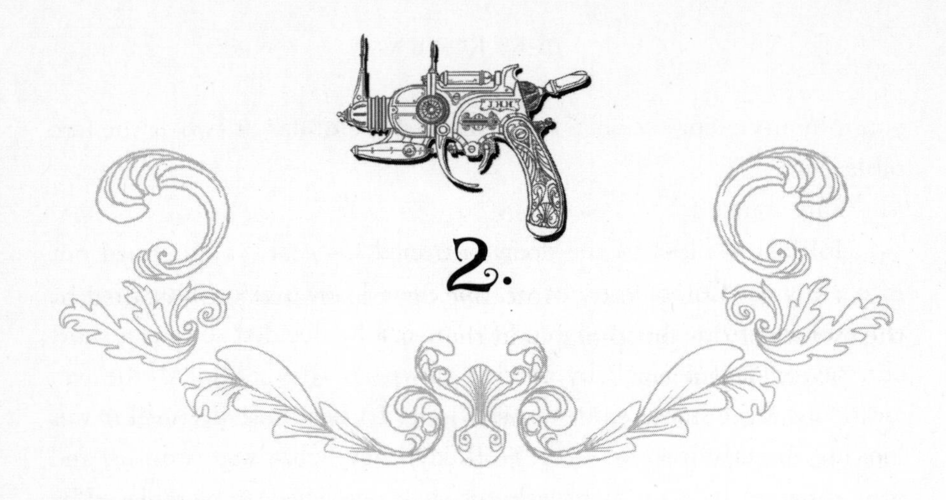

2.

HOLLIDAY HAD ORIGINALLY BEEN BOUND FOR THE MONARCH, but after his encounter with the phantom Apache he changed his course and went directly to the large building with the super-hardened brass walls across the alley from Shale's General Store. He stared at the electric sign that proclaimed it was the *Buntline Manufacturing Plant* and wondered how Ned Buntline was handling the fact that just about everyone in town called it "Edison's Lab."

There was a mangy-looking dog stretched out on the ground by the front door, gnawing on a bone. Holliday paused and stared at it until he was certain that it wasn't going to morph into another of Geronimo's message-bearers. The dog stared curiously at him for a moment, then went back to its bone.

Holliday approached the impenetrable brass door that reflected the light of the sign, keeping a wary eye on the dog. After all, it didn't have to be a mystic Indian to feel threatened and decide to bite, but the dog decided that the bone was far more interesting than the emaciated dentist/gambler.

"Friend or foe?" demanded a voice that didn't belong to Thomas Edison or Ned Buntline.

"That depends on who you are," responded Holliday warily, his fingers gliding down to the top of his pistol.

"I am one of the many protective devices created and installed by the owners of this building," said the voice.

"Then I'm a friend."

"Advance, friend, and be recognized," said the voice, as a small circular lens he hadn't seen before began to glow.

"Goddamnit, Tom, it's colder than a witch's tit out here!" growled Holliday. "Are you going to keep me standing here all night?"

He heard Edison utter a hearty laugh and then order the door to swing open. "Good evening, Doc," said the inventor, standing in the doorway. "Just testing out the latest addition to my security system." He smiled at Holliday. "Come on in."

Holliday walked past the dog and entered the brass building, joining Edison as they walked to his study, a wood-paneled room with books and scribbled notes everywhere—on a desk, on tables, tacked to the wall, crumpled on the floor. Suddenly Holliday stopped and stared at his host. "Where the hell's your arm?"

Edison glanced briefly at the stump on his right shoulder, all that remained of his original arm. "Ned is making some improvements to it."

"It already spins, cuts metal, weighs things to the closest ounce, could lift all of the Earps tied together, and can probably outdraw me in a gunfight. What else does it have to do?"

"It's too good a conductor of electricity, and it actually becomes a hazard during some of my experiments. I'm tired of removing it every time I'm working with positive and negative charges, so Ned's trying to negate its conductivity."

"I think I may introduce you to a British visitor I met tonight.

He'd love to write you up in song and story for the stage." A pause and a cynical smile. "Well, he'd love to write your arm up, anyway."

"Mr. Wilde?"

"I was going to ask how you knew," said Holliday. "Then I remembered that he's probably the only writer currently on tour in Leadville."

"Well, the only playwright," agreed Edison. "Miss Anthony has written some powerful articles. I hope to meet both of them before they leave town."

"If you want to meet Mr. Wilde, come over to the Monarch. He'll be there pretty soon."

"I can't," said Edison regretfully. He wiggled his stump. "I'm being, ah, *re-attached* in another hour."

Holliday shrugged. "Suit yourself."

Edison sat down at his desk, gestured to a wooden chair with a cushioned back, and Holliday seated himself. "Now, my friend, to what do I owe the honor of this visit?"

"Have you got any business with Geronimo or the Apaches?" asked Holliday. "Did you promise them anything, or offend any of them, before you left Tombstone?"

"No to the first, and I hope not to the second," answered Edison, frowning. "Remember, it was Hook Nose and the Southern Cheyenne who got Curly Bill Brocius to try to kill me—and wound up blowing away my arm—back in Tombstone, not the Apaches."

"Good," said Holliday.

"Why?"

"Because I was just visited by one of Geronimo's representatives, so he obviously knows I'm here—and if he knows that, he knows you and Ned are here too."

"What did he want?"

"Damned if I know."

"Geronimo's warrior just walked up, said 'Hi, Doc,' and went away?" said Edison sardonically.

"In essence." Holliday's brow furrowed in puzzlement. "He told me to remember that I had once made a deal, long since consumated, with Geronimo. Before I could ask what kind of deal the old bastard wants this time, he was gone." The gambler grimaced. "I'll take war chiefs to medicine men any day. I still can't get used to magic."

"That's pretty difficult to believe at this late date," said Edison. "It's their magic that's stopped the United States from extending to the Pacific, and it's what I'm being paid to study and counteract."

"Geronimo knows that. That's what I came to tell you: He knows you're here."

"Well, he probably knew it last night and last week as well, so let's assume he has some other reason for contacting you."

"I wish he'd choose some other way," complained Holliday irritably. "I just hate giant snakes turning into braves before my eyes."

"If he wanted to kill you, he could have," offered Edison. "So if I were you, I'd wait until he decided to say what he wanted. You're not going to be leaving town, are you?"

Holliday shook his head. "I'm here for the duration."

Edison frowned again. "The duration of what?"

"Of my life." Another grimace. "You'd think they could have built the damned sanitarium a few thousand feet lower, where nothing but dogs pant and gasp for breath."

"I hear they're building one a few hundred miles south of here in Arizona," said Edison. "You might consider that."

"Too many men in Arizona want to save the sanitarium the trouble of burying me," answered Holliday with a wry grin. "No, I've set twenty thousand dollars aside for my upkeep. At five thousand a year, the place will run out of me before I run out of money."

"Try not to be such an optimist," said Edison dryly.

"I'm just being a realist. When you've been dying as long as I have, realism gets easier every day." He turned toward the door. "I think I'd better be going. Nobody'll ever remember a consumptive gunfighter, so I want to impress the illustrious Mr. Wilde and have him write me into a book or a play." He paused, then smiled. "I'm going to stop by Kate's office and pick up my bankroll, just so I can flash it and impress him."

"Let me make absolutely certain first I understand the purpose of this visit," said Edison. "The only reason you came here is to tell me Geronimo knows I'm in Leadville—or, rather, that we can assume he knows it?"

"Right," said Holliday. "And to accept a drink, if you hadn't forgotten your manners."

Edison chuckled, opened a desk drawer, and pulled out a bottle.

"No sense getting a glass dirty," said Holliday, taking it from him. He took a long swallow, then another, put the top back on, and handed it back. "My best to Ned."

"You may see him later," said Edison. "He's working on another of Kate's robots. I think he should have it—or should I say, her?—in working order by midnight."

"Must be nice work, field-testing metal whores," said Holliday.

"You know he doesn't do that."

"More's the pity," remarked Holliday. "I won't see him, though. Once I get my money, I'm off to the Monarch until sunrise."

He walked out the door, which closed automatically behind him, and headed toward Kate Elder's establishment. The dog got up and began walking beside him.

"You sure you're not from Geronimo?" asked Holliday.

The dog made no reply, which seemed almost as odd to Holliday as an affirmative would have been. He walked the two blocks to Kate

Elder's whorehouse on Second Street, pausing three times to catch his breath, and cursing the thin night air.

Finally he arrived at the large two-floor frame building, one of the holdouts against Buntline's impervious brass, climbed the three steps to the broad veranda, and entered. There were four scantily clad girls and two robots positioned around the parlor, talking to a trio of local men. The girls, none of whom were as young as they looked, all smiled and nodded to him, while the robots, whose feminine appearance always surprised him, ignored him and continued their pre-programmed flirting with the men. Holliday walked through the room, proceeded down a long corridor, and opened the door to Kate Elder's office.

Kate was a busty woman in her early thirties, with a proboscis that had earned her the sobriquet of Big-Nose Kate. She sat at a desk, staring at him, her head framed by a large painting on the wall of a passionate Leda and a highly motivated swan. "Well, you're back early," she said dryly. "Did you shoot all the customers, or did the saloon burn down?"

"Only in your dreams," said Holliday, walking over to a safe in the corner, kneeling down, and dialing the combination.

"What do you think you're doing?" she demanded.

"Taking my bankroll out for an airing," answered Holliday as the lock clicked and he was able to open the door.

"You're not touching that!" she snapped.

"Don't be silly," replied Holliday, pulling it out. "Whose money is it?"

"What if someone shoots you and takes it?"

"Then, my love, you will be shit out of luck when they read the will," answered Holliday in amused tones. "You know, it's difficult to feel sorry for the proprietor of the biggest whorehouse in the territory."

"I thought you needed it for that place where they're going to lock you away to die," said Kate.

"Ah, the mistress of the delicate phraseology," said Holliday. "I told you—I'm just taking it out for a few hours to impress someone who may very well immortalize me."

"I thought all those dime novels did that."

"There's immortality, and then there's immortality," replied Holliday with a wry smile. "The money and I will both be back here before you wake up."

"It had damned well better be," she said, glaring at him. "If you lose it, or get robbed, or get killed, don't come running to me for any money."

"Kate, light of my life, if I get killed I promise not to come to you for more money," Holliday responded.

"I'm not kidding, Doc," she said, suddenly serious. "You come back without it, and you can cough your life out in some goddamned stable or toolshed."

He closed the safe, riffled the money as if it were a deck of cards, placed it in a vest pocket, walked over, and kissed her on the cheek.

"I love you too, my angel," he said, trying to suppress a grin.

She glared at him for a moment, and then her expression softened. "Why do we put up with each other, I wonder?" she asked almost wistfully.

"There's an easy answer to that."

"What is it?" she asked, honestly puzzled.

Holliday smiled. "Who else would?"

He picked up his cane, and a moment later he was out in the street. He looked around for the dog, couldn't spot it, couldn't decide whether that was a comforting sign or a bad omen, and finally shrugged and headed toward the Monarch.

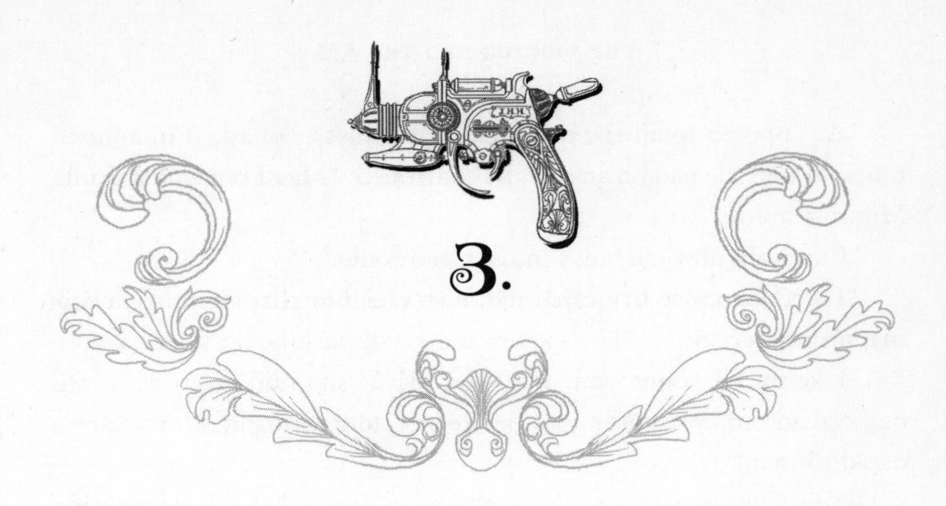

3.

As Holliday approached the saloon he saw a well-dressed woman carrying a parasol approaching from the opposite direction. As she came closer he recognized her from the posters around town as Susan B. Anthony. When they were a few feet apart he took off his hat and bowed low.

"Top of the evening, Miss Anthony," he said.

"Do I know you?" she asked curiously.

"No, Miss Anthony," replied Holliday. "But I know you. Or *of* you, anyway."

"If we haven't met, why such a fancy bow?"

He shrugged. "Why not?"

"Well, let's make the introduction official," she said, extending a gloved hand. "I am pleased to meet you, Mister . . . ?"

"Doctor," he replied, taking her hand. "John Henry Holliday."

"Dr. Holliday," she concluded.

"Doc Holliday," he corrected her. "Why stand on formality?"

Her eyes widened and she pulled her hand back as if it had been touching a rattlesnake. "The notorious *Doc Holliday*?"

"As opposed to all the other Doc Hollidays?" he asked in amused tones. When she had no answer, he continued: "May I buy you a drink, Miss Anthony?"

"Certainly not!" she said in outraged tones.

"I'd offer to play five-card stud with you, but that seems somehow inappropriate."

"I know all about you, Doc Holliday!" she said angrily. "I was hoping not to encounter you before my tour continued. You are a dreadful man!"

"True," he agreed. "But I'm a very good dentist." A self-deprecating smile crossed his once-handsome face. "Or at least, I used to be."

"I will not stand here conversing with a terrible killer!"

"Actually, I'm quite probably the best killer you will ever encounter," replied Holliday. "You're sure I can't buy you a drink?"

"You are a drinker and a shootist!" she snapped. "You represent everything I am campaigning against. You are the enemy!"

"If the enemy is composed of drinkers and shootists, you should be thanking me rather than condemning me," said Holliday easily. "I've eliminated more of your enemies than I think you can imagine."

"Murderer!" she yelled.

Suddenly his demeanor changed. "I have never shot a man in cold blood. And I do not call half the human race my enemies before judging each of them in his turn." A very brief pause. "Excuse me. I meant each in *her* turn."

She glared at him in silent rage.

"Well, it's been a pleasure, Miss Anthony. But if you'll excuse me, you are standing in the doorway to my office," he concluded, indicating the saloon's swinging doors.

She walked past him without another word.

Holliday looked at his reflection in the Monarch's glass window.

"That went about as well as usual, you old charmer, you," he said sardonically, then walked to the swinging doors, pushed them open, and entered the saloon.

The robotic bartender, a gift from Buntline, nodded to him, then went back to pouring drinks. Edison's latest phonograph, running on the same electrical circuit that powered the overhead electric lights, was playing a Viennese waltz, which seemed very out-of-place here. There was a brass roulette wheel at a large table, a dozen smaller tables for poker and blackjack, and a faro table in the corner. Holliday had considered building a stage and importing some dancing girls, but decided against it on the reasonable assumption that his clientele couldn't watch the girls and gamble at the same time, and if it were a choice between the two, he knew which was the more lucrative.

"Howdy, Doc," drawled a tall, burly man wearing a frock coat and sporting a ten-gallon Stetson.

"Hello, Jack," replied Holliday. "I see you've saved my seat for me."

"Ain't no one whose money I'd rather win," said Texas Jack Vermillion.

Holliday took his seat, joining Vermillion and the three other men who were at the table. "Has Oscar Wilde been here yet?"

"Never heard of him," said Vermillion.

One of the other men laughed. "You must have passed twenty posters of him on the way here from the Grand Hotel."

"Who looks at posters?" said Vermillion with a shrug.

"He's a British gentleman," said another. "Here on some kind of tour. I heard him speak last night. Very witty, though I'm sure half of it went over my head."

"What's he look like?"

"He'd never miss a hundred pounds," answered Holliday, "and he's got just about as much hair as Kate does."

"Nope," said Vermillion. "Ain't seen no one like that, knock wood."

Holliday signaled the bartender to bring a bottle to the table.

"How many glasses?" it asked in a mechanical monotone.

"Just one. If these gentlemen wish to partake, I'm sure they'll be happy to buy their particular poisons."

"I regret to inform you that we do not sell poison in the Monarch," replied the bartender to a chorus of laughter.

Holliday grimaced. "Ned and Tom are always telling me that I've got to be literal with it. I guess you gents will have to go to Mort Shale's store to buy poison. But if you want some fine drinking stuff, we can cater to your needs, and it'll make losing all that much less painful."

"And winning that much more pleasurable," added Vermillion, shuffling the cards. "Ante up, gents. Five-card stud is the game."

"How much to play?" asked Holliday.

"Ten dollars."

"I approve." Holliday placed ten dollars in the center of the table.

He lost the first two hands, won the third, and lost another.

"Not your night, Doc," said Vermillion as he won his second pot. "I can't tell you how happy that makes me."

Holliday filled his glass, drained it, and filled it again. "This is doubtless going to come as a shock to you, Jack, but occasionally I've even lost three hands in a row."

Suddenly he became aware of a large presence standing behind him. He turned and saw that it was Wilde.

"Welcome to the Monarch," he said. "Pull up a chair and I'll show you how this game is played."

"Poker, isn't it?" said Wilde, seating himself just to Holliday's left.

Holliday nodded. "You know the rules?"

"I read up on it," answered Wilde.

"What do you play in England?" asked Vermillion.

"Three-Card Brag," said Wilde.

"Never heard of it," said Vermillion. Suddenly he smiled. "Is it anything like Six-Gun Brag? Doc's a master at that."

"There's a difference between recounting and bragging," said Holliday, taking another drink. "I don't brag."

"I'd love to hear you recount some of your adventures," said Wilde, pulling out a pen and a notebook.

"Not if you're going to write it down," said Holliday. "It'll come out like recounting, but it'll read like bragging."

"As you wish." Wilde put the notebook back in his pocket. "Tell me about the O.K. Corral."

"Damned thing's been written up in half a dozen dime novels," replied Holliday.

"How about Johnny Ringo, then?"

"Johnny Ringo was my friend."

Wilde frowned. "I thought I read that you killed him."

"I did," said Holliday, draining and refilling his glass.

"But—"

"He was my enemy too."

"Sounds like a strange relationship," said Wilde.

"It was complicated," agreed Holliday.

"If you think the *relationship* was complicated, you should have seen Ringo himself!" laughed Vermillion.

Wilde turned to him. "Why?"

"Because a dead man takes more killing than most."

"I don't understand."

"One of the medicine men brought him back from the dead to kill Tom Edison and Doc."

"Where I come from, we call that a zombie," said Wilde. "How do you kill one?"

"Carefully," said Holliday. "Is anyone going to deal, or am I moving to another table?"

Vermillion began dealing the cards. "Draw poker this time," he announced. "Ante up."

One of the players reached for his cards, and found himself looking down the barrel of Holliday's gun.

"Forgot a little something, didn't you?" asked Holliday.

"What?" asked the player nervously.

"You pay to play *before* you look at your cards."

The player tossed ten dollars onto the table, waited for Holliday to holster his gun, and then picked up his cards. "I'm out," he announced, laying his cards on the table, getting to his feet, and walking off.

"You frighten 'em all away and you and me are gonna wind up cutting cards for money," drawled Vermillion.

Holliday drained his glass again. "He knows the rules," he said at last.

"That was positively frightening," said Wilde.

"He didn't pull the trigger," said Vermillion. "Can't compare to people getting their heads blowed off in all your Limey wars."

"Mr. Wilde is a writer, not a soldier," remarked Holliday. "I would guess that he's never seen a man killed."

"But I've written about them," replied Wilde with a smile.

"Probably reads better than the real thing," offered Vermillion.

"Neater, anyway," said Holliday.

"Do you mind if I ask you some questions?" said Wilde, as Holliday pushed fifty dollars to the center of the table.

"Go ahead."

"What was Clay Allison like?"

"Never met the gentleman," answered Holliday.

"And Ben Thomson?"

"Same answer."

Wilde frowned. "I'd have thought—"

"The West is a mighty big place, Mr. Wilde," said Holliday. "And contrary to the dime novels, it's populated by more than gunslingers, a term we don't use much."

"What *do* you use?"

"Shootists."

"How many cards, Doc?"

"Two, please," answered Holliday, sliding two cards, face down, across the table to Vermillion.

"I *know* you knew the Earps," continued Wilde. "What were they like?"

"Morgan was a sweet man with a wonderful sense of humor. If I'd had a brother, I'd have wanted him to be like Morgan Earp."

"And Virgil?"

"He and Wyatt were cut from the same cloth," answered Holliday. "Humorless men, hard men. Their word was their bond, and there was nothing they were afraid of."

"They didn't have to be afraid of anything with *you* there," said Vermillion. He turned to Wilde. "Doc was their enforcer, just like Ringo was for the Clantons."

"Tell me about it," said Wilde eagerly.

"Up to you, Doc," said one of the players.

"How much?"

"Two hundred to stay in."

Holliday pulled out the wad of money he'd taken from Kate's safe, peeled a pair of hundred-dollar bills off the top, and shoved them into the pot in the middle of the table.

"Two hundred dollars!" said Wilde, clearly impressed. "Translate that into pounds and it's more than my advance for *The Nihilists*."

"That's one of the advantages of being a successful gambler," replied Holliday. "Do you know how many teeth I'd have to pull for two hundred dollars?"

"Another fifty to stay in, Doc," announced Vermillion.

Holliday pulled a fifty out of the wad.

"Don't you want to look at the two cards you drew first?" asked Wilde.

"If there's another raise, I may very well do that," said Holliday. He looked at the empty bottle in front of him, frowned, and snapped his fingers to get the robot bartender's attention. "Another bottle over here," he ordered.

"Since you are the proprietor there will be no charge," announced the robot, walking out from behind the bar and carrying the bottle over to the table.

"Damned generous of you," said Holliday sardonically.

"Thank you, sir," said the robot.

"Call me Doc."

"Thank you, sir Doc."

"I've got to talk to Tom about you," said Holliday. He gestured to the bar. "Go back to making money."

"I do not make money, sir Doc," replied the robot. "I serve drinks."

"I stand corrected."

"You *sit* corrected."

"Whatever."

"Call," said one of the players.

"Three ladies," announced Vermillion.

"Shit," muttered the man who had called. "Beats two pairs."

Vermillion turned to Holliday. "What have you got, Doc?"

"Let's see," said Holliday, laying down two aces and a jack. He turned up the two cards he'd drawn, an eight and a six.

"Maybe I should have looked first," he said, pouring another drink.

The game continued until midnight, at which time the other two players had left, and Holliday and Vermillion were waiting for someone to join them. Suddenly there was a loud *"Yahoo!"* from the far side of the room, and a well-dressed man stood up from a table. He surveyed the room, saw that the crowd had thinned down to perhaps twenty men, and announced that he was buying drinks for the house.

"Here it comes," said a grinning Vermillion to Wilde.

"The house cannot drink, sir," said the bartender. "Only humans can."

Wilde chuckled in amusement.

"All right," said the man. "Drinks for all the humans." He walked over to the bar and slapped a bill down on it. Then his gaze fell on Holliday, and he walked over. "You gents still playing?"

"Care to join us?" said Holliday.

The man sat down at the table. "My name's Wilson," he said. "Henry Wilson. Selling ladies' dresses, corsets, and shoes town-to-town."

"John Henry Holliday," said Holliday, "and this is Jack Vermillion."

"I've heard of you both," said Wilson. He smiled at Wilde. "And I was at your lecture last night. You're a fine speaker, sir."

"Thank you," said Wilde. "I'm even a better writer. I hope you'll consider buying my book before you leave town."

"Why not?" said Wilson. "It gets mighty lonely riding the stage from town to town, especially since Mr. Buntline created that damned horseless coach."

"Why would that make you lonelier?" asked Wilde. "You get to where you're going faster."

"Ah, but you don't stop to rest and water the horses a few times a day, so you don't get to visit along the way."

"Man's got a point," agreed Vermillion.

"Well, gentlemen, I feel lucky tonight," announced Wilson. "What's the game?"

"Been playing draw for the past hour," replied Vermillion.

"That suits me fine," said Wilson. "And how much to play?"

"As long as you're having a good night," said Holliday, "let's make it a hundred."

"That's a lot of corsets and unmentionables," said Wilson thoughtfully. Then he shrugged. "What the hell. I'm playing with other people's money anyway. When it's gone, I'll take mine back to the hotel with me and dream about how I might have beaten the famous Doc Holliday."

"I like your attitude, sir," said Holliday. He noticed that his bottle was empty and called for another.

"You ought to take it a little easy, Doc," said Vermillion. "That's your third bottle tonight."

Holliday shrugged. "I'm thirsty."

"But—"

"Enough," said Holliday in a tone of voice that convinced Vermillion to drop the subject.

They played four hands. Wilson won two, Vermillion won the other two.

"Let's up the ante to two hundred," said Holliday. "I've got to start winning some of my money back."

"No objection," said Wilson.

"Me neither," added Vermillion.

Wilde studied Holliday closely. The man was starting to smell like a distillery, he had a little trouble picking up and fanning his cards, and whenever he looked at his cards he blinked his eyes several times as if trying to focus them. Vermillion opened with one hundred dollars, Holliday raised him with a pair of eights, Wilson dropped out, and Holliday drew a third eight to win the hand.

It was Holliday's turn to deal. He shuffled the cards awkwardly, poured yet another drink to steady his hands, shoved his ante into the middle of the table, and dealt. Wilde looked over his shoulder as he picked up his cards and slowly fanned his hand. He had two kings, a jack, a three, and a deuce.

Wilson shoved a thousand dollars into the center of the table. Vermillion took one look at his hand and folded. Holliday pulled out his bankroll and peeled off a thousand.

"How many cards, sir?" he asked Wilson.

"None."

"Dealer takes two," said Holliday, discarding his deuce and three, and dealing himself two more cards. He picked them up and slowly fanned his hand to reveal a third king and a six.

Wilson counted the pile of money in front of him and pushed it all into the center of the table. "Sixty-three hundred dollars," he announced.

Wilde was sure Holliday would fold, but the gambler pulled out his bankroll and put it down next to Wilson's bet. "See you and raise you."

"How much?" asked Wilson.

Holliday shrugged. "Whatever's in the pile," he slurred.

Vermillion counted it and turned to Wilson. "It'll cost you eleven thousand one hundred and fifty to see him."

"I haven't got it."

"I will not accept the marker of a corset salesman," said Holliday.

"We'll get it," said Vermillion. He signaled seven or eight of the patrons over. "Look at his hand, gents. Who wants to buy in?"

It took ten minutes, but finally they'd collected enough to match Holliday's bet, and Wilson laid down his hand, face up. It contained four queens and an ace.

"Nice try," said Holliday, laying out his own. "Four kings."

"What are you talking about?" demanded Wilson. "That's three kings and a jack."

"What are *you* talking about?" Holliday shot back angrily. He got unsteadily to his feet, placed his hands on either side of his cards, and lowered his head until it was mere inches above the table. He stared at the cards, blinked furiously, then stared again. "Well, I'll be damned!" he muttered, and collapsed.

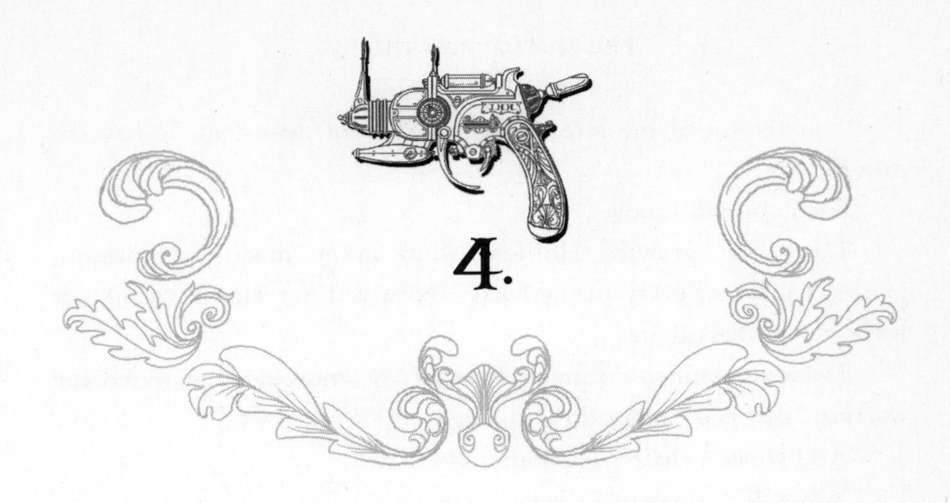

4.

THE MONARCH WAS EMPTY, except for the bartender, when Holliday awoke. It took him a few minutes to remember what had happened, and another to realize that he was now all but penniless, every dollar he had saved for the sanitarium gone because he'd been too drunk to tell a jack from a king.

He got to his feet, steadied himself for a moment, and then staggered out into the night. Harrison Street was empty except for a single coyote that stared at him, unafraid.

Holliday pulled out his gun and aimed it at the animal.

"It will have no effect," said the coyote.

Holliday tried to focus his eyes as it grew into an Apache warrior, the same one he had seen earlier.

"Goyathlay knew this night would come," said the warrior.

"Bully for him," muttered Holliday. "Did he send you here to gloat?"

The warrior shook his head. "To remind you that you have worked together once before."

"You reminded me already. What kind of deal does he have in mind?"

"Soon you will know."

"Damn it!" growled Holliday. "I'm in no mood for guessing games. I just lost every penny I have. Now tell me what he wants, or leave me the hell alone."

"He wants you to do precisely what you must do," answered the warrior. "But you cannot do it alone."

"And what is that?" demanded Holliday.

"You will know when the time comes."

"And when will that be?"

Suddenly he was facing a coyote again.

"Soon," promised the animal, and ran off into the night.

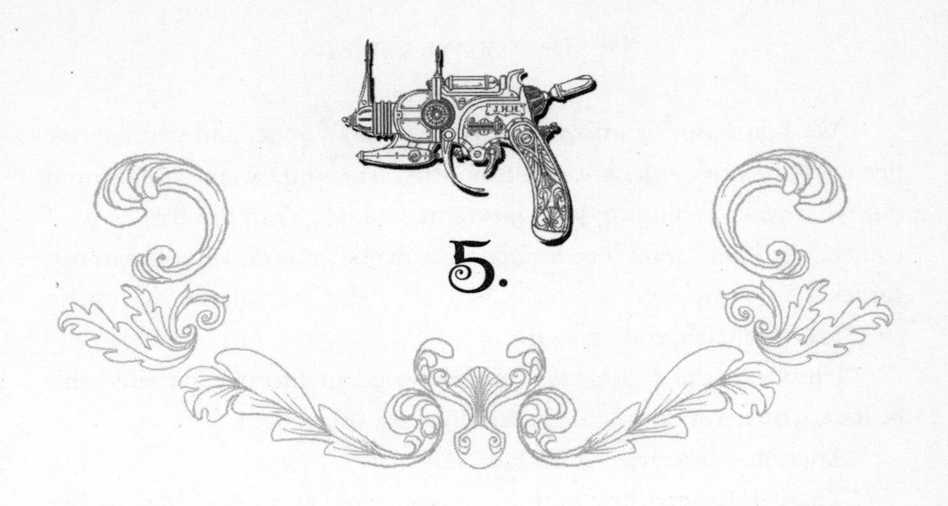

5.

"YOU LOST IT *ALL*?" demanded Kate Elder.

"Every last cent of it," said Holliday. "I have about two hundred dollars left in the world."

He was standing before her desk in her office, trying not to sway as he stood there facing her.

"This isn't another of your damnfool jokes?"

He was about to shake his head, decided that would precipitate a headache, and settled for saying, "No."

"What now?"

An almost-amused smile cross his face. "Now I find a new place to die."

"I could shoot you right now," said Kate.

"If anyone else said that, I'd think they were kidding," replied Holliday. A pause. "I've got to sit down, Kate." He walked over to a chair and half-sat, half-sprawled in it.

"Well, you can't gamble if all your money's gone, and you haven't been able to work as a dentist for months," she said. "Have you figured out what you're going to do to raise some money? You can live here, of course, but if you want a newspaper or a drink, how do you plan to pay for it?"

"I'll have to go out and earn it."

"I just explained: you can't gamble without money, and you can't be a dentist if you keep coughing blood on your clients."

"There's a third way," said Holliday.

"There'd damned well better be." She stared at him, and finally her expression softened. "Come on to the kitchen and I'll cook you up some eggs."

"You haven't cooked in all the time we've been in Colorado," noted Holliday. "Am I *that* much a figure of pathos?"

"I plan to have Annabelle do the cooking."

He frowned. "Do I know her?"

"You'd damned well better not. She's one of your friend's robots." She walked to the door and turned to him. "Well?"

"Give me just a minute for the world to stop spinning," said Holliday. "I'll be along."

"Damned well better be," Kate muttered and walked down the hall to the kitchen.

Holliday sat perfectly still for a long minute, then got to his feet and went to the kitchen. The world seemed a little steadier, and he was pretty sure he wasn't going to vomit.

Annabelle—super-hardened brass, huge-breasted, tiny-waisted, and expressionless—was scrambling some eggs as he took a seat at the table.

"Thank you," said Holliday as she slid the eggs onto a plate and handed it to him.

"Oh, baby, you're the best," said Annabelle. "Want to do it again?"

"It would have been nice," said Kate caustically, "if your friends had given her more than three sentences or one topic of conversation."

"I'm sure if you order a cook instead of a whore, they will," said Holliday.

"Those look pretty good," said Kate, indicating the eggs. She turned to Annabelle. "I'll have some too."

She seated herself opposite Holliday. "So how *are* you going to get your money back?"

"I do have another talent," he said.

She studied his face for a moment. "You're going to be a gun for hire?"

He shook his head. "I've never worked for anyone in my life. I don't intend to start now, so close to its end."

"Then what?" she asked, puzzled.

"I hear Wyatt's in Denver. I'll take the Bunt Line over there tomorrow morning, and—"

"Morning?" she interrupted him with a disbelieving look.

"When I get up," he amended. "Wyatt's still a lawman, last I heard. He'll know who has the biggest prices on their heads. If he can find a gang where they *all* have prices, maybe we'll go after them together and split the reward."

"It's always Wyatt," she said contemptuously. "Wichita, Dodge, Tombstone, now here. What's his hold over you?"

"He's my friend," said Holliday.

"Big deal."

"A man like me hasn't got many friends, so I cherish the ones I have."

"Have you ever noticed that you're always helping him, that it's never the other way around?"

"That's enough, Kate," he said, and something in his tone convinced her to stop talking and concentrate on eating her eggs.

They ate in silence, they walked to Kate's bedroom in silence, and Holliday collapsed on the bed and spent the next eleven hours sleeping in silence.

6.

HOLLIDAY HATED TRAVELING on the horseless Bunt Line at night. He knew that Edison had installed what he called spotlights on the front of the coach, but seeing a hole or perhaps a buffalo corpse in the trail didn't mean avoiding it. Horses would find a way, but with no horses the coach's safety depended on the driver, and Holliday had very little confidence in his fellow man.

The one thing he knew was that the brass coach was safe from attack. He'd been attacked twice by Apaches, and their bullets and arrows simply bounced off the exterior of the coach. In the old days, which, he reflected wryly, meant two years ago, attacking Indians would simply kill the horses that were pulling the stagecoach and that would be that. But the Bunt Line was powered by an electrical engine and battery that Edison had designed and Buntline had built, and while he expected to break an axle—and his neck—on the hazardous road, he knew he was safe from attack.

Soon it was completely dark, and he lit the little battery-powered lamp next to his seat and continued reading the dime novel he'd picked up on his way to meet the coach. It was a rootin' tootin' shoot-'em-up about, of all people, himself. In this ridiculous story he faced a gang of twenty-two and killed them all, which was a pretty good trick with a pair of six-guns. Then he saw the illustration, and realized he was firing Buntline's Gatling pistols that carried about two dozen bullets apiece. He'd actually tried one out back in Tombstone, and realized that in his condition he was too weak to hold the weapon up and aim it. Evidently no one had told the illustrator, who'd put an extra fifty pounds of muscle on him and had him looking like a normal human being.

There was a *Where Is He Now?* feature on John Wesley Hardin. Easy answer: He was in jail, studying for a law degree. But the magazine had him hiding out in Mexico, killing any stranger who approached his *hacienda*.

Next there was a *Great Jail Breaks* section. This issue featured the daring escape from the Lincoln County Jail by Henry McCarty, who was fast becoming known as Billy the Kid. He'd killed two deputies and made his getaway in broad daylight. Holliday wished they'd run a photo of him, rather than a drawing of him shooting the deputies by an artist who had clearly never been west of the Mississippi and had no idea of how people dressed or even what kind of gear the horses carried. The Kid was making quite a name for himself; he'd have liked to see what he really looked like.

Finally there was an annoying article on *The Fastest Guns*, as if that meant anything. The six fastest guns Holliday had ever seen all died young, beaten by *accurate* guns.

When he was done he put the publication on the seat beside him, lay a small suitcase on his lap, and started playing solitaire. Before long he was so engrossed in it that he barely noticed that the coach was slowing down.

"Denver in ten minutes!" announced the driver from his protected cab atop the coach.

"Thanks," said Holliday, gathering up his cards and putting them in a pocket. "You'd think more people would want to come here from Leadville."

"Miss Anthony and Mr. Wilde are both speaking today," answered the driver. "They tell me we're full tomorrow." He paused. "You got a place to stay, Doc?"

"Not yet."

"Try the Nugget," said the driver. "That's where I always stay. Clean and cheap."

"Sounds good," said Holliday.

"Stick around five minutes after we stop and I'll take you there myself. I just have to turn the rig over to the guy who's taking it back to Leadville."

Holliday pulled out his watch, which was attached to his vest by a gold chain. "That'll be fine. The man I'm here to see won't be going to bed for another three or four hours."

"A gambler like you?"

Holliday shook his head, though of course the driver couldn't see it. "Not a gambler, and not like me," he replied.

The coach began slowing down as it reached the outskirts of town, and finally came to a stop at the small building serving as the Bunt Line station. Holliday emerged carrying his small suitcase, and waited a few minutes for the driver to climb down. Two women and a man boarded the coach, and after changing batteries the new driver turned it around and headed back toward Leadville.

Holliday checked in to the Nugget, left his bag in his room, and was soon walking toward the Greenback Saloon and Casino. It was far larger than his own establishment, and it took him a couple of minutes to spot the man he was looking for.

A trio of women were carrying drinks and cigars to the forty gaming tables, and Holliday stopped one as she walked by.

"I wonder if I might ask a favor of you," he said.

She stared at him suspiciously.

"Do you see that tall man at the table in the corner, the one with the brocaded silver vest?"

"Yeah?"

He thrust a dollar bill into her hand. "Please tell him that his dentist is waiting for him at the bar."

She looked at him like he was crazy, but she walked off and delivered the message, and a moment later the tall man walked over to the bar and approached Holliday.

"How the hell are you, Doc?" he said. "I got the impression you were in Leadville to stay."

"Hello, Wyatt," said Holliday. "I had planned to stay there, but conditions have changed."

Wyatt Earp smiled. "Kate throw you out again?"

Holliday made a face. "No more than once a week. Then she remembers that the whorehouse is a pretty peaceful place when people know I'm living there."

"So what brings you to Denver?"

"You."

"Should I be flattered?" asked Earp. "Or should I be looking for the nearest exit."

"I just need to pick your mind, Wyatt."

"I don't know if I like the sound of that."

"Buy us a drink and with a little luck we'll be done before I ask for a second one."

Earp signaled to the bartender, held up two fingers to indicate the number of glasses he wanted. When the bartender delivered them, he turned to Holliday. "Okay," he said. "What now?"

"Let's find a table where everyone can't overhear us," said Holliday, heading toward an empty table by a window.

"This is terrible stuff," said Earp, taking a sip and grimacing. "I've tasted better cow piss."

"Not better," said Holliday. "Just younger."

Earp laughed. "Damn! I've missed you, Doc! Now seriously, what can I do for you?"

"I lost my stake for the sanitarium in a poker game," said Holliday. "I don't know how long I'll stay healthy enough to live on my own. I need a lot of money very fast, just to be on the safe side."

"I don't think they're hiring any deputies in Denver this month," said Earp.

"I said money, not chicken feed," retorted Holliday. "You were still in the marshal business until a month or two ago. Who's got a nice price on his head?"

"You're going to turn bounty hunter?" said Earp, arching an eyebrow.

"What's so surprising?" said Holliday. "I am not entirely unacquainted with firearms."

"Doc, they say a bounty hunter rides a hundred miles for every shot he takes," replied Earp. "Are you sure you're up to it?"

"I can be uncomfortable now, or when I'm too weak to feed myself," said Holliday. "It's an easy choice."

"All right," said Earp. "Last I heard there's seven hundred and fifty dollars for Bob Olinger, dead or alive."

"Isn't he a deputy?"

"Yes."

"Well, then?" asked Holliday.

"You never heard of a deputy murdering anyone?" replied Earp.

"Who else?"

"There's Black Jack Ketchum and El Tigre Sains at five hundred apiece."

Holliday shook his head. "I could spend five hundred just tracking them down. Isn't there anyone with a *real* price on his head?"

"You already killed Johnny Ringo."

"Once."

"John Wesley Hardin's in jail."

"What about this kid everyone's talking about?" asked Holliday. "Got a bunch of aliases."

"You don't want any part of him, Doc," said Earp seriously.

"What's he worth?" persisted Holliday.

"Forget it. He's you, a dozen years younger and in perfect health."

"Damn it, Wyatt," said Holliday irritably.

Earp took a deep breath and stared into his old friend's eyes. "Ten thousand."

"Ten thousand," repeated Holliday, impressed. "I guess most of those rumors weren't rumors after all."

"He's killed between fifteen and twenty men," said Earp. "And if he lived on the other side of the Mississippi he wouldn't be old enough to vote. Leave him be, Doc."

"Well, he figures to be good for ten thousand dollars."

"Doc, he just killed two really good men—good with guns, I mean—when he broke out of the jail down in Lincoln. I knew them. I don't think *you* could have taken them both at once."

"If you're that worried, come with me and we'll split the money," replied Holliday.

Earp shook his head. "Governor Lew Wallace posted that reward."

"He could afford to. *Ben-Hur* is the best-selling novel in the country."

"Ben *what*?"

Holliday sighed. "I forgot. Only one of us has an interest in literature."

"Anyway," continued Earp, "half the goddamned territory's out looking for the Kid. They haven't turned him up yet.

"That money will pay for two years in the sanitarium."

"I thought you were planning on four years."

"I figure I'll take two years off my health just hunting him down," answered Holliday. "Come along. Don't tell me you can't use five thousand dollars—and we can treat ourselves to Olinger and the others along the way."

"I'm not a lawman any more, Doc," said Earp.

"I never was," said Holliday. "So what?"

"Yes you were," said Earp. "Virgil deputized you on the way to the O.K. Corral."

"I never thought it was legal," replied Holliday. "Did you?"

"It was legal enough."

"We're getting off the subject. Come down to New Mexico with me."

"Doc, I'm a married man."

"So what?"

"Josie doesn't want me looking for trouble," said Earp uncomfortably. "We're planning on going up to Alaska and looking for gold instead.

"You can make more in ten seconds facing the Kid with me than you can make in two years of busting your back in a mine," said Holliday. "Josie is your third wife, Wyatt. You never listened to the first two. Why change now?"

"This one's different."

"This one's Jewish," said Holliday. "Comes from a long line of killers, dating all the way back to what her people did to Jesus. She should approve of killing the Kid."

"Tread easy there, Doc," said Earp.

"You think they're not killers?" said Holliday. "Go read the goddamned Bible sometime."

"I'm warning you, Doc."

"You can stand up to a sick consumptive man, but you won't stand up to a damned Jewess," complained Holliday.

"That's it," said Earp, getting to his feet. "From this minute on we're no longer friends."

He walked out of the building, leaving Holliday sitting alone at the table.

"Now why did I say that?" muttered Holliday. "Hell, Josie is the only Jew I've ever met, and I *like* her." He held up his glass and stared at it. "Someday I really have to give you up. I wish to hell you weren't the only thing that makes life bearable."

He downed the drink, left the Greenback, stopped at the Bunt Line station, bought a ticket to New Mexico for the next morning, and went back to the Nugget after picking up the latest dime novel, which featured a cover story about the invincible Billy the Kid.

7.

THE BUNT LINE STOPPED at the edge of the New Mexico Territory, and Holliday transferred to a horse-drawn stagecoach. The ride was rougher, the odor and flies suddenly prevalent, and the possibility of an Indian attack greater.

Their surroundings became flatter, with nothing but the occasional cactus to break the even horizon. It seemed too hot and dry even for snakes and spiders, and they passed occasional stark-white cattle skeletons along the way. Holliday stared out the window, unable to comprehend why the Indians would fight to hold onto this bleak land, or why the United States coveted it.

They stopped twenty miles into the territory at a stagecoach station to rest and water the horses, and Holliday clambered down from the coach and decided to stretch his legs. The stretching was cut short when he saw there was a bar inside the station, and he walked inside for a drink.

"What'll it be?" asked the station master, who doubled as bartender and ticket salesman.

"Just whiskey."

"I can make something fancier if you like."

Holliday shook his head. "I'm not a fancy kind of man."

The station master shrugged. "Whatever you say. I'm not about to argue with Doc Holliday."

Holliday stared at him. "Do I know you?"

"Never had the honor of meeting you."

"Then how—?"

"Came over the telegraph," was the answer. He picked up the message and read it aloud. "'Doc Holliday will be on the next coach. Show him every courtesy, and whatever you do, don't rile him.'"

"They must think I kill someone before breakfast every day," remarked Holliday, draining his glass.

"If you say you don't, I believe it," said the station master. "Hell, if you say cows can fly and pigs can piss beer, I'll believe you."

Holliday couldn't repress a grin. "How about if I just say this is damned good whiskey and I'd like a refill?"

"It's yours, on the house," said the station master, pouring him another.

"That's very generous of you," said Holliday. "I'll remember you in my will."

"They say you can't die."

Now that I'm broke, wouldn't that be ironic if it were true?

"Oh, everything dies," he said aloud.

The station master leaned on the bar. "How many men have you killed, Doc?"

"One or two," answered Holliday.

"They've credited you with twenty-five."

"One of those damned McLaury brothers must have come back to life," said Holliday with an amused smile. "Last I heard it was twenty-six."

"So it's twenty-six?"

Holliday shook his head. "You can't believe everything you hear."

"Okay," said the station master, who sensed he had pushed enough. "It'll be your secret."

"Mine, and a bunch of dime novel writers who can't count," agreed Holliday, walking out the door.

He adjusted his hat to keep the sun from his eyes, and unbuttoned his jacket. He didn't remember New Mexico being this hot; it could just as well have been Arizona. A hot breeze was blowing sagebrush and sand across the flat ground. A snake seemed content to remain in the shade cast by the coach. The horses had slaked their thirst, but were drenched in sweat.

"Welcome to New Mexico," said the driver, grinning as he noticed Holliday's discomfort. "Hot enough for you."

Holliday took a deep breath. "At least the air's a little thicker than up in Leadville."

"I imagine most of the men you killed are where it's a little hotter right now."

"Only the first four or five thousand," said Holliday, forcing a smile to his lips. *What the hell kind of maniac do you people think I am?*

"Well, we've got our share that needs killing," said the driver. "Got one right now."

"Oh?" said Holliday, trying not to look too interested.

"Well, maybe," hedged the driver. "They say he's killed twenty men, maybe thirty. But they also say he's a really nice, polite, thoughtful kid, so who knows?"

"Who are you talking about?"

"Billy Bonney," was the answer. "Just busted out of jail a couple of months ago. Killed eight or nine deputies in the process. Maybe twelve."

"I don't believe I've heard of any desperado named Bonney," said Holliday, hoping the driver could tell him more details.

"Maybe you've heard of Billy the Kid?"

"Here and there."

"Don't know why he permits it. Who'd want to get famous as being a kid?" continued the driver.

"Sounds to me like he's chosen a profession where he's not likely to get much older," answered Holliday. "What else can you tell me about him?"

"They say he's got a Mexican ladyfriend," was the answer. "I hear he's left-handed, but I don't put much stock in it, since I figure anyone who's seen him draw ain't around to report on it."

"Makes sense."

Suddenly a horse-drawn buckboard pulled up, and a woman in her fifties climbed down, tipped the man at the reins, walked over to the stagecoach, handed a ticket to the driver, and entered the coach.

"I guess we can go now," said the driver. "She's what we were waiting for. Climb aboard, Doc."

Holliday entered the coach and sat down opposite the woman.

"I'm Charlotte Branson," she said, extending a gloved hand.

"John H. Holliday at your service, ma'am."

She frowned. "I heard the driver call you Doc."

"Yes, ma'am. I'm a dentist."

"You're Doc Holliday, aren't you?"

"I've been called that, yes, ma'am," he said, tipping his hat.

"I want you to know that I'm not the least bit afraid of you," said Charlotte Branson.

"I'm terrified of you, ma'am," replied Holliday.

She chuckled. "I do believe we're going to get along famously, Doc." Then: "May I call you Doc?"

"Why not?" said Holliday with a shrug.

"Well, how shall we kill the time, Doc?" she continued. "Have you got a deck of cards, or would you rather regale me with stories of the Gunfight at the O.K. Corral."

"How does canasta sound, Miss Branson?" said Holliday.

"It's *Mrs.* Branson, and please call me Charlotte."

"Very well, Charlotte. Shall we play a friendly game of canasta?"

"How about a friendly game of blackjack, dollar a hand?" she countered.

Suddenly Holliday grinned. "You're right, Charlotte. We're going to get on well together." He paused. "And when you hear stories about the gunfight, you can tell them that it was in the alley leading up to the O.K. Corral, and your source for that is Doc Holliday."

"I shall do that," she promised. "Was Ike Clanton as ugly as they say?"

"Uglier," replied Holliday, putting his suitcase on his lap and starting to deal.

They played and exchanged stories until the horses came to another watering station three hours later, at which time Holliday was seven dollars ahead.

"Well, I guess I didn't do so badly," said Charlotte.

"Charlotte, around Tombstone and elsewhere, they say that an outlaw named Johnny Behind-the-Deuce is the best cardplayer in the West." He smiled at her. "I never had to work this hard beating him at the card table."

"I'm flattered," she said, beaming. "Seven dollars poorer, but flattered."

"Let me spend some of that seven dollars buying you a drink," offered Holliday.

"Just one," she said as he climbed down and then held out his hand to her. "I can't get used to—what do you call it?—rotgut."

"I call it wet," answered Holliday, offering her his arm and escorting her into the station.

"Welcome," said the station master. "What can I get for you and the missus?"

"The missus is from back in the States," said Holliday. "You got anything from east of the Mississippi?"

"Almost," was the answer. "Is St. Louis close enough?"

Holliday looked questioningly at Charlotte, and she nodded.

"That'll be fine," he said. As the station master was hunting up the bottle, Holliday added, "It's been a long trip. You got an outhouse around here?"

"There's one out back."

Holliday turned to Charlotte. "Ladies first."

"I'm fine, Doc," she said.

"Then if you'll excuse me . . ."

He turned and walked back out the door, then circled the station until he saw the outhouse and began approaching it. Then a prarie dog caught his eye. It was sitting on the ground a few feet from the outhouse, staring unblinking at him.

He pulled out a handkerchief and waved it at the prarie dog. "Shoo!" he growled, taking a step toward it—and suddenly he was facing what was becoming the familiar Apache warrior.

"What now?" demanded Holliday irritably.

"He knows why you have come."

"He sent you here to tell me that?"

"No," said the warrior. "He sent me here to tell you that you will never conquer Henry McCarty who is known as Billy the Kid on your own."

"We'll see about that," said Holliday.

"It will be best if you listen to him. McCarty who is called Billy is protected."

"By a gang?"

The warrior shook his head.

"By another medicine man?"

The warrior nodded.

"Maybe so," said Holliday dubiously, "but I haven't come all this way just to turn around and go back to Leadville."

"He does not expect you to."

"Can he answer a direct question?" said Holliday. "Just what the hell *does* he want?"

"A service."

"Why should I do Geronimo a service? He's an enemy of the United States."

The trace of a smile played about the warrior's lips. "Do you really care about that?"

Holliday shrugged. "No, not really. But my question remains: Why should I do him a service?"

"Because then he will do one for you."

"One having to do with the Kid?"

"Yes."

"He'll help me kill him?"

The warrior shook his head. "Only you can do that, if you are capable, and neither he nor anyone else knows if you are."

"Then what?"

"He will make it possible for you to find McCarty who is called Billy without his protector."

Holliday frowned. "Just possible, not certain? That's not much of a service."

"It is *impossible* right now."

"All right. What does he want in exchange?"

"He will tell you."

"He's talking to me right now, isn't he?" demanded Holliday.

"He will tell you himself," said the warrior.

"When?"

"Soon."

"Why not now, damn it?" growled Holliday, but suddenly he was talking to the prairie dog again. "I'd like it a lot better if you'd use one of Tom Edison's new-fangled telephones," he muttered. "It's getting to where every time I see a goddamned animal I think it's one of your braves."

He entered the outhouse and emerged a moment later. The prairie dog, if it actually existed, was nowhere to be seen, and he went back into the station.

"I didn't know you were an animal lover, Doc," said Charlotte when he had rejoined her.

"I can take 'em or leave 'em," he said. "Why?"

"I looked out the back window and saw you talking to a prairie dog."

"For how long?" he asked.

"Maybe two minutes."

"And that's all you saw?"

"Should I have seen something else?"

Holliday frowned and shrugged. "Beats the hell out of me."

8.

THE COACH PULLED INTO LINCOLN, a town that seemed apiece with its surroundings: brown, flat, dry. No building, not even the church or the courthouse, was more than three stories high, and except for a pair of hotels, the vast majority were low, flat, single-story structures. The Bunt Line hadn't made any inroads here, and horses still provided the most common means of transportation, but it was too hot to leave the animals tied to hitching posts, and they passed a number of stables along the way to the center of town.

Holliday opened the door and did his best to help Charlotte down to the dirt street, though she outweighed him, as did almost any woman who stood more than five feet tall.

When they had retrieved their luggage and the coach had pulled away, Holliday looked up at the hotel. Three windows were cracked, some siding had fallen off and been rather clumsily nailed back, the building hadn't been painted or stained since it had been built and the dust and the sun had both taken their toll of it.

"The Grand Hotel," he read, and grimaced. "Is there a town anywhere west of the Mississippi that doesn't have a Grand Hotel, almost none of which have more than a nodding acquaintance with the concept of 'grand'?"

"Do I detect a Southern aristocrat beneath the scowl of the shootist?" asked Charlotte with an amused smile.

"'*Way*' beneath," came the sardonic reply. "The war buried it pretty deep."

"I'm sorry," she said. "I meant no offense."

"None taken," replied Holliday. He looked around. "We can stand here gathering dust all day, or we can go inside and register."

She nodded, he picked up his suitcase with his right hand, and was about to lift hers with his left when she beat him to it and carried her luggage inside before he could protest.

"Got any rooms?" asked Holliday, walking up to the desk.

"That's our business," said the elderly clerk pleasantly. "One for you and the missus?"

"One for each of us," said Holliday. The clerk looked surprised, and he added, "She's a missus, but she's not *my* missus."

The clerk turned to the rack of keys behind him and pulled a pair down. "206 for the lady, 215 for the gentleman," he announced, handing them over. "How long will you be staying?"

"I'll be here ten days," answered Charlotte promptly.

"I don't know," said Holliday.

The clerk stared at Holliday for a long moment. "You're *him*, ain't you?"

"Probably not," replied Holliday with no show of interest.

"You're him," repeated the clerk, nodding his head with conviction. "You're Doc Holliday, come to town to kill someone."

"I'm a dentist and a gambler," said Holliday.

"You're Doc Holliday, and you're here on business," insisted the clerk.

"My business is pulling teeth and playing cards."

"Who are you going to kill?" asked the clerk, oblivious to Holliday's answers. "The bank president, maybe, or perhaps the mayor?" He lowered his voice to a whisper. "Are you working with the Kid?"

"What kid?" asked Holliday, trying to hide his interest.

"Why, Billy Bonney, of course!" exclaimed the clerk. "Billy the Kid! Our claim to fame!" He looked at the front door, as if he expected someone to enter and interrupt him at any moment, then turned back to Holliday and lowered his voice. "You're in cahoots with him, right?" he said conspirationally.

"I guess I can't fool a sharpie like you," said Holliday. "Yeah, we're partners. Where can I find him?"

"Hell, he's *your* partner," replied the clerk with a chuckle.

"I'm new to town. I just want to let him know I'm here."

"The marshal and his deputies have been looking high and low for the Kid for a couple of months. If *they* can't find him, *I* sure as hell don't know where he is."

"That's okay," said Holliday, forcing a nonchalant shrug. "But pass the word that I'm in town and I've got some business to discuss with him."

"I'll do that," promised the clerk. "But it could be a month or more before he shows his face. That reward is up to twelve thousand dollars. There's more than a few men, including those who call themselves his friends, that'd like to put a bullet between his pale blue eyes."

"Thanks," said Holliday, flipping him a quarter. "And now I think the lady and I will go to our rooms to unpack and freshen up."

Charlotte was again too fast for him and lifted her own luggage. He sighed, wondering how he would manage both suitcases if he *had* beat her to it, picked up his own, and together they climbed to the second floor. As she was unlocking her door, he stopped and pulled out his watch.

"Two-thirty," he said. "May I escort you to dinner?"

"I'd like that very much, Doc," replied Charlotte. "What time?"

"Seven o'clock?"

She nodded. "I'll meet you in the lobby, such as it is."

He tipped his hat to her and walked down the hall to room 215, where he inserted the key and opened the door. The room was small, but reasonably clean and serviceable. There was a small wardrobe, a single narrow bed with a torn bedspread, a nightstand next to it, a table that had seen better days and was currently doubling as a desk, and a straight-backed wooden chair. One corner held a washstand with a pitcher of water and a basin, and as he looked out the window he could see a quartet of outhouses.

He opened his suitcase on the bed preparatory to hanging up his clothes in the wardrobe. Then he decided the room needed a little fresh air, so he walked over to the lone window and opened it. A small bird immediately perched on the sill, staring curiously at him.

He closed the suitcase, slid it under the bed, turned back to the window—and found an Apache warrior sitting on the sill.

"He wants you," said the intruder.

"You were the bird," said Holliday, surprised that he was no longer surprised at the warrior's comings and goings.

"Now," said the warrior.

Holliday looked out past the warrior. "Is he out there?"

"They would kill him if they saw him."

"He's in the hotel?"

The warrior shook his head. "I am to bring you to him."

Holliday shrugged. "All right," he said. "Let's go and get this over with."

He walked to the door.

"Not that way," said the warrior.

"Then how—?" He was going to say more, but he suddenly found himself surrounded by darkness. He had a sensation of movement, though his legs remained motionless. He was sure he wasn't flying, for no wind whipped through his clothes and hair. He tried to analyze whether he was warm or cold, dry or wet, but his senses simply couldn't respond. The only conclusion he could reach was that he was *elsewhere* . . . and then, seconds after it began, it ended.

He knew he wouldn't still be in his room, but even though he knew the powers of the medicine men, he was surprised to find himself as far from *anything* as he was. He was in a vast valley, surrounded by cactus and tumbleweed and not much else, except for a handful of teepees. Sitting behind a fire before the nearest of them was Geronimo, surrounded by shadowy, ethereal shapes of writhing python-type creatures. He had not changed in the year since Holliday had last seen him: thick, muscular, broad of face and body, unsmiling.

"Goyathlay welcomes you," said the warrior, who Holliday realized was standing next to him.

"Goyathlay can speak for himself," said Holliday.

"Goyathlay speaks through me."

"Why? He understands every word I say. You don't expect me to believe that he can't speak my language."

"He chooses not to speak the tongue of his enemies."

Holliday stared into Geronimo's eyes. "If I'm your enemy, what am I doing here, and why should I do you any favors?"

Geronimo stared back, silently, and after a full minute it became obvious that neither man would turn away first.

"I will speak to you," said Geronimo at last, rising to his feet.

"Good," said Holliday. "Just remember that I am not the enemy."

"There is only one member of your race who is not the enemy, White Eyes," replied Geronimo, "and he is on the far side of the great river that his nation may not cross. You are but a killer."

JSG

"If that's the case, why am I here?" responded Holliday. "Surely you do not lack for killers."

"There are killings for which the notorious Holliday is better suited."

"I appreciate what you doubtless think is a compliment, but I'm not a hired gun."

"No," agreed Geronimo. "But you are a *traded* gun."

"Explain."

"A favor for a favor," answered Geronimo. "We have done it once before, you and I, a year ago, in the place you call Tombstone."

"Lawyers call your trade a *quid pro quo*," said Holliday. "Why should I do you a favor, other than the fact that I'm captivated by your charming personality?"

"I know why you are here, Holliday," said Geronimo. "You are a drunken fool who lost all his money, and you are dying."

"I appreciate your sympathy," interjected Holliday sardonically as a coyote howled in the distance.

"You need money to die in peace, and you have decided to get it by killing the one you know only as Billy the Kid."

"I don't know him at all."

"Do not play word games with me," continued Geronimo harshly. "You are here for the White Eyes' reward for killing the man McCarty who is called Billy the Kid."

"All right," conceded Holliday, "I'm here to kill him."

"You cannot."

"Suppose you tell me why not?"

"He is protected."

"So your messenger told me," said Holliday. "Who is protecting him, and why?"

"He is protected by Woo-Ka-Nay of the Southern Cheyenne," answered Geronimo.

"Hook Nose?" repeated Holliday, surprised. "I thought you two were partners, the two most powerful medicine men on the continent, the two men whose magic stopped the United States from expanding past the Mississippi."

"We *are* partners in that enterprise," Geronimo assured him.

"But McCarty called Billy the Kid operates under his protection."

"Why? What kind of deal has he made with the Kid?"

"None. McCarty called Billy the Kid does not even know he *is* protected."

"Then I repeat: Why?" said Holliday, trying to understand.

"Woo-Ka-Nay hates the White Eyes. McCarty called Billy the Kid kills White Eyes. He has never killed one of the People, and until he does, he is protected."

"And you'll lift his protection?"

Geronimo shook his head. "I am not more powerful than Woo-Ka-Nay."

"Then why are you telling me all this?" demanded Holliday.

"I probably cannot defeat Woo-Ka-Nay. And if I could, I would not, not to help any White Eyes." Geronimo paused. "But I *can* negate him, so that you will kill McCarty called Billy the Kid *if* you can kill him."

"That's not wildly encouraging," replied Holliday. "I'm a dying man, going up against a kid who is killing men at a faster rate than even John Wesley Hardin, and you not only can't guarantee a win, you can't even be sure you can hold Hook Nose off since he's as powerful as you. Maybe he's even a shade more powerful, and take my word as an experienced shootist, most of the time a shade is all it takes."

"All this is true," agreed Geronimo. "But you will agree to a trade anyway, because while you *might* fail with my help, you *will* fail without it."

Holliday stared at him for a long moment, then spoke. "All right. That's what you're doing for me, such as it is. What do you think I'm going to do for you? Who am I supposed to kill?"

"You will not kill anyone," answered Geronimo.

"I won't?" asked Holliday, surprised.

"Unless it is necessary."

Holliday grimaced. "Let's have it."

"A day from here—" began Geronimo.

"I don't know where *here* is," interrupted Holliday.

"You will," Geronimo assured him. "A day from here is a valley very much like this one. There was a time when the two valleys were sisters, when it was clear that the same hand had created them both."

"But no longer?" suggested Holliday.

"Today a track runs through the valley, and there is a building where people await the train or depart from it."

"OK, there's a valley with a train station. What about it?"

"You will destroy it," said Geronimo as a trio of bats flew overhead. Holliday wondered where they came from in this desolate landscape, or if they were actually bats at all.

"Why?"

"It desecrates an Apache burial ground."

"You're the medicine man," said Holliday. "Why don't you destroy it?"

Geronimo frowned. "I cannot."

"Hook Nose is protecting it, too?"

"I do not know. He swears he is not, and we are allies now. But we have been enemies before. This is Apache holy ground, so there is no reason why he should care about it, but there is also no reason why he should protect it. But someone or something is protecting it."

"I assume the Apaches have other enemies?" said Holliday.

"Like grains of sand when the wind blows across the desert," answered Geronimo.

"Suppose you tell me what's special about this station, or the men defending it, what you've tried to do and failed."

"We tried to burn it. It will not burn. We have captured three cannons from your cavalry. We know how to use them. We fired at the building and could not even shatter the window. Our arrows bounce off the men who guard the station. We fire bullets into them, and they do not fall or even flinch."

Holliday was silent again for another moment. Finally he looked into Geronimo's cold, unblinking eyes.

"Let me see if I've got this straight," he said. "All I have to do is destroy men and buildings that are impervious to arrows, bullets, cannonballs and fire, and in exchange for that, a sick, dying man gets to face the greatest killer in the West on even terms, is that your offer?"

"That is my offer."

"Give me a minute to think about it," said Holliday, staring down at the ground.

Geronimo nodded his assent.

Holliday stood motionless for awhile, then looked up at the medicine man.

"What the hell," he said. "If he kills me, I don't need the money anyway."

"We will trade," confirmed Geronimo.

"We will trade," agreed Holliday. "But before I attack your station I have to send for two friends who are currently in Leadville."

He looked to Geronimo for his consent, but found that he was back inside his room, and a small bird was flying off into the night.

9.

HE HAD JUST RETURNED from the telegraph office when he ran into Charlotte Branson in the lobby of the Grand Hotel.

"I was starting to worry about you," was her greeting.

"No need to," replied Holliday. "He's not going to kill me as long as he needs me."

"*Who?*" she asked sharply.

Suddenly he realized what he had said and who he had said it *to*. "I apologize. I must have been preoccupied."

"Who's not going to kill you?" she persisted.

"I think that statement can apply to everyone in the world," he said with a lame attempt at flippancy. "How late am I?"

"About half an hour. Are you all right?"

"Don't I look all right?" he responded.

She stared at him for a moment, then smiled. "I'm beginning to understand why you get into so many gunfights," she said. "You can be an infuriating man to talk to."

"Then why not see if I'm less infuriating to eat with?" He offered her his arm. "Shall we go scout out the restaurants?"

"There ain't but four," said the desk clerk.

"Which do you recommend?"

"The Silver Steak," answered the clerk.

"Silver steaks sound hard on the teeth," remarked Holliday, as Charlotte chuckled.

"Take it from me," said the clerk. "It's the best."

"What makes it the best?"

"My cousin owns it."

"I suppose we can't go wrong with a testimonial like that," said Holliday. He turned to Charlotte. "Shall we go?"

"Where is it?" she asked the clerk.

"Out the front door, and two blocks to your right."

They left the hotel, walked along the raised wooden sidewalk, crossed the dirt street, repeated the process a block later, and finally came to the Silver Steak.

"Sounds more like something you'd find in Tombstone," remarked Holliday.

"Oh?" said Charlotte. "Why?"

"Town was built around a big silver strike," replied Holliday. "It was almost played out when I left. Should be just about empty now."

"You've traveled all over, haven't you, Doc?"

"I've spent most of my adult life looking for a place with air I can breathe where not too many people want to shoot me." He paused, then offered her a self-deprecating smile. "I'm still looking. For both."

"Are you considering Lincoln?"

He shook his head. "I'm just here on business."

"Where were you before this?"

"Leadville, Colorado."

"Are you going back there when you're done with your business?"

He shrugged and uttered a sigh. "I don't know. They've got the medical facility I want . . ." His voice trailed off.

"But?"

"But the air is so damned thin there even the birds prefer to walk."

"Then you really should consider staying down in the flatlands here, or in Arizona."

Another smile. "That runs smack dab against the other consideration."

She frowned, confused. "*Other* consideration?"

"Finding a place where not too many people want to shoot me," he replied.

"It's none of my business, Doc," said Charlotte, "but Lincoln's not known as a gambing center, and we passed a dentist's office on the way in, so I assume you're here for some other reason. Something to do with *that*," she concluded, pointing to his gun.

"It's possible," he admitted.

"Well, then?"

"I'm a dying man. I'm just trying to raise enough money so that I can die under competent medical care." A sudden smile. "With my boots off."

"Damn you, Doc!" she complained. "Why do you have to be so honest? Now I'm not going to enjoy my dinner at all!"

"Then we'll demand a refund from the guy who recommended this place."

A waiter approached them nervously.

"Excuse me, Doc," he began. Then: "You *are* Doc Holliday, aren't you?"

Holliday nodded his head. "Is that a problem."

"Absolutely not, sir," the waiter assured him. "The management, that is to say, my boss, would like to treat you and the lady to the specialty of the house if he can post a sign saying that you ate here."

"Tell him he's got a deal," said Holliday.

"Thank you, sir!" said the waiter, rushing off.

"Does this happen a lot?" asked Charlotte.

"From time to time." He smiled across the table at her. "They got away cheap."

"I don't understand."

"If I stay in town another two or three days, the undertaker will offer me ten dollars if I write a note saying he's got the right to bury me, and he'll make it twenty-five or even fifty if I give him permission to display me in his window for a few days first."

"That's horrible!" said Charlotte.

"What's horrible," explained Holliday in amused tones, "is that whether I take the more expensive deal or not, he's going to display me anyway."

"That's all you mean to him—a body to display?"

He nodded. "And one to bury."

"I don't know how you shootists can live like that."

"It's dying like that that upsets us," replied Holliday wryly.

Their steaks arrived.

"Well, nothing's going to change you," said Charlotte. "So you might as well regale me with tales of other shootists you know or knew. It'll keep my mind off how overcooked the steak is."

"I can tell you about Wyatt Earp and his brothers," offered Holliday. "Or Curly Bill Brocius. Or Bat Masterson."

"I've heard of all of them," she said. "Do you know Wild Bill Hickok?"

"No, I regret to say I've never had the pleasure. But I knew Clay Allison and Ben Thomson and the McLaury Brothers."

"They say you killed the McLaurys," said Charlotte.

"It's possible."

"You're a walking dime novel," she said with a laugh. "Who was the most memorable?"

"Johnny Ringo," said Holliday without hesitation.

"An interesting man?"

Holliday nodded his head. "The most interesting man I ever met. And as good a friend as I ever had."

"Is he still around?" she asked.

"No."

"Who killed him?"

"I did," said Holliday.

10.

THE BUCKBOARD STOPPED at the top of the rise and three men looked down at the train station in the middle of the barren valley.

"It doesn't seem remarkable or unusual in any way," remarked Edison, adjusting the polarity of his goggles to keep the sun from affecting his vision.

"No super-hardened brass," added Buntline, studying the walls of the station.

"Geronimo says it's more than the station and the railway," said Holliday. "He says even the people are immune to bullets and fire."

"*Any* people?" asked Edison. "If you were to drop me off there so I could wait for a train, would *I* be invulnerable?"

Holliday shrugged. "I *think* so, but don't know for sure, and I didn't know how to test it out. I mean, if it *doesn't* affect passengers, then I could kill an awful lot of them."

"Sensible," said Edison.

Buntline nudged him. "Wind's starting to blow from the west, Tom," he announced.

"Bad?"

"Could be. There's not much to stop it, and there's an awful lot of sand."

Buntline reached down and grabbed a cloth bag from the floor of the buckboard, then pulled out three round metal objects an inch in diameter, handing one each to Edison and Holliday while keeping the third for himself.

"What the hell is this?" asked Holliday, examining it. "It's got a hundred little holes in it, but I can't see any use for it, and unlike most of Tom's inventions it doesn't seem to plug in anywhere."

"It's powered by one of these," said Edison, reaching into his pocket and withdrawing a tiny battery.

"Powered to do *what?*" said Holliday suspiciously.

"To filter the sand out of the air so you don't have to hide during a dust storm," answered Edison. "Put it in your mouth like *this*, and remember not to breathe through your nose until the storm passes."

Buntline pointed toward the goggles that hung around Holliday's neck. "And put those damned things over your eyes if you don't want to go blind, Doc."

While Holliday was inserting the filter and donning the goggles, Buntline climbed down and put a contraption that seemed half-net and half-glass over the horse's head.

"Now the horse won't choke or go blind either," he announced when he'd climbed back onto the buckboard.

Holliday clucked to the horse and the animal began pulling the wagon down to the station.

"The tracks are just about covered," he noted. "How do they get the sand off?"

"The wind that covered them will uncover some of them," answered Edison. "And along with cow-sweepers, the trains out here are equipped with kind of a brush that moves the sand off the tracks as the wheels approach it."

"One of your inventions?" asked Holliday.

Edison shook his head. "A Mr. Glover from Chicago. Contrary to what you read in the papers," he added with as much of a smile as he could manage with the filter in his mouth, "I am not responsible for every invention of the past dozen years."

When they were within one hundred yards of the station, the wind died down as quickly as it had spring up, and Holliday immediately took the filter out of his mouth and stuck it in a pocket. "Damned difficult to talk with that thing."

"My problem isn't talking," said Edison. "It's remembering not to breathe through my nose."

"Place looks deserted," remarked Buntline.

"No reason why not," said Holliday. "There's only one train every two days, and it passed through yesterday."

"Where does this damned thing go?" asked Buntline.

"From what I hear, it goes to Tombstone and the other five towns in Arizona, then continues on to California."

"Where in California?"

Holliday shrugged. "Beats me. I've never ridden it. Never been to California either."

Holliday reined the horse to a stop, and the three men climbed awkwardly down from the buckboard. Edison returned the filter to Buntline, who replaced it in the bag.

"What about *those*?" asked Holliday, indicating Edison's and Buntline's goggles.

"We'll keep them a bit longer," replied Edison.

"Doesn't look like it's going to blow again for awhile," said Holliday. "And besides, you'll be inside."

"Doc, do you see that little button on the left temple of your goggles?" asked Buntline.

"I don't *see* it, but I can feel it."

"Press it."

Holliday did so, and suddenly his vision was so blurry he could barely see. "What the hell happened?" he demanded.

"You just turned the two lenses into magnifying glasses. If you press the button on the right temple, they'll become spyglasses. Not powerful ones, but far stronger than your eyes."

"We don't know what we're looking for," added Edison, "and it may be that we'll need the goggles to spot anything unusual."

"And if not, we have other methods," added Buntline.

The three men walked into the station building. There was a bearded middle-aged man in a railroad jacket standing in the kiosk where tickets were sold, and a young man who had barely enough stubble to make his chin look dirty was sitting on a bench, reading a dime novel.

"Still blowing?" asked the stationmaster.

"Just finished," said Holliday.

The stationmaster studied the three men. "Damnedest spectacles I ever saw," he said at last.

"They're all the rage in New York," said Holliday sardonically.

The young man looked up. "New York?" he said. "I knew someone from there once."

"Bet he wishes he was back there every time he found himself in a dust storm," said the stationmaster.

"I don't know," said the young man. "I never asked."

Edison turned to Holliday, "Ned and I are going to take a good, thorough look around."

"I'll help you," offered Holliday.

Edison smiled. "You don't know what you're looking for."

"Neither do you," said Holliday.

"True," admitted Edison. "But we'll know it when we find it."

"Grab yourself a drink, Doc," added Buntline. "We won't be that long."

Holliday pulled his goggles down until they hung around his neck again, and walked up to the stationmaster. "I assume that's a service you provide?"

The man nodded. "It gets mighty dry out here, waiting for the train to come." He reached down, found a bottle and a glass, and poured Holliday a drink.

Holliday laid a dime on the counter, then turned to see which bench he wanted to sit on, and became aware that the young man was staring unblinking, at him.

"Is something wrong, son?" asked Holliday.

"You're *him*, ain't you?" said the young man. He got to his feet, still staring with an expression of total awe on his face. "They called you Doc."

"I *am* a doctor. Well, a dentist, anyway."

"A *dentist*!" exclaimed the young man. "Then you *are* Doc Holliday!"

Holliday tipped his hat. "At your service."

"Doc Holliday!" repeated the young man excitedly. "I can't believe it!" He held up the dime novel. "I been reading about you all year!"

"Am I in that one?"

"No, this one's about the Younger Brothers." Suddenly the young man blushed furiously. "Where are my manners?" He held out his hand. "I'm Henry Antrim." Holliday took his hand. "Damn! Now I can say I shook Doc Holliday's hand!"

"Come on over and share a drink with Doc Holliday," said Holliday. "My treat."

"Are you sure?" said Antrim. "I mean, I should be buying one for you!"

"Someday, Henry, when you have money, you can return the favor."

"What makes you think I don't have money?" asked Antrim defensively.

"The train doesn't come until tomorrow," answered Holliday. "There's only one reason to be waiting for it now. You've got no money to buy a room back in town."

The young man's face displayed a guilty smile. "Truth to tell, I couldn't have bought you a drink. But I felt I had to offer."

"Loan me that book for a minute, Henry," said Holliday, stretching out his hand. Antrim gave it to him, and Holliday turned to the stationmaster. "You got a pen?" The man supplied it, and Holliday signed his name on the cover, then returned the pen. "Here," he said, handing the book back to Antrim. "Wait a year or two until I'm in the grave, and you can sell that thing, with a genuine Doc Holliday autograph, for half a dollar. Maybe a dollar if you're lucky."

Antrim clutched the dime novel to his chest. "I'm never going to part with it. Never!"

Holliday smiled. "Never's a long time, Henry. You'll grow a little older, someone will offer to trade you some of those French postcards I've seen and you've probably at least heard about, and you'll jump at the chance."

"Not me!" Antrim assured him.

"Well, it's nice to have such an admirer," said Holliday. "Now how about that drink?"

"Sure," said Antrim, walking over and waiting for the stationmaster to pour him a glass. He lifted it to his lips, took a swallow, and made a face.

"A little strong for you?" asked Holliday.

"A little!" Antrim whispered as he gasped for breath.

"You'll grow into it."

Buntline entered the room just then.

"Well?" asked Holliday.

Buntline shook his head. "Seems absolutely normal to me. Some of the wood even has termites."

Edison joined them a moment later.

"You're sure *this* is the station he was talking about?"

"Absolutely."

"Very strange," muttered Edison. He stood up and looked around. "Well, at least it's empty." He walked up to the stationmaster. "I want to buy you a new window. How much will it cost?"

"Don't need one."

"You may. How much?"

The stationmaster scratched his head. "Including labor, a dollar and a half."

"It's a deal." Edison turned to Holliday, "Doc," he said, pointing to a window, "shoot that damned thing out of its frame."

Holliday drew his gun and fired in one motion.

Nothing happened.

Buntline walked over and examined the glass. "Not a mark."

Antrim, who had ducked when Holliday fired, was on his feet now. "Where's the bullet? I didn't hear or feel anything ricochet."

They all spent a couple of minutes looking, without success, for the spent bullet.

"It's like magic!" said Antrim.

"Exactly," agreed Edison, his face lighting up with excitement. "Doc, stand six inches away from that wooden wall and put a slug into it."

Holliday did as requested. The result was the same: no mark on the wall, and no spent bullet.

"This is wonderful!" enthused Edison. "Simply wonderful!" He turned to his companions. "Come along! It's time to go back to town and get a couple of rooms for the night." He walked over to the stationmaster. "Are there seats available on tomorrow's train?"

"Always," was the reply.

"Good! We'll want two tickets to Tombstone."

"Three," said Holliday. Edison looked at him questioningly. "I told you about my trade. The sooner we get this over with, the better."

"So I'll see you tomorrow, Doc?" asked Antrim.

Holliday nodded. "We'll be here."

"Could we maybe . . . maybe sit together on the train?"

"Sure," said Holliday. "How far are you going?"

The young man shrugged. "I don't know. As far as my money will take me."

"See you tomorrow," said Holliday, turning and joining his companions. They walked out to the buckboard, then climbed onto it one by one.

"There's a horse out behind the station," said Buntline. "But before we shoot it, we should make sure it belongs to the stationmaster."

"It won't matter," said Holliday. "Geronimo sounded like it's the area that's protected, that it doesn't make any difference if you work there or are a customer—or his horse."

"And we can't just walk up and slap it," added Edison. "If we're not trying to kill it, my guess is that nothing will happen except that we'll spook the poor dumb creature. God damn, this is lucky! Thanks for calling us in on it, Doc!"

"What's so lucky about finding a place where bullets and cannonballs and fire don't work on wood, on people, on *anything*?" demanded Holliday as the horse began pulling the buckboard.

"Don't you see?" said Edison happily. "This is *magic*!"

"I know it's magic," replied Holliday. "So what?"

"The government brought me out here to see if I could find a way to combat the medicine men's magic, which is what has stopped us from expanding beyond the Mississippi," answered Edison. "Here's a kind of magic that William Tecumsah Sherman's entire army probably couldn't defeat or destroy. If I can find a way, we're that much closer to finding a way to combat *all* their magic."

"I never looked at it that way," admitted Holliday. "I suppose that's why you're the genius, and I'm the shootist."

Edison turned to Buntline. "There's no sense unpacking. We'll be back here tomorrow."

"Right," agreed Buntline.

"Just out of curiosity, why are we going to Tombstone?" asked Holliday, idly wondering if there was still a warrant out for his arrest.

"That's where my first factory is," said Buntline. "And once Tom figures out and designs what we need, I'll have to make it—and along with being better-stocked, Tombstone is a lot closer than Leadville."

"It's still operating?" asked Holliday.

"Why not?" replied Buntline. "After all, the government is paying for it, and I've got your friend Henry Wiggins overseeing it."

"Doc?" said Edison.

"Yes?"

"We're halfway out of the valley. See that prairie dog there?"

"I see him."

"Shoot him. Let's see how far this protection extends."

Holliday pulled his pistol and aimed it at the prairie dog without firing, while the little animal stared at him curiously.

"What's the matter?"

"I may know that particular animal," replied Holliday. "I want to give him time to warn me off." Finally, when no transformation took place, he squeezed the trigger. The prairie dog fell backward, jerked spasmodically once, and lay still.

"Okay, there's a limit," said Edison. "Good."

As they continued on their way out of the valley, Holliday looked at the body of the little animal that couldn't do him any harm, and realized that he felt worse about shooting it than about most of the men he had killed.

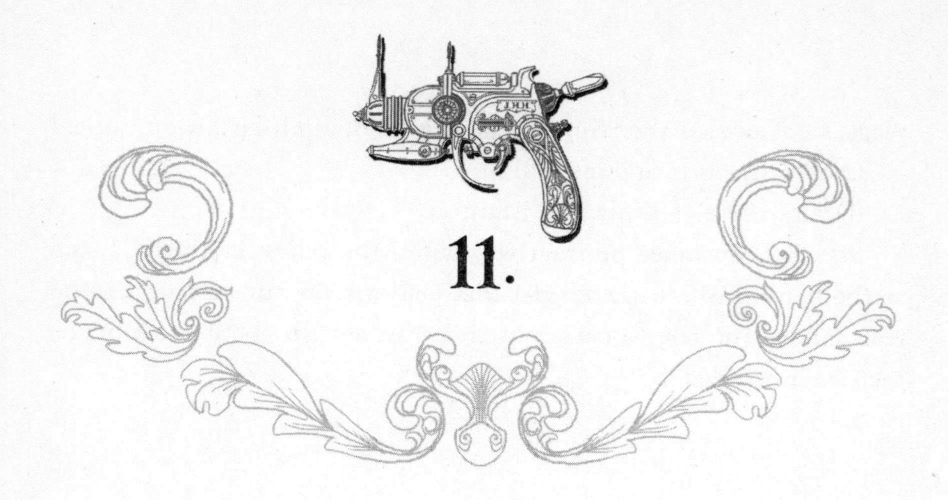

11.

"SO DID YOU TWO MEN of the world enjoy your talk?" asked Edison as he, Buntline, and Holliday climbed down from the train and walked the hundred feet to the terminus of the monorail. The station was new, clean, made of the super-hardened brass that was now omnipresent in Tombstone, and there was a bar and a restaurant in the interior.

Holliday smiled. "The poor kid slept just about all the way. He couldn't have gotten two winks on that rock-hard bench back at the station."

"I don't see him around," said Buntline.

"Probably still asleep," said Holliday. "I gave him a quarter to spend in the dining car. If he doesn't wake up before the train pulls out, it'll have to last him through to California." He looked around. "I don't think an innocent country boy like that could handle what Tombstone's become, anyway."

As he spoke, he gestured to a monorail with bullet-shaped brass cars that were just pulling up to the station.

"This was my pride and joy before we left for Colorado," remarked Buntline, staring lovingly at the brass cars. "Circles the whole city, and cuts across the middle, right in front of the Oriental Saloon."

"That place saw a lot of action when you and the Earps were here," added Edison at the mention of the Oriental. "I understand that it's just about empty these days."

The cars came to a stop and their tops popped open. "Climb in," said Buntline. "No sense walking. One to a car."

"You should have made them bigger," said Holliday, tossing his suitcase into a car.

Buntline shrugged. "A lot of people don't want to ride with strangers, especially out here. But everyone's willing to ride alone if the alternative is walking. Saves a lot of wasted space."

"Where are you staying?" asked Holliday.

"We have connected houses here, remember?" replied Buntline.

"Well, I can't stay at Kate's whorehouse any more," said Holliday. "She sold out when she left. I suppose I'll get a room at the American Hotel. Josie Marcus used to stay there before she married Wyatt; it seemed a nice enough place. At least their restaurant's got a well-stocked bar."

"Nonsense!" said Edison. "You'll stay with me, as my guest."

"I've got a nicer guest room," said Buntline. "And"—he leaned forward for the kill—"*indoor plumbing*!"

Holliday shook his head. "I appreciate the offers, but usually you're just waking up about the time I'm going to bed, and whiskey doesn't seem to be in abundance in either of your houses."

"Check in with us once a day," said Edison. "That way we'll know you're still alive, and you'll know when we're done."

They climbed into the coaches, the tops popped down, and they began to circle the entirety of Tombstone. Holliday had almost forgotten how totally Edison and Buntline had transformed it. There were street lights every ten yards, most of the buildings were made of Buntline's impervious brass. The self-propelled stagecoaches of the Bunt Line had made horses almost superfluous and only two were hitched along the street. More than one man had the brass handle of a specially made twin-barreled pistol peeking out above the top of its holster.

After a few minutes, the monorail turned up Fremont Street and shortly thereafter came to a dead stop, though there was no platform and the tops remained closed. Then Holliday looked out the window and saw a huge sign identifying the O.K. Corral, and half a dozen vendors selling souvenirs, everything from false badges and toy guns to dime novels by writers who swore they'd been eyewitnesses to the shootout.

"It wasn't even *at* the goddamned corral!" muttered Holliday to his window. "It was in the alley next to Fly's Photo Studio *near* the corral." He took a flask out of his vest pocket, unscrewed the top, and took a swig. "They turned the damned place into a shrine!" he growled as the monorail began moving again.

He got off a few minutes later, grabbed his suitcase, and walked to the American Hotel.

"Got a room?" he asked.

"We've always got one for you, Mr. Holliday," said the clerk obsequiously.

"Doc," Holliday corrected him.

"Will you be with us long, Doc?"

"I've no idea."

"Room 112," announced the clerk.

Holliday shook his head. "Nothing on the ground floor. If someone's going to stick his gun through my window and shoot me while I'm sleeping, I want him to at least have to climb a tree first."

The clerk checked the rack behind the front desk. "327."

Holliday shook his head again. "I'm a sick man who has limited physical resources. The second floor is more than enough climbing."

"210," said the clerk, making an effort to keep smiling.

"Fine," said Holliday. "Have someone take my bag up there. I'll get the key later."

"Uh . . . sir . . ." said the clerk uneasily.

"Doc."

"Doc," amended the clerk. "This is very awkward, but . . ."

"Spit it out," said Holliday.

"You are not without your enemies in this town. If someone calls for you or asks if you're in . . . ?"

"If it's Henry Wiggins, send him up or tell him where I am," said Holliday. "Same with Tom Edison and Ned Buntline. Anyone else," he continued, holding up a one-dollar gold piece, "you never heard of me."

"Yes, sir."

"Now I think I'll see if your restaurant's as good as I remember," said Holliday, tossing him the coin, then turning and walking across the lobby to the restaurant. He thought he spotted a familiar face, took a couple of steps toward it, and peered at it through all the cigar smoke.

"Doc?" said the object of his attention. "Is that you?"

"Hi, Henry," said Holliday, extending his hand and stepping forward.

"Well, I'll be damned!" said Henry Wiggins, a small, wiry man in a neatly tailored suit. "I never thought I'd see you back here again."

"And I thought you were going to be selling Tom and Ned's inventions and weapons and robots all over the frontier," replied Holliday.

"This is just temporary," said Wiggins as Holliday sat down at his table. "I'm no manager. I'm a salesman. But when your friends ask for a favor . . ." He paused and stared at Holliday. "Damn, it's good to see you again, Doc! What the hell are you doing here?"

"I came to town with your two employers."

"They're here too?"

"I'm sure you'll see them soon. Mind if I help you kill the bottle?" added Holliday, indicating a fifth of whiskey that sat on the table.

"Be my guest," said Wiggins. He pointed to the small "*HW*" scribbled on the label. "That's how they identify that it's mine. I'm not the kind of drinker you are. It takes me three or four nights to kill one of those bottles."

"That's because you dilute it with food," said Holliday, filling an empty glass. "How have things been since Wyatt and I left?"

"Johnny Behan's still a crook, and he's never forgiven Wyatt for taking Josie away from him. John Clum still uses the *Epitaph* to campaign for law and order. Most of the Cowboys are dead or gone. Most of the silver mines have been played out. To be honest, things are getting a little dull around here. Not," Wiggins added quickly, "that this town couldn't do with a little dullness."

"Nothing wrong with dull," agreed Holliday.

"Of course, it won't *stay* dull if Fin Clanton or a few others I could name learn you're back in town."

"Fin Clanton will live a lot longer if he stays right where he is. Has he learned how to walk again since I blew his knee away?"

"He doesn't leave the ranch, so I don't know," answered Wiggins. "I'll be damned if I know why he stays there. There's no profit any more in stealing horses from Mexico and selling them up here, not since Tom and Ned's machines have replaced most of the need for horses."

"Fin was always a slow learner," replied Holliday.

"You staying here at the American?"

"Yes, I am," said Holliday. "And you?"

"Too expensive for my taste. I save all my money to spend at the Wildcat."

"I'm not familiar with that name," said Holliday, draining his glass and pouring himself another. "Is it a gambling establishment or a tavern?"

"Neither," said Wiggins. Suddenly he smiled. "It's Kate's old place."

"Oh?"

Wiggins nodded. "Still got all the metal chippies, too. Along with some flesh-and-blood ones. And the new owner has redecorated it. There's all new beds, they serve good whiskey—well, if you know to ask for it—and they've even got red velvet wallpaper, just like they say is in all the top New Orleans bawdy houses."

"You know," said Holliday, "it's been awhile. Maybe I'll go over there with you."

"And with Kate in Colorado, you can finally sample one of the metal ladies," added Wiggins with a grin.

"The thought has crossed my mind," answered Holliday, returning his grin.

"Hell, we can go right now if you want, Doc."

Holliday shook his head. "Finish your dinner, and let me at least get started drinking mine. It's been there for three years; it'll be there for anther hour or two."

Wiggins ate, and Holliday drank, and they talked about the past few years. Holliday was surprised at how well his friend had adapted to life on the frontier. Wiggins, for his part, hadn't believed Holliday could become any more gaunt and remain alive until he saw him. He noticed that the shootist's hair was rapidly turning gray, despite being in his early thirties, and marveled at the life force within the emaciated body.

Finally they finished and made their way over to Fifth Street.

"As often as I've been here," remarked Wiggins, "I can never get used to all the lights going on at once. We had gas lights back in St. Louis and a couple of other towns I've lived in, but we always had to light them one by one, and put them out the same way. But here Johnny Behan just throws a switch, and suddenly the whole town is lit up."

"I'm glad he does *something* for his pay," was Holliday's only comment.

They were within sight of the Wildcat in another couple of minutes, and could hear the noise and the laughter when they got to within one hundred feet of it.

"Sounds like everyone's having a good time," remarked Wiggins.

"Why shouldn't they?" replied Holliday, striding forward and wishing he'd brought his cane with him.

Suddenly a single gunshot rang out, and both men froze.

"It came from inside," noted Wiggins.

"Must have done its job," remarked Holliday. "No one's shooting back."

"Maybe it was just one of the men feeling happy," said Wiggins hopefully. "Place like this tends to give you high spirits."

"Maybe," said Holliday noncommittally.

They climbed the three steps to the broad veranda. Wiggins seemed hesitant to enter, so Holliday opened the door and walked in. He was greeted by a pair of gleaming robotic whores, who each took him gently by an arm and led him in.

"Welcome to the Wildcat," said a totally human woman, walking up to him. "My name is Dorcas, May I show you around?"

"It's not necessary," replied Holliday. "I've *been* around."

She stared at him with a puzzled frown. "I don't remember you, sir."

"You may very well live longer that way," said Holliday.

"You don't know him?" said a familiar voice from across the room. "Why, that's the world-famous Doc Holliday!"

Holliday turned and saw his traveling companion from the train ride to Tombstone sitting on a chair with a number of human, cyborg and robotic whores behind him, stroking his arms and neck.

"Henry?" said Holliday. "Henry Antrim?"

"Hi, Doc," said the young man pleasantly. "I guess you figured to turn up here sooner or later."

"I thought you were too broke to eat," said Holliday.

A quick smile. "Who's eating?"

"Well, enjoy yourself," said Holliday.

"You too, Doc."

Holliday held out his hand, palm up.

"What's that supposed to mean?" asked Antrim.

"I want my quarter back."

"Sorry, Doc, but I already spent it, and a lot more, on these lovely ladies."

"I'll expect it tomorrow, Henry," said Holliday.

"I'm afraid you're doomed to be disappointed," said Antrim. "And I've got to tell you something, Doc."

"Oh?"

"My name's not really Henry Antrim. At least, not all the time. And I'm not broke, and I'm not shy. I was just having a little fun with you."

"And what *is* your name?" said Holliday, tensing.

"Oh, I got a lot of 'em. Henry McCarty's one. So's William

Bonney." A huge grin spread across his face. "You can guess the other one."

"I suppose I can," said Holliday.

"Doc, together you and I can *own* this town," said the Kid. "We split everything down the middle, including these chippies. What do you say?"

"What do I say?" replied Holliday. "I say keep the quarter."

The Kid frowned. "What are you talking about?"

"It'll be a down payment for your coffin," said Holliday, drawing his gun. He fired four quick shots, two between the Kid's eyes, two into his chest, as the whores screamed and dove for cover.

"You know, he never out-and-out said it, but I *thought* Woo-Ka-Nay was watching over me," said the Kid with an amused smile when the smoke from Holliday's barrel has dissipated. "After something like that, I think we'll have to make it a sixty–forty split in my favor. Or," he added, leisurely pulling his own gun and aiming at Holliday's heart, "maybe I'll just keep one hundred percent instead."

He squeezed the trigger.

The sound of the explosion was deafening.

12.

"NOT A MARK," said Edison, frowning as he examined Holliday's chest. "Not even a scratch."

"Did you feel it hit?" asked Buntline.

Holliday shook his head. "As skinny as I am, even if the damned thing bounced off me it would have sent me flying back against the wall."

He was standing in Edison's lab, his jacket, vest, and shirt off, his pale, undernourished torso being scrutinized by the inventor and the manufacturer. There was an old, scarred desk, a worktable that had been stained by chemicals and seared by electricity, two chairs, and books everywhere—in cases, on window ledges, and piled up against the wall. The floor was littered with discarded notes.

"Did it ricochet?" asked Edison.

"I can't imagine it did," replied Holliday. "They had quite a crowd there. It would have hit *someone*."

"And nothing bounced off the Kid either?"

"No. He just kind of . . . I don't know . . . *absorbed* it."

"Okay, you can put your shirt and coat back on," said Edison.

Buntline pressed a button on Edison's desk. "Bessie, bring us three beers."

"Bessie?" asked Holliday.

"One of the robotic prostitutes I made for your ladyfriend a year ago," explained Buntline. "When you and Kate left town, I took her back and reprogrammed her—well, *it*, really—as a maid."

"This is a *really* interesting problem," said Edison.

"I'm invulnerable," said Holliday. "There's got to be a way to use that to our advantage."

"You think so?"

"Absolutely."

"Come over here and stick your hand out."

Holliday did as he was asked. Edison picked up a pin from his lab table, held Holliday's hand steady, and jabbed the pin into it.

"*Damn!*" growled Holliday, surprised. "That *hurt!*"

"I guess you're not invulnerable after all," said Edison with a smile.

"You *knew* that would hurt, even though the Kid's bullets bounced right off me," said Holliday.

"I had a feeling," said Edison. "And his bullets *didn't* bounce off you. Or go through you. Or flatten out against you. They just vanished."

"What am I missing, Tom?" asked Buntline. "How did you figure out that you can break his skin and hurt him?"

"Just put your mind to work, Ned," said Edison. "Why are we here at all? Only because Doc can't make a dent in that station back in New Mexico. It's immune to bullets, cannonballs, fire, and probably everything else anyone can throw at it. Again why? Because it's protected by a medicine man—and given the level of protection, it's a fair guess that Hook Nose is behind it. As far as we know, only he and Geronimo wield that kind of power."

"I know that," said Buntline. "But how did that lead you to guess that you could jab his finger and break the skin, when the Kid's bullets couldn't do that?"

Edison turned to Holliday. "Doc, why did you agree to destroy the station?"

"Because the Kid is protected by some medicine man," answered Holliday. "And Geronimo wouldn't make it possible for me to meet the Kid on even terms until I did him this service. A favor for a favor, so to speak."

"Well?" said Edison.

"I still don't see it," said Buntline.

"*Think*, Ned!" said Edison, as Bessie the robot, wearing a shapeless garment over her exotic if metallic curves, delivered the beers on a tray and immediately returned to Buntline's house through the fortified walkway between the two buildings. "The Kid is protected by Hook Nose, or someone with Hook Nose's kind of power. Geronimo wants Doc to destroy a railway station that's protected from him but not necessarily from Doc. He knew the Kid was in the vicinity, and with his powers he had to know the Kid would go to Tombstone when the three of us did. Now, protected or not, the Kid is one hell of a killer, everyone knows that. And it was very likely Doc would confront him sooner or later. I mean, hell, Geronimo *had* to know they rode out here together." He paused and smiled. "Do you see it now?"

"He's protected by Geronimo," said Buntline, frowning. "But that's obvious. It doesn't explain why you could hurt him with a pin."

Edison's smile grew broader. "Because I'm not Billy the Kid."

"Damn it, I'm not following it any better than Ned is!" said Holliday in frustrated tones.

"Think it through, Doc," said Edison. "You're here because you can't destroy the train station until we come up with a methodology.

All the warrants against you have been quashed, you were found not guilty of the charges stemming from the O.K. Corral, the Cowboys are dead or dispersed, the only man with a grudge against you is Fin Clanton, who's crippled and never leaves his ranch . . . so what could possibly harm or threaten you in Tombstone? Only the Kid."

Holliday and Buntline stared at Edison, still uncomprehending.

"Doc, you're not fighting for the glory of the Apaches any more than the Kid is in the service of the Southern Cheyenne," continued Edison. "There is a *reason* why you're protected, and that's because Geronimo can't destroy the station and he needs you—or *us*. But he's only protecting you against Hook Nose's magic, which means against the Kid, who is, for reasons we don't know yet, Hook Nose's client. If he protects you against *everything*, why should you ever do him the service that he wants of you, and how can he get rid of you if you break your bargain?"

"He can just take the spell or curse or whatever it is off," said Holliday.

"No, he can't."

"How do you know?" demanded Holliday.

"Empiricism," answered Edison.

"What are you talking about?"

"If I'm wrong, you'd be protected against anything, not just Hook Nose's magic. But then I couldn't have pricked your finger with the pin. The mere fact that I could do it would seem to prove that I'm right. Which means," he added with a smile, "if you're going to get into a gunfight with anyone but the Kid, make sure you shoot first."

"Then fuck Geronimo!" said Holliday. "He's trading a dead horse for a live one. He wants me to destroy the station that's on his burial ground, but he's supposed give me an even chance against the Kid, and making it impossible for either of us to kill the other is a bullshit way to go about it. I need the reward money, not a harmless draw. So to hell with his goddamned station!"

Edison sighed deeply and shook his head. "You're not thinking it through, Doc."

"What am I missing?"

"You *have* to destroy the station, if we can come up with a way for you to do it. Because the second he decides you're not going to do it, he doesn't have to protect you from the Kid any longer. And I don't think you want to go up against him when he can't be harmed and you can."

"Shit!" muttered Holliday. "I hadn't considered that."

"So I guess we're back to figuring out how to destroy the station," said Buntline. "Nothing's changed."

"Something's changed," Edison corrected him.

"Oh? What?"

"We don't know if the Kid is protected against everyone, or just Doc. Given that the protection was afforded before Doc got to New Mexico, I'd guess everyone. And we know Doc is protected only against the Kid." He turned to Holliday. "It means if the Kid takes a dislike to you, all he has to do is pay some confederates to backshoot you."

"This is getting very complicated," growled Holliday. "I liked it better when all I had to do was come south, find him, and shoot him."

"There's something further to consider," said Edison.

"*More?*" demanded Holliday.

"I don't know what kind of deal, if any, the Kid has made with Hook Nose in exchange for his protection," said Edison. "But it could be that Ned and I are at risk, since Hook Nose knows who we are and has doubtless figured out why we were inspecting the station."

"I doubt it," said Holliday. "He had plenty of opportunity to kill you on the train."

"Let's hope you're right, because if I'm correct and the Kid's invulnerable to *everything*, there's no way we can stop him."

"He can't have been this way for long," said Buntline. "I mean, hell, he was in jail just a few months ago."

"That figures," said Holliday. "Hook Nose and Geronimo were partners a year ago."

"Well," said Edison with a shrug, "we can't worry about it. We'll just have to keep working until we can come up with a solution."

"I just wish we'd been able to break off a board, a window, *some* part of the damned station so we'd have something to work with—or on," said Buntline.

"If we could have broken it off, we wouldn't be back here in our labs trying to figure out how to destroy it," said Edison logically.

"One thought has occurred," said Buntline, "but I don't think Geronimo will permit it."

"Oh? And what was that?"

"The Brass Mole, that we use to dig down in the silver mines. We could dig under the station and tracks and sink them into the earth and out of sight. But," added Buntline with a grimace, "that might constitute our damaging consecrated ground. I mean, that is the reason he wants the station gone."

"It would work, no question about it." He turned to Holliday. "I don't suppose you could ask him?"

"*He* contacts *me*. I've no idea how to get hold of *him*."

"Isn't he located half a day's ride south of here?"

Holliday shook his head. "He was, a little over a year ago. But it didn't look like a permanent camp then, and I'm sure it hasn't become one. Hell, he *owns* the Arizona territory; he can set up shop anywhere he wants. We're here on sufferance. If the Indians ever find any use for silver or cattle, they'll push us back to the other side of the Mississippi."

"Until Tom finds a way to counteract their magic," added Buntline.

"*Unless*, not until," Edison corrected him.

Holliday walked to the door. "Thanks for the beer. No thanks for the explanation; I was a lot happier a few hours ago."

"Yeah, truth can do that to you," said Edison with a grim smile. "You off to gamble now?"

"If I could afford to gamble, I wouldn't have turned bounty hunter," answered Holliday.

"Have a good night's sleep," said Buntline.

"I'm not going to sleep."

"And you're not gambling. Going back to the Wildcat, then?"

Holliday shrugged. "It all depends."

"On what?"

"I'm off to find Mr. McCarty-Bonney-Antrim-whoever," replied Holliday. "What better time to study the face of mine enemy than when neither of us can do the other any harm?"

And with that, he walked out into the warm Arizona night.

13.

HOLLIDAY STOPPED BY THE WILDCAT, and when there was no sign of the Kid, he went over to the Oriental Saloon, which had been the Earps' property until Wyatt and Virgil left town. It still felt like home to him. He walked through the swinging doors and looked around, half-expecting to see Wyatt or Morgan sitting at a table, or perhaps Ike Clanton, or one of the McLaury brothers, or Curly Bill Brocius standing at the bar. He smiled ironically as he remembered that of them all, only Wyatt was still alive, a mere year after he'd last set foot in the place.

He nodded to the bartender, whom he didn't recognize, paid for a bottle and a glass, wandered over to an empty table, sat down, filled the glass, and pulled a deck of cards out of his pocket. He began playing solitaire, sipping his drink, studying each man who entered the place, very aware of the fact that he was invulnerable only to the Kid's bullets. He idly wondered how he'd do against the shorter Kid in a fistfight. Suddenly his body was wracked by a coughing seizure, he placed a handkerchief to his mouth, and when he had finished ninety seconds later the handkerchief was soaked with blood, as usual, and he admitted to himself that he probably couldn't beat a ten-year-old in a fistfight.

He was on his third game of solitaire, and his second glass of whiskey, when a voice said, "Black ten on the red queen." He'd been concentrating so hard on the game that he'd lost track of his surroundings, and the comings and goings of the clientele. He looked up and found himself facing the Kid, who stood across the table from him.

"Black tens go on red jacks, not queens," replied Holliday.

"You're Doc Holliday and I'm Billy the Kid," came the answer. "Who can tell *us* where they go?"

"Can't argue with that," said Holliday pleasantly.

"But you still haven't moved it."

"To quote the most famous desperado in the West, I'm Doc Holliday," said Holliday with a smile. "Who can tell *me* how to play?"

The Kid threw back his head and laughed. "Damn! I liked you from the start, Doc!" Then: "I *can* call you Doc, can't I?"

Holliday shrugged. "It's my name." Another smile. "My *only* one. You seem to be collecting them."

"The other names were my real one and my stepfather's and a bunch of aliases I had to dream up on short notice. But Billy the Kid is *me*." He grinned. "At least until I'm a few years older."

"How old *are* you?"

"Twenty-one."

"Well, you've had an interesting start," said Holliday. "If you're as good as they say, you might make it all the way to thirty. Now stop looming over me and have a seat."

"Why thirty?" asked the Kid as he sat down opposite Holliday.

"That seems to be the expiration date for shootists."

"How old are you?"

"Thirty-two."

"Then you were wrong."

Holliday shook his head. "You're the desperado. Me, I'm just a dentist with a cough."

The Kid laughed again. "How many men have you killed, Doc?"

"Less than you've heard, I'm sure."

"Forty? Fifty?"

"Now you're in John Wesley Hardin territory,"

"How many, then?"

"A lot less," said Holliday. "And I never killed anyone who didn't deserve it."

"Neither did I," replied the Kid. "In fact, I never killed anyone who wasn't trying to kill me."

"Including the deputies who were taking you to court?"

The Kid flashed him a quick abashed smile. "Well, *almost* anyone."

"What the hell brought you out here in the first place?" asked Holliday. "I understand you're from New York City. That's a mighty long distance to travel."

"I don't remember a damned thing about New York," answered the Kid. "We moved to Kansas when I was three or four. Then my dad died, and the guy my mother married next moved us to New Mexico."

"Good for longevity," said Holliday. "They'd never let you kill so many men in New York."

"They don't *let* me," said the Kid irritably. "I just *do* it." He frowned suddenly and shook his head. "That sounds wrong. I'm not an assassin or a madman. Hell, I never killed anyone until I was fifteen, and close to half the men I killed were in the Lincoln County War."

"I heard about that," said Holliday. "They say it got pretty vicious. They also say you were absolutely fearless, and a damned good shot."

"Not as good as I should have been—or at least not as smart," said the Kid. "I killed a sheriff and his deputy." Then he shrugged. "It was their own fault for interfering in the War."

"Don't be modest," continued Holliday. "Most of our notorious shootists are lucky, not accurate. The only ones I'd trust to hit what they were aiming at would be Wild Bill Hickok, John Wesley Hardin, and Johnny Ringo. Of the three, two died young and one's in jail."

"You mean the only ones besides you and me," the Kid corrected him.

"We shot each other at point-blank range last night," noted Holliday. "Are you dead? Wounded? Scratched?"

"We're both protected by our medicine men," said the Kid. "You know that." He paused. "Or anyway, you know it now. So do I."

"But you didn't know it when you fired at me," said Holliday.

"I suspected it. Remember: you fired first, and nothing happened."

"Who's your sponsor, if I may use the word?" asked Holliday. "I suspect that it's Hook Nose."

The Kid shook his head. "Some old geezer named Woo-Ka-Nay."

"That *is* Hook Nose," said Holliday. "Medicine man of the Southern Cheyenne. They say he and Geronimo of the Apaches are the two most powerful medicine men around. I've seen some of what they can do."

"Geronimo," repeated the Kid. "I thought he was their war chief."

"No, he's a hell of a warrior, but his official job is medicine man. Their best war chief is Vittorio, though if he could do it full-time I'd wager Geronimo would be just as good, maybe even better."

"Well, you live and learn," said the Kid. "What does Geronimo want from you? He must want *something* to make bullets bounce off you."

"They don't bounce off; they vanish. Check your clothing. There are no holes."

The Kid shrugged. "Whatever."

"He wants me to do a favor for him."

"Something he can't do himself, no doubt?"

Holliday nodded. "Yes."

"And he's paying you by making you *in* . . . *inv* . . . what the hell's the word?"

"Invulnerable."

"Big goddamned word. So is that the deal?"

Holliday looked at the Kid for a long minute. *You haven't figured it out yet, have you?* Finally he spoke: "Yes, that's it." Then: "How about you?"

"Seriously?" said the Kid. "I think he just wants me to kill more white men."

"Nothing more explicit?"

"What's 'explicit'?"

"Exact," said Holliday, certain the Kid wouldn't know "precise."

"Not that I know of," replied the Kid. "It's a fair enough deal. I'm in the cattle trade these days."

"Stealing cattle?"

"Do I look like a farmer?" said the Kid with a laugh. "Anyway, my line of work gets dangerous from time to time, and I think he's protecting me so I can keep killing white men—and especially white lawmen." Suddenly his boyish expression darkened. "And I've got one at the top of my list right now. It'll be the only time I've ever gone out hunting for someone; usually they call *me* out, or come after me when I'm working, either as a soldier or a cowboy."

"Soldier." "Cowboy." I love the way you rationalize, even though you have no idea what rationalize means. "Who's the man you're after?" Holliday asked aloud, more to be polite than out of any serious curiosity, since he knew almost no one in New Mexico.

"A man I used to ride with," said the Kid. "Then he became a lawman. I trusted the bastard, and he arrested me. I could have killed him when he approached me, and because I thought he was my friend I didn't." His face clouded over. "I won't make *that* mistake again, you can bet your ass on it."

"Has he got a name?"

"Pat Garrett," said the Kid. "*Sheriff* Pat Garrett," he added contemptuously.

"I'd heard, or maybe read, that Lew Wallace pardoned you," said Holliday.

"The governor?" said the Kid. "Yeah, he did, provided I give him evidence on some other killers. Since I didn't ride with them, I gave it."

"So if you were pardoned, why did this Garrett arrest you?" asked Holliday.

"I shot a few more lawmen," said the Kid nonchalantly. "A couple of reporters were in court when I got sentenced. Didn't you read about it?"

"That you were sentenced?"

"What I said *when* I was sentenced."

"I must have missed it," said Holliday.

"The judge said to me, 'William Bonney, you are sentenced to be hanged by the neck until you are dead, dead, dead!'" The Kid grinned. "And I said, 'Judge, you can go to hell, hell, hell!'"

"Sounds like an interesting, if redundant, conversation," remarked Holliday.

"Didn't you ever talk back to a judge when you were sentenced?"

"I know it's going to come as a shock and a profound disappointment to you, but I've never been convicted of anything."

"You just love them big words, don't you?" said the Kid, not without a touch of admiration. "I'll bet you've had a lot of schooling."

"I'm a doctor. Well, a dentist."

"I envy that kind of book-learning," admitted the Kid. "I know they write me up in the dime novels, but I can barely wade through the first page before I give it up." He frowned. "And I'm never *on* the first page!"

"We all have to live with disappointment," said Holliday. "At least you live to the end of the story."

"Other people read 'em and tell me about 'em," said the Kid. "Some bastard wrote one last month that has Garrett calling me out and shooting me down in the street at high noon." He frowned. "I think I'll kill both the writer *and* Garrett for that."

"I'm sure Woo-Ka-Nay will be thrilled," said Holliday dryly.

"So who are you here to kill?" asked the Kid, signaling to the bartender for another glass. "I hope you don't mind if I share your poison?"

"Not at all," said Holliday, filling his glass when it arrived. "As for why I'm here, I lived here for more than a year."

"Yeah, everyone's heard about the Gunflight." The Kid leaned forward. "Was it as bloody as they say?"

"Nine people showed up. Three died, two ran away, three were wounded."

"And Wyatt Earp got off Scott-free!" said the Kid. "I heard that." He paused. "Were all nine of you really in that little alley?"

Holliday nodded. "According to the *Tombstone Epitaph*, which measured the place, the farthest any of us could be from the men on the other side was nineteen feet."

"Sounds crowded."

"It was," answered Holliday. "One of the McLaurys even had his horse there."

"I wish I'd been there," said the Kid wistfully. "They'll be talking about that shootout a century from now."

"I doubt it," said Holliday. "The whole thing was over in half a minute, tops, and there was so much smoke from the gun barrels that you couldn't see half of what was happening anyway."

"Still, ain't no one ever gonna remember the Lincoln County War."

"Sure they will," said Holliday. "It was a war, it's got Lincoln's name, and the notorious Billy the Kid fought in it. What more does it need?"

"You really think so?" said the Kid eagerly.

"I really do."

"I *like* you, Doc Holliday!" said the Kid, draining his glass. "I think we're going to be great friends."

"Might as well be," said Holliday. "After all, we can't shoot each other even if we want to."

And I've got to get Tom working on that.

"Let's finish the bottle and then go straighten our backs at the Wildcat," suggested the Kid.

"I don't know if they'll let us in after last night," said Holliday with a smile. "We frightened away half their clientele."

"Who's going to stop us?" said the Kid.

"A telling point," agreed Holliday, finishing the whiskey and getting to his feet.

"I'll tell you true, Doc," said the Kid, also rising. "I'm sure glad I can't kill you."

"Me, too," said Holliday, swaying just a little as a wave of dizziness passed over him. He coughed into his bloody handkerchief.

But I'm going to have to find a way to kill you, *and before too much longer, or I'll be too damned weak to make it back to Leadville.*

14.

HOLLIDAY WALKED DOWN THE DIRT STREET past all the empty hitching posts. *Ned adds a few more carriages to the Bunt Line and they might as well get rid of these damned hitching posts*, thought Holliday. *Hell, they might even pave the streets.*

He turned a corner and saw Edison's and Buntline's houses. From the outside, they appeared to be normal residences. Only the brass-enclosed connecting passage between the two gave any indication that they weren't what they seemed to be, but Holliday knew from previous demonstrations that these were the best-protected buildings in Cochise County.

He approached Edison's house. Before he could knock on the door, the security system had identified him and the brass portal swung inward.

"Hello, Doc," said Edison's voice. "I'm in the lab."

Holliday made his way through the foyer and the book-lined corridor to the laboratory, which was almost devoid of chemicals and test tubes but abounded in electrical and brass devices. "Making any progress?" he asked.

"I wish I knew," said Edison.

"You're Thomas Alva Edison," replied Holliday. "How can you *not* know?"

"It's not that simple, Doc," said Edison, looking up from his notepad, where he had been furiously scribbling. "I may be close to the solution, I may be on the wrong track. It's impossible to know for sure until I test it out. For example, we know the Brass Mole can bore through three thousand feet of rock . . . but I don't know if it can move an eighth of an inch into the station." He held up a strange-looking device that was shaped like a cylinder with a button at one end and a tiny hole at the other. "I can melt anything short of Ned's super-hardened brass with this, and I suppose if I kept it trained on the brass I might even make a dent in it before the battery wore down. But I don't know if it can make that same dent in the station, or the track, or even the people who are waiting for the train, if you and Geronimo are right that they're all protected."

"Maybe there's a way to kill two birds with one stone, to borrow an expression I heard up in Denver," said Holliday.

"I'm open to suggestions."

"I'm sure I can get the Kid to come over here to meet the great Edison. Once he's here, let's see if you've got anything that can kill him."

"And if the first attempt fails, you think he'll just sit still for the next?"

"Absolutely," said Holliday.

Edison stared at him. "That doesn't make any sense, Doc."

"He knows he can't be hurt. Once you prove that even *you* can't hurt him, what has he got to fear from staying?"

"First, he'll probably kill us," said Edison. "Well, *me*, anyway. I forgot: he can't kill you. And more importantly, even if I can hurt him, even kill him, that won't prove a thing."

"The hell it won't," said Holliday. "If you can kill him, you can destroy the station."

"Why?"

"They're both protected by Hook Nose. If you can break through his magic on the Kid, you can break through it on the train station."

"But *are* they both protected by Hook Nose?" asked Edison. "You told me Geronimo didn't know who was protecting the train station. It might be Hook Nose, it might not. If it's a different medicine man, it's probably a different magical spell."

Holliday frowned as he considered what the inventor had said. "I hadn't thought it through," he admitted. "But if we can kill the Kid, then I don't *have* to destroy the station. I can take the reward and go back to Colorado."

"Geronimo didn't have any trouble finding you there before," noted Edison. "I don't think he'd have any trouble this time—and if we can kill the Kid and we leave the station alone, I think he'll make certain that you don't die fast, or peacefully, or in a sanitarium."

"Shit!" spat Holliday. "I thought I had something there."

"A man who can hold the United States at bay on the other side of the Mississippi River doesn't ask for easy favors," replied Edison.

"When you put it that way, I realize the full magnitude of what he's asking," said Holliday. "*Can* it be done?"

"All problems are capable of solution," said Edison. "Some just take longer."

"*All* problems?" repeated Holliday dubiously.

"*All* problems," said Edison emphatically. "I know it's hard to believe, but someday we're going to reach the Moon, and the planets, and even the stars. We're going to replace old, diseased, used-up organs like the heart and the lungs with new ones." He peered wistfully into the future. "We'll eradicate every disease. We'll even create machines that think." He blinked his eyes rapidly and brought himself back to the present. "So of course we'll figure out how to counteract the spell and destroy the station, and we'll do it without trying—probably unsuccessfully—to kill the Kid."

Holliday shrugged. "You're the genius. I'm just a card-playing dentist."

Ned Buntline wandered over through the enclosed passageway between the two houses, crossed through an unused bedroom that stored more books and equipment, and entered the lab.

"Hi, Doc," he said. "I thought I saw you come in." He turned to Edison, "I've been playing around with that compound I mentioned. It may have some promise. At least, it'll make a hell of a big bang."

"Keep at it if you want," said Edison, "but I just don't think a stronger explosive is the answer. Don't forget: cannonballs didn't make a dent in the place." He shook his head. "I'm convinced the way to break through that spell is with something Hook Nose, or whoever cast it, has never encountered before."

"No one's ever seen an explosion like this one," said Buntline. "In theory, anyway."

"The order of magnitude may differ, but he's seen explosions, and if the place is protected against small ones, it'll be protected against big ones—or at least it figures to be."

"What do you have in mind?" asked Buntline.

"I'm not quite sure," answered Edison. "But I'll bet he's never encountered an electric charge before."

"Where do you apply it?" asked Holliday. "If the body of the spell is half a mile in each direction, where's the heart?"

"I don't know," said Edison. "Yet." He grimaced. "First I have to come up with a weapon, something that's not only beyond Hook Nose's experience, but also totally beyond his ability to imagine and prepare for. *Then* we'll worry about where to apply it." He paused thoughtfully. "*Weapon* is the wrong word. What I need, what *we* need, is a *device*."

"Comes to the same thing in the end," said Holliday.

"Not so," insisted Edison. "If I do it right, the device won't harm anyone. All we want to do is counteract the spell that's made the station impregnable."

Suddenly Holliday grinned.

"What is it?" asked Buntline.

"A new word for the Kid," replied Holliday. "Just about the time he learns 'invulnerable' I'll hit him with 'impregnable.'"

"That's a rather infantile joy," commented Buntline.

"I can't hurt him, he can't hurt me," said Holliday. "I'll take my triumphs where I can."

"What's he like?" asked Buntline.

Holliday shrugged. "He's a nice enough kid, I suppose."

"For a crazed killer," added Edison.

"I've rubbed shoulders with crazed killers," replied Holliday. "He's not like them."

"He's got more of a reputation than any of them, and he's barely old enough to shave," said Buntline.

"He's good at his trade," said Holliday. "I don't know what got him started. I suppose I'll ask him one of these days. Doesn't make any difference, though. I'm here to kill him, so I'll be just as happy if I don't find myself liking him too much."

"It didn't stop you from killing Johnny Ringo," noted Buntline.

"Ringo was out to kill me. The Kid isn't."

"I seem to remember you saying that it was inevitable that you and Ringo would face off, that you both sought the highest level of competition," said Edison. "Doesn't the Kid qualify as the highest level too?"

"Circumstances have changed," said Holliday. "With Ringo it was the competition. He was the Clantons' enforcer, I was the Earps'. But the only reason I want to kill the Kid is so I can die in comfort in a Colorado sanitarium." He paused and smiled wryly. "It's actually not a bad situation to be in. If I win, I get the best medical care available for what remains of my life, and if I lose, I'll be dead two seconds later and at least I won't have to cough myself to death in total poverty."

"And you find that a cheerful situation?" asked Edison, frowning.

"I wouldn't call it cheerful, but there are worse."

"Remember what I told you a few minutes ago?" said Edison. "Eventually they'll cure every disease, including consumption."

"I don't doubt you," said Holliday. "But no one's going to cure it in time to save me."

Edison stared at him for a long moment. "No, almost certainly not," he agreed.

"You know," continued Holliday, "this conversation has given me an idea."

"Oh?"

"Whatever the hell device you create, you're going to need someone to carry it to the station before activating it. And if it works, you can be sure Hook Nose is going to be mightily pissed off. He'll almost certainly take his anger out on the guy with the device. You and Ned are too important to lose, and there's every chance Geronimo will protect me, not out of any love for me but just to get even with Hook Nose for screwing up the Apache burial ground. So," he concluded, "I'm the one who should take the device to the station."

"We're ahead of you, Doc," said Edison.

"We are?" asked Buntline, surprised.

Edison nodded. "We've got the perfect conduit for the device. And if Hook Nose goes on a rampage, no one gets hurt."

"Oh?"

"She even knows she's expendable, and it won't bother her a bit." He pressed another button, and a moment later a large-breasted narrow-waisted gleaming brass woman entered the room.

"Bessie!" said Buntline and Holliday together.

"Sirs?" asked Bessie.

"It has to be more useful than bedding cowboys or making our dinner, wouldn't you agree?" said Edison.

"It occurs to me," said Holliday, "that there's a lot more to being a genius than I thought."

15.

HOLLIDAY SPENT A BAD NIGHT, half-drunk, half-sick, coughing up blood every few minutes. He was almost glad when the sunlight came through his window at the American Hotel. He couldn't feel much worse and still be alive, so he had to start feeling better.

Halfway through the night he'd made up his mind to return to Lincoln, that, with no money to gamble at the Oriental, he was just wasting his time here. By the time another hour had passed he had decided to stay in Tombstone. After all, he couldn't gamble in Lincoln either. He didn't know anyone there, and this way he could at least check on Edison's and Buntline's progress every day. Also, he actually had another friend here in Henry Wiggins, and he'd be able to spend some time with the Kid and probe for weaknesses.

Of course, all of that presupposed that he would have the strength to climb out of bed, which was by no means a certainty or even a probability until he did it. Finally it was a need to pass what remained of the whiskey he'd drunk the previous night that got him out of bed and onto his feet. The American had two large privies on each floor, one for men, one for women, and by the time he returned to his room he was ready to face the day.

He ran his hand over his cheek, decided he needed a shave, realized he was hungry, and put the trip to the barber off until he'd stopped by the restaurant and had some breakfast.

He picked up his cane—he'd done without it since arriving in Tombstone, but he knew he'd need it today—and made his way down the stairs and through the lobby to the restaurant. He sat down at a table, read the menu, realized that the thought of food, which was so vital to him not two minutes ago, made him sick, and ordered a bottle of whiskey instead. When it arrived he took one look at it, felt queasy, and moved it as far away as he could reach.

"For me?" said a voice. "How thoughtful."

He looked up and saw the Kid approaching his table.

"I saw you through the window as I was walking by," said the Kid, sitting down across from him. "You look like hell warmed over."

"I wish I felt that good," muttered Holliday.

"It's a little early in the day for me," said the Kid, opening the bottle and pouring an inch into the glass, "but what the hell."

A waiter noticed him and brought a second glass to the table.

"Are you sure I can't bring you anything to eat, Doctor Holliday?"

"Doc," said Holliday irritably.

The waiter turned to the new arrival. "And you, sir?"

"Cook up half a dozen eggs," said the Kid. "I'll eat what he doesn't."

"How do you want them?"

"Fast and without questions."

The waiter looked at him, nodded, and rapidly retreated to the kitchen.

"So what have you been doing with yourself?" asked the Kid.

"Drinking, coughing, sleeping, not much else," replied Holliday. "How about you?"

"Mostly I've been admiring all the things your pals have done to the town. Electric lights at night, stagecoaches with no horses, and all that brass!"

"Yeah, they've pretty much remade it," agreed Holliday.

"And the metal whores are the best part of it!" enthused the Kid. "You know," he said confidentially, "I know a whore's probably heard and tried everything, but there are things I was always too shy to suggest to one. But not to a machine! I've been having the time of my life at the Wildcat!"

"I'm very happy for you," said Holliday, wishing the room would stop spinning.

"They tell me you used to actually live there," continued the Kid. "Is that so?"

"Yes."

"Did you ever make it with three of the metal whores at once?"

"I never even made it with one."

The Kid looked his disbelief. "Why not?"

"Did anyone tell you *why* I lived there?"

"Something to do with the madam."

Holliday nodded delicately. "Kate Elder."

"Big-Nose Kate. I've heard of her. They say she broke you out of jail."

"Once, a few years ago," said Holliday. "She felt that put me under an obligation of fidelity to her."

The Kid made a face. "Big words again."

"She felt that if she was willing to bust me out of jail, I shouldn't touch another woman—even a metal one." He shrugged. "So I didn't."

"But you're Doc Holliday!" said the Kid.

"And she's Kate Elder. She could probably beat the shit out of both of us at the same time."

"A woman?" snorted the Kid contemptuously.

"Not a lot of frail flowers bloom in Tombstone," said Holliday.

"I'm sure glad I didn't choose you for my hero when I was a kid."

"You're still a kid," replied Holliday. "Just out of curiosity, who *was* your hero?"

"George Armstrong Custer."

"Seems to me he ran into some difficulties at the Little Bighorn a few years back."

"He went out with his guns blazing," said the Kid.

"You know that for a fact, do you?" asked Holliday.

"Of course he did," said the Kid heatedly. "The Sioux don't take no prisoners." He stared across the table at Holliday. "Who was *your* hero?"

"Hippocrates."

"Is that a person, or an animal that lives in the water?" asked the Kid with a smug, self-satisfied grin.

"Fella from Europe," replied Holliday. "And before you ask, he wasn't much with a gun."

"Don't sound like much of a hero to me."

At least he didn't blunder into Sioux headquarters, thought Holliday. Aloud he said, "How long are you planning to stay in town?"

"I don't know," answered the Kid. "I'll probably be heading back to Lincoln County one of these days. I've got friends there." His face darkened. "And I've got someone who needs killing there, too—Pat Garrett." He looked at Holliday. "You ever plan on going back, or were you just passing through?"

"It seemed a pleasant enough place," answered Holliday. "I suppose

I'll pay it another visit one of these days."

"If you do, I'll be pleased to show you around."

"I'll take you up on that," said Holliday.

The waiter arrived with a large plate of scrambled eggs. Holliday expected to be sickened by the sight and smell of them. Instead he found himself getting hungry, and he moved about a third of the contents onto his own plate.

"You don't mind if I eat the rest?" asked the Kid.

"Be my guest," said Holliday. "After all, you're a growing boy."

"You know, you're the only man who can get away with teasing me like that and not get shot."

"Wouldn't do you any good anyway," said Holliday with a smile.

The Kid chuckled. "I forgot. Still, you know what I mean."

"Yes," said Holliday. "You mean you kill people for teasing you."

"A man's got to be treated with respect," said the Kid. "I mean, hell, you demanded that at the O.K. Corral."

"It wasn't quite like that," said Holliday.

"I was right, then," said the Kid. "I figured you were going easy on them."

Holliday frowned in puzzlement. "Easy on them?" he repeated.

"Yeah," said the Kid. "I went over there yesterday, just to see where it happened. Didn't take much to figure it out."

"I don't think I follow you."

"You couldn't miss from that distance. Five men, five shots, five seconds tops, and it's all over. I figure you held back until you saw the Earps were getting all shot up."

"You think you could have taken all five of them out in five seconds?"

"Why not?" said the Kid. "You couldn't miss, not from that distance."

"There was a lot of smoke from the guns," said Holliday. "One of the McLaurys was hiding behind his horse, and Ike Clanton was running all the hell over. They weren't just standing there being targets. They were firing at *us*, too. Virg and Morgan went down in the first five or six seconds."

"If you'd been firing from the get-go, you could have saved them."

"They were wounded, not killed."

"I wish I'd been there," said the Kid.

"Why?"

"It was the most famous shootout ever. I'd like to have been a part of it."

"Billy Clanton and the McLaury brothers were part of it. I don't think they'd agree with you."

The Kid threw back his head and laughed. "I like your sense of humor, Doc!"

"I didn't know I was being funny."

"That makes it all the funnier," said the Kid, leaving Holliday mystified by what passed for the young man's sense of humor.

They finished their eggs, Holliday had another half-glass of whiskey, checked the bottle, decided there was enough left not to throw it out, and told the waiter to label the bottle so he could have it ready for dinner. He left some coins on the table, and then, picking up his cane, he and the Kid walked out into the hot, sunny Arizona morning.

"What are your plans for the day?" asked the Kid.

"I have no idea," said Holliday, pulling the brim of his hat down to shield his eyes from the sunshine. "It's been a long time since I was awake before noon. I don't remember what people do in the morning."

"I've got a suggestion," said the Kid.

"It's too damned early for the Wildcat," said Holliday. "You go alone and give them my regards."

The Kid shook his head, "No, I didn't mean that."

"*That's* a relief."

"I thought we'd mosey over to the corral and you could show me exactly how it happened."

"It was all over in half a minute, even if you think we were loafing," said Holliday. "There's just not much to show."

"You know how many dime novels have been written about it?" asked the Kid.

"All by Easterners who haven't been within five hundred miles of it," replied Holliday.

"Next you're gonna be telling me that there wasn't any gunfight at all, that some newspaper made it all up."

"There was one," said Holliday. "I just don't know why everyone's still talking about it."

"Why don't you show me and let me make up my own mind?" said the Kid.

"What the hell," said Holliday. "It's only a few blocks away. We might as well go and get this over with."

"Thanks, Doc."

They walked a couple of blocks and came to Fremont Street.

"This is where I met them," said Holliday, pointing up the street with his cane.

"Them?"

"The Earps. All three of them were dressed in black. Virgil was carrying a shotgun, and he traded it to me for my cane. Not that he thought I needed it, but he didn't want to antagonize the Clantons and McLaurys by holding the damned thing." A sudden smile. "I never understood why he thought they'd feel safer if *I* was carrying it. Anyway, I fell into step with them, and we walked the rest of the way to Fly's Photo Studio."

"You mean the O.K. Corral."

"Six of one, half a dozen of the other," said Holliday with a shrug. "Truth to tell, they weren't in either place. They were between the photo studio and an assay office in an alley that backed up to the corral." Suddenly he smiled. "I can see where calling it Gunfight in the Alley Near the Photo Studio lacks a little something."

There was a small crowd at the site of the gunfight, while a guide explained where each of the participants had stood, and his partner was selling souvenirs at the entrance to the alley.

"Well, I'll be damned if it ain't one of the survivors," said the guide. "Here he is, folks—the legendary Doc Holliday!"

There was polite applause, and a few expressions of awe, and Holliday tipped his hat.

"I was just about to give the details of the Gunfight," said the barker. "But perhaps you'd like to do it?"

"You go ahead," said Holliday. "You probably know the details better than I do. I was a bit preoccupied at the time."

"I'll be happy to," said the barker. "Now, according to the eyewitness accounts, Wyatt Earp stood here, Virgil here, Morgan here, and Doc was over there, toting a shotgun."

He walked over to show where the Clantons, McLaurys, and Billy Claiborne had positioned themselves, and as he did so the Kid walked over to where Doc had stood at the onset of the shootout. He pointed his finger at the guide and fired five quick, imaginary shots, then walked back to Holliday's side.

"Five seconds, tops," he said softly.

Let's find out how good you really are, thought Holliday. He stepped forward and got the guide's attention.

"My young friend is a rodeo sharpshooter," he said. "I think if we encouraged him with some applause, he might be happy to give you a demonstration of marksmanship."

"Certainly," said the barker enthusiastically. "How would you like to do it?"

"Give me five targets," said Holliday, "one to represent each of the Clanton gang."

The guide's partner supplied five souvenirs, carved statues of Wyatt Earp, and Holliday positioned them around the alley, two high, two on the ground, one on a small barrel.

"All right," said Holliday, stepping back. "The remarkable Henry Antrim will now take the place of myself and the Earp brothers."

Now let's see if you're good enough to hit even three of the targets.

The Kid looked so relaxed Holliday thought he might have misunderstood, might be waiting for someone to yell "Draw!" or fire a pistol, but then, so quickly that the eye could barely follow him, he drew his pistol and fired five shots in rapid succession, twirled it once when he had finished, and slid it back into its holster.

"Amazing!" said the guide, picking up the shattered pieces of the targets. "He hit every one!"

The Kid bowed to a new round of applause, then fell into step beside Holliday as they walked back up Fremont Street.

"So am I as good as you?" asked the Kid.

"You're damned good, and you know it."

"But am I as good as you?" persisted the Kid.

"There's only one way to find out," answered Holliday, "and it seems Hook Nose and Geronimo have denied us that ability."

"Maybe someday," said the Kid.

"Maybe."

They walked another block in silence. Then the Kid spoke again.

"I was wrong."

"About what?" asked Holliday.

"It only took four seconds."

And here I am, waiting for Tom and Ned to find a way to blow up the station so that I'm vulnerable to your gunfire again. A wry smile played on Holliday's lips. *Maybe I should be thinking of offering my services to Hook Nose instead.*

16.

"HI, DOC," said Henry Wiggins as he entered the Oriental Saloon and walked over to Holliday's table. "I was hoping I'd find you here."

"Aren't you supposed to be minding the store, so to speak?" asked Holliday.

Wiggins shook his head. "They're working on something *big*, and they say I'd just get in the way. I don't know whether to feel relieved or insulted."

"Enjoy your vacation, such as it is. With a little luck it won't last too much longer." Holliday gestured to the bottle on the table. "Pour yourself a drink."

"I don't know how you can handle this stuff," said Wiggins.

"If you feel that way, don't drink after all."

"Oh, a sip now and then can't do me much harm. But you put it away like there's no tomorrow."

"For some of us, that's a pretty accurate description," said Holliday.

"Damn it, Doc, don't talk like that!" complained Wiggins. "You thought you were dying a year ago, when we met, and you're still here. If you'd just stop abusing your body . . ."

"The consumption's abusing my body," replied Holliday. "The whiskey's just making it tolerable."

Wiggins sighed. "Okay, I give up."

"I appreciate your concern, Henry," said Holliday. "Truly I do. Most people either actively want me dead, or else don't give a damn. You actually want me to live."

Wiggins pulled out a thin cigar. "You mind if I smoke?"

"Not a problem. Just blow it in the other direction." Holliday lifted his glass and took a swallow. "How have you been?"

"Like I told you, it's been the best job I've ever had," said Wiggins. "I made a good living selling ladies' corsets, and I did all right selling laudanum and other pharmaceuticals, but they were nothing like selling Tom's and Ned's inventions."

"Everyone wants electric lights and phonographs?" suggested Holliday.

Wiggins nodded. "But you know what I make my *real* money from? Ned's metal women!"

"That's hardly surprising," responded Holliday, turning his head away for a moment as Wiggins inadvertently blew some smoke toward his face. "Men outnumber women ten-to-one out here."

"You want to know the crazy part? A quarter of my customers are women!"

"Either we've got a lot of degenerate females out here, or we've got a lot of exceptionally unattractive husbands."

"The latter. They buy them so they won't have to mingle with their husbands."

"Interesting word: mingle," mused Holliday. "The metal women have to be expensive as all hell. You'd think if a family could afford one, the husband's already got a flesh-and-blood woman or two stashed around the landscape."

"Probably," agreed Wiggins. "But a husband who's got a mistress or two isn't the kind of man who's inclined to share that information with his wife."

"Makes sense," admitted Holliday. "Kate can't be the only woman who gets into killing rages." He took another swallow. "Well, I'm glad you're making money, Henry. How many kids have you got now?"

"Just the three. I've hardly been home a month, total, since I started working for Tom and Ned."

"Damned lucky for you traveling salesmen that someone isn't criss-crossing the country selling metal men."

"Tom says that someday almost all our work will be done by machines," said Wiggins.

"Not the work his metal chippies do, I hope," replied Holliday. "How far afield have they sent you?"

"I've hit most of the major settlements out here on this side of the Mississippi," answered Wiggins. "I've seen a lot of interesting folks and things along the way. I saw where they buried Jesse James. I saw Cole Younger and Clay Allison having a drink together. I even saw Bill Hickok's grave, and the table where he was shot while he was playing cards."

Holliday smiled. "Henry, you sound like an Easterner who's read too many dime novels."

"I suppose I do at that," said Wiggins, returning his smile. "At least someday I'll be able to tell my kids that I saw all these desperados—and that I saw the Gunfight at the O.K. Corral."

"Speaking of desperados, have you met the latest?"

"I've been meaning to ask you about that," said Wiggins. "He says his name is Henry Antrim, but people say he's really Billy the Kid."

"I think they've got it backward," said Holliday. "They call him Billy the Kid, but his real name is Henry Antrim, or if you prefer, Henry McCarty."

"I don't follow you."

"His father was McCarty, his stepfather was Antrim—or so he tells me."

"So where does Billy Bonney come from?"

Holliday shrugged. "Beats me. I'll ask him next time I see him. In fact, he usually stops in here about now."

"For someone with his reputation, he doesn't look very formidable," said Wiggins.

"I saw him put on a little impromptu exhibition a couple of hours ago," said Holliday. "Trust me—he's formidable."

"Of course I trust you," said Wiggins. "You were the first man to befriend me when I came out here, and you were the one who made sure I never got in anyone's line of fire."

"There *were* a lot, weren't there?" said Holliday.

"There were," Wiggins affirmed. He looked at Holliday, "You sound almost wistful."

Holliday sighed deeply. "At least I knew what I was up against."

"And now?" queried Wiggins. "I thought you were just here to gamble."

"You haven't seen me at a table, have you?"

"Come to think of it, no," admitted Wiggins. "So why *are* you here?"

"It's complicated."

"Does it have anything to do with what Tom and Ned are working on?"

Holliday nodded. "It does."

"If there's anything I can do . . ."

"Just continue being my friend," replied Holliday. "I have few enough that I can't spare any."

"Of course. I'll be as staunch a friend as Wyatt Earp."

Holliday grimaced and took another drink.

"Oh my God!" said Wiggins, his eyes widening. "You two were the closest friends there were, always protecting each other's back. What the hell happened?"

"I said something foolish," answered Holliday.

"I'm surprised he cared."

"It wasn't about Wyatt," said Holliday.

"Then who—?"

"It's over," said Holliday. "The subject is closed."

"Whatever you say, Doc."

"Hey, Doc!" cried a voice from across the saloon. "Got an empty chair if you'd like to sit in."

"Perhaps later," Holliday called back.

"You really *aren't* gambling," noted Wiggins, frowning. "I don't believe I ever saw you turn down a game, even one with Ike Clanton or the McLaurys."

"Call it maturity," said Holliday ironically.

"Is it?"

Holliday smiled and shook his head. "Or poverty," he added wryly.

"If you're tapped out, I can loan you some money," said Wiggins, pulling out his wallet and thumbing through the contents. "It's only a hundred and ten dollars, but it's yours if you want it."

"You'd do that for me?"

"That's what friends do for each other."

"I'm touched, Henry," said Holliday. "I truly am." He pushed the proffered wallet back toward Wiggins. "You keep it. Buy those kids something special with it."

"You're sure?"

Holliday nodded. "I'm sure."

Wiggins got awkwardly to his feet. "Well, I guess I'll be moving along," he said. "I've got some things to buy, and I don't know when Tom or Ned will need me."

"Take care," said Holliday.

Wiggins walked out through the swinging doors just as the Kid entered. He nodded to Holliday, but made a beeline to the poker table with the empty seat. He slapped some bills on the table, and they began dealing him in.

A bearded man wearing a deputy's badge entered next, looked around, and walked over to Holliday's table.

"Mind if I join you?" he asked.

"Suit yourself, Deputy Breckenridge," said Holliday.

"Call me Billy, damn it," said Breckenridge. "I just took this job because when Johnny Behan is the sheriff, *somebody* ought to be enforcing the law."

"Hell," said Holliday, "for all I know, I'm still a deputy myself."

"I think that ended with the Gunfight, Doc," said Breckenridge. "Or at least with all the murder charges."

Holliday nodded his agreement. "Probably."

"I hope you don't mind my sitting here," continued Breckenridge. "I'm just here to keep an eye on young Antrim there. Word has it he's really Billy the Kid."

"So arrest him."

"I don't care what he's done anywhere else. I'm only concerned with whether or not he breaks a law in Tombstone."

"My understanding is that there's only one law he ever breaks," remarked Holliday.

"It's what he's famous for, but word has it that he's also a cattle rustler."

"He picked a lousy place for it," noted Holliday. "Not much grows on this desert, and certainly not cattle."

"Hell, Doc, I hope I'm wrong. I hope he's not the Kid, or if he is, I hope he wins a bundle, buys drinks for everyone, and goes home happy. I know enough about his reputation to know you're the only man in town who might have a chance against him."

Breckenridge hung around for twenty minutes, then got up, walked out into the street, and started making his rounds. Holliday stayed at the table for another half hour, then got up and walked to the door.

"Hold on, Doc!" cried the Kid. Lowering his voice, he told the dealer to cash him out. He stuffed some bills in a pocket and walked rapidly to the swinging doors, where Holliday was waiting for him.

"How'd you do?" asked Holliday with no interest whatsoever.

"Won about fifteen dollars," answered the Kid. "I just had a feeling my luck was about to turn." Suddenly he smiled. "I saw the deputy speaking with you, as if he was interested in anything except seeing me shoot a man down in cold blood."

"Night like this, you'd have to shoot him down in warm blood," said Holliday. "Must still be close to a hundred degrees."

"I wouldn't want to live back in New York or even Kansas," said the Kid. "I *like* heat."

"Just as well," said Holliday. "You've probably got a seat reserved for you in hell."

"Won't be so bad," replied the Kid. "All the great gunfighters go there."

A bat fluttered overhead, then flew into the eaves of the church.

"I hate those things," said the Kid.

"They're just animals."

"You know what I heard?" continued the Kid, lowering his voice confidentially.

"What?"

"They say Geronimo turned Bat Masterson into a *real* bat."

Holliday shrugged. "People say a lot of things."

"He was *your* friend," persisted the Kid. "Don't you know if it's true or not?"

Before Holliday could answer, the same bat—or at least a similar one—flew overhead again. The Kid drew his gun and fired at it, all in one motion. The bat screeched, veered crazily, and flew behind Mason's General Store.

"You'd better head off to wherever you're staying before they arrest you for firing your gun within the city limits and disturbing the peace," said Holliday.

"Yeah, I guess so," agreed the Kid. "See you tomorrow."

He walked off to the north, and Holliday decided to take a shortcut to the American Hotel, one that led him through the alley behind Mason's store.

When he reached the alley he found an Apache warrior writhing on the ground, a bullet wound in his neck. His thrashings grew weaker, and finally he lay still.

"I know you are working with the magician of the White Eyes," said a familiar voice, and he turned to see Geronimo standing behind him. "Do not wait too long. My people cannot ascend to the Great Hunting Ground until the offending structure and tracks are gone."

"It's not up to me," said Holliday. "I know nothing of how his magic works."

"Then you will urge him to make haste," said Geronimo. "My patience is not infinite, and neither," he added, staring coldly at Holliday, "is your protection."

Holliday was about to reply when he realized that he would be speaking only to empty air.

17.

"DID HE GIVE YOU A DEFINITE TIME LIMIT?" asked Edison when Holliday stopped by his house to report his encounter with Geronimo. For a change, the inventor was in his parlor, sitting in a deep leather chair while Holliday seated himself in its counterpart.

"No, just that he's losing patience."

"Well, I suppose we'd better test what we have."

"Here or at the station?" asked Holliday.

"Here. The lab's here, and so is Ned's manufacturing plant. If we try it out at the train station and it doesn't work, we'll have to come back here anyway. This'll save two days of traveling."

"But you won't know if it works," noted Holliday.

"True," agreed Edison. "But at least I'll know if it's not working at all."

"When do you want to try it out?" asked Holliday. "And probably just as important: Where?"

"If Geronimo is getting impatient, I suppose the sooner the better."

"Tonight?"

"Well, tomorrow morning, anyway. I think Ned turned in early. I'll tell him when he wakes up. I suppose one of the abandoned silver mines is the safest site." He bent his artificial arm and held his wrist up in front of his face. "Be here at nine o'clock."

"What the hell's *that*?" asked Holliday, pointing to the object in question.

"I call it a wristwatch," answered Edison, extending his arm so Holliday could get a close look at it, a brass clock the size of a gold dollar affixed to his metal wrist. "It's going to replace pocket watches in your lifetime," he added proudly.

"In *my* lifetime?" said Holliday dubiously.

"Well, in your or my normal life span, anyway."

"I don't know," said Holliday. "I like having my watch on a chain, where no one can steal it. Besides, not everyone's going to let you attach it like that. In fact, almost no one will."

"They can't steal a wristwatch either, unless they cut your hand off," said Edison. "And it won't be *attached* to the wrist. With me it's just a convenience since I have an artificial arm, but most people will just use a leather band, exactly the way some of the cowboys out here wear wristlets, although the band will be much narrower."

"It could be a distraction or an annoyance if I have to go for my gun in a hurry."

Edison smiled. "If you have to go for your gun in a hurry, you won't even remember you're wearing a wristwatch."

"Maybe," admitted Holliday. "But I think I'll stick with my pocket watch all the same."

"I really wasn't trying to coerce you," said Edison. "Though I'd be happy to make one for you if you ever change your mind."

"I appreciate the offer, but I won't be asking for it anytime soon."

"All right," said Edison. "If we're leaving at nine, I've got a lot of work to do. You can see yourself out."

Before Holliday could reply Edison was scribbling furiously on his notepad. Holliday made his way out to the street, considered returning to the Oriental but decided against it since he had no money with which to gamble. He thought about walking over to the Wildcat, but concluded that if he partook of its offerings he'd never wake up in time, and if he didn't then there was no sense walking the extra few blocks to get there. Leaning heavily on his cane, he reviewed his few other options, rejected them all, and returned to the American Hotel.

Sheriff John Behan was standing at the polished wooden bar when Holliday arrived, admiring the painting of the well-rounded nude that hung behind it. He turned, saw the dentist approaching the far end of the bar, and glared at him.

"This place is going downhill," muttered the sheriff. "They let just anybody in these days."

"Careful, Johnny," said Holliday pleasantly. "These days I don't have Wyatt holding me back and telling me not to cause problems for him."

"Here's what I think of Wyatt Earp!" snapped Behan, spitting on the floor.

"That's right," said Holliday, smiling. "He stole your fiancée right out from under you, didn't he?"

"Good riddance!" muttered Behan.

"That's what I'd say, too, if I couldn't keep my woman."

"I should have killed you both a year ago!" snarled Behan, reaching for his gun, but before his hand closed on it he was staring down the barrel of Holliday's pistol.

"You're a lucky lawman, Johnny Behan," said Holliday. "I've got important things to do tomorrow, more important than killing someone as unimportant as you, and I don't want to spend the day in court telling them all the many good reasons I have for ridding the town and the world of you. So don't even think of touching your gun, step back from the bar, turn away, and walk out of here."

Behan tensed, and his hand snaked down toward the top of his gun.

"Please," said Holliday. "I hope you do."

Suddenly all the tension left the sheriff's body, and he turned away from the bar and walked out the door.

"Damn!" said the bartender. "I was hoping I'd have something to tell my grandkids about."

"He's probably waiting right outside the hotel, gun in hand," said Holliday. Suddenly he smiled. "He doesn't know I've got a room here. I figure he's going to get good and tired in a couple of hours, especially after he almost shoots the next ten or twenty men who walk out that door."

The bartender laughed aloud. "Damn, this town has missed you and Texas Jack Vermillion! What the hell were the two of you doing up in Colorado?"

"Initially we were there to avoid arrest warrants," answered Holliday. "I decided I liked the dry air, and he decided he liked the type of gambler who showed up at the Leadville casinos."

"Leadville," said the bartender. "Sounds like this town."

"Tombstone suits this one better," said Holliday. He bought a drink, downed it, and painfully climbed the stairs to the second floor, where he went directly to his room. He leaned his cane against the door so he wouldn't forget it when he left in the morning. Then he slipped out of his boots, put his hat on the desk, hung his shirt and vest on a chair, folded his pants over them, and hung his coat in the wardrobe. He slung his holster over the headboard, the handle of his gun within easy reach.

Then, secure in the knowledge that no one could see into the room, he lit the lamp by his bed and lay back to read the latest adventure of the notorious Billy the Kid, killer of more than fifty lawmen and an equal number of rival desperados.

He woke up when the sun beat in through his window, found the dime novel spread open on his chest, and realized that he'd fallen asleep somewhere on page six. He got up, rinsed his face off with the pitcher of water that was on the sink, and got dressed, then paid a visit to the privy down the hall. His pocket watch (which suddenly seemed awkward and bothersome to him) said that it was a few minutes after eight in the morning, so he decided he had time for a shave before he was due at Edison's.

He stopped at the barber shop that was across the street from the American, waited for the barber to spread a cloth over him, gently pulled his gun out of its holster, and held it in his hand just in case any of his many local enemies saw him sitting helplessly in the chair and decided it might be a good time to kill him. When the barber was done, he holstered the gun, paid the barber a dime—a nickel for the shave, a nickel for the tip—and began walking to Edison's combination house and lab.

As he approached his destination, he saw a large wagon with a team of four horses sitting just beyond Buntline's house.

"Good morning, Doc!" called Buntline. Holliday didn't see him at first, but then he appeared from behind the wagon and waved. "Lovely day, isn't it?"

Holliday muttered an obscenity.

"Well, trust me, it is," said Buntline. "Tom should be joining us in a few minutes."

"You created the horseless coaches," noted Holliday. "Why aren't we riding a Bunt Line out to the mine?"

"Ground's too rough," answered Buntline. "The horses can negotiate it better, and we've got some pretty delicate equipment."

"Such as?"

"A number of prototypes."

"Whatever *that* means." Suddenly Holliday half-snorted, half-chuckled. "Makes me sound as ignorant of the language as the Kid."

"They're experimental devices," answered Buntline. "Even if they don't work on the station, some of them may be of use to the army."

Holliday frowned. "The army can't cross the Mississippi. You know that. So how the hell can it help them against the Indians?"

"We've already fought two wars against the British," replied Buntline. "I'd say, based on history, that we're more likely to be attacked from the east than the west."

Holliday shrugged. "Okay, you've got a point."

"Ah!" said Buntline. "Here comes Bessie!"

The robot emerged from Edison's house, carefully carrying something Holliday couldn't quite make out. "She's coming with us?" he asked, surprised.

Buntline shook his head. "No, she's just bringing lunch out to the wagon. We could be all day."

The robot delivered the picnic basket, then stood still, waiting for further instructions.

"Thank you, Bessie," said Buntline. "You may return to your duties now."

"Thank you, sir," she said in a low, mildly feminine monotone.

"Henry tells me he's getting rich off those things," remarked Holliday.

"Rich is a relative term," answered Buntline. "To my way of thinking, Andrew Carnegie and J. P. Morgan are rich. As for the machines, one of these days I plan to make them without a gender at all. There are so many services a mechanical being can provide, I feel guilty creating them to perform just one."

"Adam Smith would point out that this is the nature of capitalism," said Holliday. "There's a need out here for mechanical women. If you don't supply it, someone else will."

"You've read Adam Smith?" said Buntline, surprised.

"Despite my ignorance of prototypes, I wasn't born a consumptive shootist," replied Holliday. "I've had the benefits of a classical education. Even if," he added wryly, "I haven't applied them."

"You are constantly surprising me, Doc."

"I almost surprised Johnny Behan last night," said Holliday. "I regret missing the opportunity."

"If that means what I think it means, it's just as well you didn't shoot him," said Buntline.

"Why? He's a liar and a coward. You have no more use for him than I do."

"In case it's slipped your memory, you are the reason Tom and I aren't in Colorado right now. If you go to jail, we've wasted the trip."

"Actually, it *had* slipped my memory," admitted Holliday. "Old age will do that to you."

"Doc, you can't be thirty-five," said Buntline.

"Thirty-two," Holliday corrected him. "But that's old age for a shootist."

"You're a dentist by profession. You're only a shootist by circumstance."

"The reason doesn't matter," answered Holliday. "I've still lived longer than most."

"How old is the Kid?" asked Buntline.

"I can't pin him down. He says twenty-one. That's probably pretty near right." Holliday paused. "*He* might make it to thirty. He's good enough." Another pause. "I don't know if he's smart enough, though."

"Does he have to be?"

"The ones who make it to thirty usually are," answered Holliday.

"Hickok. Allison, Ringo. Masterson. Wyatt and Virgil. The Younger brothers. Well, a couple of them, anyway."

"And you."

"And me."

"And you think the Kid might make it?"

"He might. I hope not. If he makes it to twenty-two, you'll be burying me here or in Lincoln County—and I've got my heart set on gasping my last breath in Colorado."

"You're not the cheeriest person in the mornings, are you?" commented Buntline.

"This is one of my friendlier days," replied Holliday.

Edison finally emerged from his house and walked briskly to the wagon.

"All ready?" he asked.

"Been ready for a few minutes," replied Holliday.

The three men climbed aboard, and Buntline handled the reins.

"This damned seat wasn't built for three men," remarked Holliday uncomfortably.

"I can stop by the livery stable," suggested Buntline." You could rent a horse and ride alongside."

"It's not *that* uncomfortable," replied Holliday, who hated horses.

"We're carrying some interesting inventions here," said Edison, as the wagon turned onto Allen Street. "Let's hope at least one of them works as planned."

Buntline clucked to the horses, and they began heading toward the west end of town.

"I got permission to use the old *Silver Spoon* mine," continued Edison. "It's not perfect, but then, nothing that isn't protected by Hook Nose is."

"I have a thought," said Buntline. "Doc, can you get Geronimo to duplicate whatever Hook Nose did to the station? Then we'd know if any of our ideas are working."

"Think it through, Ned," said Edison. "If Geronimo could create the conditions, he'd also know how to eradicate them, and he wouldn't need Doc or us."

Buntline nodded his head. "Sorry. Wishful thinking."

"Let's concentrate on *useful* thinking," said Edison. He turned to Holliday. "We don't have anything out here that's as impervious to weaponry as the train station, but before we're done today we'll have a pretty good idea what these inventions can do. I can't believe at least one of them won't solve the problem."

Holliday turned and looked at the back of the wagon. "I can't see through the tarp," he said, "but it sure doesn't look like you've got anything as big as a cannon back there."

"We don't," answered Edison.

"I don't know," said Holliday dubiously. "We already know cannonballs bounced right off it."

"Never mistake size for strength," said Edison, as they passed out of town and headed toward the mines.

"I know you're the genius and I'm the shootist," said Holliday, "but that whole damned valley is resistant to cannons, guns, fire, everything. It's going to take a whole train to carry a weapon that can make a dent in it."

Edison merely smiled.

"Aren't you going to answer me?" demanded Holliday.

"When I'm sure no one can see us," replied Edison.

They went another four miles, and the landscape, which was never colorful, became a duller brown. There were a few stray cactus plants and the occasional bush. Trees were few and far between, and it was hot enough that the lizards, the snakes, and the insects all chose to remain in their lairs below the ground. What had been occasional rocky outcroppings as they first left the city limits became more common. Edison finally nodded to Buntline, who pulled the team to a halt.

"Do you see that rocky ridge off to the left?" asked Edison.

"Of course I do," said Holliday.

"Ned, can you climb down and pull out that device we came up with Thursday—no, Friday—afternoon?"

Buntline got off the wagon, went around the side, lifted the tarp, found what he was looking for, and carried it around to the front, where he handed it up to Edison.

"That looks like about half of a metal broom handle," remarked Holliday.

"Oh, it's a little bigger than that," replied Edison, fiddling with some buttons and knobs at one end of it. "Three inches in diameter, twenty-four inches long." He pointed to a bulge beneath the knobs. "Can you give me the cord, Ned?"

Buntline handed him a heavy rubber-coated wire that he attached to two thick metal pins.

"And it's plugged into the battery in the wagon?" asked Edison.

"Yes, it is, Tom."

"Okay, it's a *big* metal broom handle," said Holliday, staring at it. "What has all this got to do with the ridge over there?"

"Watch," said Edison, pointing the device toward the ridge. He fiddled with the buttons, cursed when nothing happened, then touched them in a different order. Holliday thought he heard a very soft whining for perhaps ten seconds. Then it stopped, but not before the rocky ridge had turned entirely to rubble and a cloud of dust.

"This little thing did *that*?" demanded Holliday.

Edison nodded. "I'm thinking of calling it a Deconstructor."

"It *really* did it?"

"Really," replied Edison, looking very pleased with himself.

Holliday turned to Buntline. "Whip the hell out of these horses, Ned! I've seen Hook Nose's magic. Now I want to get to the mine and see what kind of magic we've got in the back of this wagon!"

18.

THE WAGON MADE ITS WAY past half a dozen abandoned mines until it came to the *Silver Spoon*, where Buntline pulled the horses to a halt, and the three men climbed down.

The mine looked like all the others, a large rocky outcropping with a cave entrance, enhanced and widened by the miners, with abandoned cart tracks leading to the interior. Buntline and Edison untied the tarp that was covering their equipment. Holliday was about to help when he experienced another coughing seizure. It was when he was putting his blood-soaked handkerchief away in a pocket that Edison turned and stared at him.

"Is there *anything* you can do about that, Doc?" he asked. "I don't know how much blood a man carries around, but you're ridding yourself of it at an alarming rate."

"The body reproduces blood," noted Buntline.

"Not as fast as he's coughing it up, I'll wager," said Edison.

"I'll take that wager," said Holliday with a sardonic smile. "After all, if I lose, I won't be around to pay off."

"Well," said Buntline, "I suppose it's a better attitude than being morose."

"I have my morose moments," said Holliday. "I just don't choose to share them." He walked around to the back of the wagon. "So what have you got here?"

"Just about everything we could come up with on short notice," answered Edison as the sun glinted off all the bronze objects, some looking like weapons, others looking like nothing Holliday had ever seen or imagined. Even after staring at them for a long minute, Holliday couldn't determine how more than half of them would be used, or what their functions were. "The problem is that even if something works here, it doesn't mean it'll work on a station that's protected by Hook Nose's magic—and conversely, if it doesn't work here, that doesn't mean it *won't* work on the station."

Holliday frowned. "Then what the hell are we doing here?"

"Testing them out," said Edison. "We won't know if *any* of them work until we give them this field test. So far these are just theories that Ned's given physical form to, but what works on paper or in theory doesn't always work in practice."

"What about that one?" asked Holliday, indicating a multi-barreled rifle. "It looks like a Gatling gun."

"Same principle," said Buntline. "I improved on Gatling a bit. It's more accurate, the barrels will turn faster, and it's considerably lighter. You could carry this one for a mile or more, whereas most Gatling guns have to be transported by wagon."

"That's all very well," said Holliday. "But when all is said and done, it's a Gatling gun and we already know the station can't be penetrated by bullets."

"Have a little faith in your partners," said Edison with a smile. He turned to Buntline, "Ned, you want to load it?"

"How many rounds?" asked Buntline, carefully pulling out a small wooden box.

"Oh, I think a dozen will do it."

Buntline opened the box, and Holliday leaned forward and stared at it. "They're just bullets, each one wrapped in cotton," he said.

"Not quite," said Edison, still smiling.

"Brass casings, and they're the right size," said Holliday as Buntline very gingerly loaded the first bullet.

"Pick one up, Doc," said Edison. "And be very careful how you handle it. Above all, don't drop it."

Holliday reached over and pulled out a bullet, then held it up to examine it. Suddenly he frowned.

"What the hell is *that*," he said, indicating the nose. "It's sure as hell not lead."

"It isn't," confirmed Edison.

"Looks like glass," continued Holliday.

"Probably because it is," said Buntline, continuing to load the weapon.

"If you thought shattering glass against the station would harm it, we wouldn't be here in Arizona testing things out," said Holliday. "What am I not understanding?"

"Instead of shooting a lead bullet, this rifle will shoot a specially made glass pellet," explained Edison. "Inside the pellet is a small amount of nitroglycerin, the same explosive that the miners have been using for half a dozen years."

"And you think one little pellet . . . ?"

"I doubt it," continued Edison. "That's why we'll be shooting them from this specially constructed Gatling gun. Each will hit the target with explosive force, and we'll hit the same spot twelve times in maybe six seconds." He paused while Holliday assimilated what he'd said. "It just might be strong enough to break through Hook Nose's magic."

"Why bother testing it here, then?" asked Holliday. "You won't know until you shoot it at the station."

"These are explosive bullets, Doc. If you drop them, or even shake them too much, they make a mighty big bang."

"So?"

"I'd like to know that the first or second time we fire the gun, with it's noise and its kick, that the other ten or eleven bullets don't blow up inside the gun."

Holliday turned to Buntline, who was loading the final bullet. "And you're going to test it?"

Buntine chuckled. "How stupid do I look?"

"Well, you're sure as hell not getting *me* to fire the damned gun," said Holliday.

"Nobody's going to fire it," said Edison. "At least, not the way you mean."

Buntline pulled a brass stand with long, thin legs off the wagon and set it up about fifty feet from the entrance to the *Silver Spoon*. Then he led the horses and wagon about one hundred yards farther from the mine, took a cord that was on a large reel, and pulled it over to the stand.

"The other end is connected to a battery and a little control switch in the wagon," explained Edison. "Now Ned will attach the rifle and aim it at the entrance of the mine."

"If it works, no one will ever get into the mine again," noted Holliday.

"We have other devices that should fix that," replied Edison.

Buntline attached the gun to the stand, and the cord to the firing mechanism, then aimed the weapon at the mine.

"Okay," he said, walking back to the wagon. Edison and Holliday followed suit.

"Doc," said Edison, pointing to a switch at the side of the wagon, "would you like the honors?"

"What do I do?" asked Holliday.

"Just throw the switch, and then protect your ears, because *something* is going to explode—either the mine or the gun."

Holliday walked over to the switch, placed his hand on it, turned so he could observe the results, and threw it.

The explosions came so close together it sounded like one long *Boom!* The rifle fell off its stand, but not before it had emptied its chambers of the nitro-filled bullets.

The smoke and dust obscured the entrance to the mine for a full minute. Then an errant breeze blew the dust cloud away, and suddenly they could see the results of their experiment. The entrance to the *Silver Spoon*, which could easily accommodate five men walking abreast, was now totally sealed off by debris from the ceiling and walls.

"What do you think?" asked Edison.

"It'll do," said Buntline.

"What about the gun?"

"I was watching it," said Buntline. "It fell after the eleventh shot. I don't know where the hell the twelfth went. So if it didn't have enough kick to fall off the stand with the first few shots, it can be handled."

"And it'll have to be," said Edison. "We keep talking about the station, but we've got to get rid of the tracks, and anything else we may have missed when we were there, like perhaps a storage shed behind the station, or whatever."

"You could get rich selling this to the army," suggested Holliday.

"We *are* rich," replied Buntline. "And before we sell it to the army, we have to make sure it does what it's supposed to do. Remember, if it won't work against the station, then it won't work against any Indians who are protected by their medicine men."

"But if it *does* work," added Edison, "indeed if anything we try out here works, then we've taken our first major step toward combating the medicine men's magic—which, when all is said and done, is why I'm not tending my garden in Ohio."

"All right," said Holliday, peering into the back of the wagon. "What else have you got in here?"

"I've never liked guns or explosives," said Edison. "Electricity is my forte."

"You used electricity to fire the Gatling gun," noted Holliday.

"Only as a convenience, until we could be sure it wouldn't blow up," replied Edison. "But *this* little item"—he pulled out a device that seemed to be all spokes and buttons, made totally of Buntline's super-hard brass—"will use electricity as a weapon, not as an ignition."

"What does it do?" asked Holliday.

"It works on the same principle as the Deconstructor, but it generates a much broader field."

"Where's the battery?"

"We'll use the same one that powered the gun," answered Edison. "It isn't depleted yet."

Another breeze came up, and the men all turned their backs and covered their faces as best they could. Then Buntline heard the horses shuffling uncomfortably, and turned them away from the wind.

The breeze died down as suddenly as it had begun, the dust settled out of the air, and the men went back to work. Buntline walked to the multi-barreled rifle, unplugged the cord, and pulled it back to Edison, who plugged it into the angular brass device.

"I've got a question," said Holliday. "This brass of yours—bullets don't dent it, you can't melt it, you can't even scratch it. So how do you mold it into all these shapes?"

An amused smile crossed Buntline's face. "Hardening it is the *last* step in the process, Doc. No way I could shape it once it's as hard as the final product."

Edison walked to the now-filled entrance to the mine, set the device on the ground, and walked back to the wagon.

"Another bang coming up?" asked Holliday.

"It should be silent as a tomb."

"Then why are you back here instead of aiming it?"

"I've already aimed it," said Edison. "Those longer spokes, the ones that curve in, will generate the field. But there's always a chance that the brass will become too hot to hold, or, more likely, that the heat generated by the field will be overwhelming, so until I know all of the unintended consequences I think it's much more intelligent—to say nothing of being safer—to stand back here and observe."

"It isn't doing a damned thing," said Holliday.

"I haven't activated it yet," replied Edison. "I wanted to be sure I was out of harm's way—well, as far from potential harm as possible—before generating the field."

"You say that as if I know what it means to generate a field," said Holliday.

"Don't worry about it," said Edison. "Just watch." He turned to Buntline, "Okay, Ned, let's see what it can do."

Buntline, who had detached the cord from the battery when the first experiment was over, now attached it again. There was no explosion, no light, no humming, nothing to indicate the device was working, and Holliday was just about to make that observation when the rocks and dust blocking the entrance to the mine simply vanished.

"Son of a bitch!" exclaimed Holliday.

"Not bad," commented Buntline.

"It's too damned bad that the landscape isn't littered with castles, and that we're not conquerors," remarked Holliday.

"Well, so far so good," said Edison. "Our luck can't last much longer."

"Why not?" asked Holliday.

"Every one of these is an experimental device that's never been tested before," replied Edison. "It's the nature of such things that most will be failures."

"What do you want to try next?" asked Buntline.

"Well, if it works, my guess is that the most effective of all of these devices will be the Imploder."

"*Im*ploder, not *ex*ploder?" asked Holliday.

"Right."

"What does it do?"

"It's my belief that everything—you, me, that bush, the wagon, *everything*—is composed of tiny particles, so small that you can't see them, not even with a magnifying glass or a microscope," said Edison. "There is space between them, just as there is between the planets. Just as an *ex*plosion blows things apart, an *im*plosion presses them together. Take yourself, for example. An explosion, if it's powerful enough, might very well spread you over two or even three acres. An implosion might reduce you to the size of an apple."

"That's pretty weird stuff," said Holliday. "Have you discussed this with anyone—I mean, with anyone who can argue the subject?"

"I've mentioned it to a few colleagues," answered Edison. "Some believe in these particles, some don't. Time will tell who's right."

"But we can go a long way toward proving Tom's right if the Imploder works," added Buntline.

"Do *you* believe in these tiny particles?" asked Holliday.

"I don't know," said Buntline. "But I'm willing to help prove it one way or the other." He reached into the back of the wagon and withdrew a device that looked like a sister to the Deconstructor—brass, cylindrical, an opening at one end, a switch at the other. Buntline attached it to the battery then handed it to Edison.

"Stand back," Edison warned them as he pointed the device at the mine.

"Why?" said Holliday. "Even if the mine collapses or does whatever it's supposed to do, *we're* not in your field of fire."

"I don't know what the effects will be," said Edison. "There could be a ton of smoke or dust, which would be especially hard on your lungs. The whole mine could implode, rather than just the part I'm aiming for, and that could loosen some of those large rocks on the mountain above it."

"All right," said Holliday, backing up another ten feet.

"Further," said Edison, as Buntline joined Holliday in retreating from the mine and the wagon. "Ready?"

"Do I close my eyes because of the brilliance of the light, or put my hands over my ears to protect them from the deafening implosion?" asked Holliday.

"No flash, no bang—*if* it works," replied Edison. "Here goes."

He pushed a button on the side of the Imploder. Holliday shielded his eyes just in case Edison had been wrong and there *was* a blinding flash of light. But there wasn't. Nor was there any noise.

"Damn!" said Edison after a totally uneventful moment had passed.

"So there aren't any tiny particles?" asked Holliday.

"Oh, they're there, I'm convinced of that," said Edison. "But either they can't be imploded, or I still haven't designed the device that can do it."

"What next?" asked Holliday.

"Next?" repeated Edison. "We have some beer to soften the blow, and then we try the next device."

Buntline reached under a blanket and brought forth three bottles of warm beer. He opened each in turn, and handed them to Holliday, Edison, and kept the last for himself.

"How the hell did you get involved with Geronimo in the first place?" asked Edison.

"I did him a favor the last time I was in Tombstone, and he did one for me," said Holliday. He grimaced. "I thought that was the end of it." Suddenly his face softened. "Still, I suppose I should be grateful that he contacted me again. He knew I needed money and that I'd go after the biggest payday, and he knew the Kid was protected." He shrugged. "So we made another trade, although this one's getting more complicated. I should have suggested to him that we go after Hook Nose together, kill him, and then go hunting for the Kid. Except . . ."

"Except?" Buntline prompted him.

"I don't think he wants Hook Nose dead. He just wants him to stop doing things that annoy him, like protecting the station that's on sacred Apache burial ground. I don't think he can hold the United States on the other side of the Mississippi by himself. I think he needs his magic *plus* Hook Nose's magic to do it."

"They can't be the only two medicine men who practice magic," said Buntline.

"They're not," said Edison.

"But they're the two most powerful," added Holliday. "There are others, and some of them don't care about the white man. They just want to be left alone."

"Have you met any?"

Holliday nodded. "One. His name was Que-Su-La, of the Hualopai tribe. Good man."

"Ever have any dealings with him?" asked Edison curiously.

"Ike Clanton killed his son. Killing Clanton was the price for getting the curse lifted from Bat Masterson so he wouldn't turn into a giant bat every night at sundown."

"But you didn't kill Clanton!" said Buntline. "Wyatt did."

"You think Que-Su-La gave a damn?" replied Holliday. "He wanted blood for blood, and he got it."

"I'll give them this, those medicine men," said Edison. "They may be our enemies, but they're honorable men who keep their word." He finished his beer. "And now it's time to go back to work and see if we can help you keep *your* word, or at least your bargain, with Geronimo."

The next five devices either didn't work, or didn't work well enough. Finally Buntline pulled out one last one, something that looked for all the world like a brass lantern.

"This is it," said Edison. "Whether it works or whether it doesn't, this is everything we've come up with."

"You've only been working on it for a few days," said Holliday. "We have more time if you need it."

Edison smiled and shook his head. "Doc, we didn't come up with all these things since arriving in Tombstone. We've been working on some of them for almost a year."

"Okay, I hadn't realized that," said Holliday. He paused and slapped at a fly that was crawling on his cheek. "So, what is this thing and how does it work?"

"It's a prototype . . ." began Edison.

"Everything in the wagon is a prototype," interrupted Holliday.

"True enough," agreed Edison. "But the ones that worked are the ones we'll use. This"—he held up the lantern—"is a miniature. If it works, Ned will have to make one about eight or ten times bigger, if my figures are correct."

"What does it do?" asked Holliday.

"It aims a burst of sound, so high-pitched that you won't be able to hear it."

Holliday couldn't repress a smile. "Are you telling me it *yells* at the enemy?"

"In essence," said Edison.

"You're pulling my leg," said Holliday.

"Not at all," said Edison. "Look, we know that bullets and cannonballs don't work against the station. We may try those nitroglycerin bullets, because that's the strongest and most unusual explosive force I could devise, but I don't think they'll make a dent in it. That's why I'm concentrating on other things, like heat and implosion, and in this case, sound. You know that sound can shatter glass. Well, take my word for it, enough concentrated sound can bring down buildings. Whether it can bring down this particular train station remains to be seen, but at least, like everything but the exploding bullets, it's something that hasn't been tried before."

"Okay," said Holliday. "It makes sense when you say it like that."

"Ned?"

"I hope we haven't drained the battery," said Buntline. "I think we'd better use the auxiliary one, just to be on the safe side."

"Yeah, I agree," said Edison. "I'd hate to think it failed, only to find out later that it simply didn't get enough power."

While Buntline was attaching the coil to a new battery, Edison positioned the lantern at the entrance to the mine.

"What do you expect to happen?" asked Holliday. "You've already turned everything to dust."

"I'm directing it at that side wall," answered Edison. "If it can put, not a dent, but a *hole* in it, then I think we'll make the full-sized model."

"Ready," announced Buntline.

"All right," said Edison. "It shouldn't generate so much heat that I can't hold it, but I think I'll wrap my hands in rags anyway."

"Right," said Buntline, reaching into the wagon, withdrawing some cloths, and tossing them to him.

"Okay," said Edison. "Let's see what this machine can do."

He flipped a switch on the side of it.

The next thing Holliday knew, Ned Buntline was kneeling next to him, gently slapping his face.

"What the hell happened?" muttered Holliday, trying to focus his eyes.

"The device worked," said Edison, who was sitting cross-legged and dust-covered on the ground a few feet away. "But unfortunately we can't use it."

Holliday blinked his eyes rapidly, and tried to clear his mind. "What are we doing on the ground?"

"The sound was directed at the mine, and that's where it did the most damage, but it clearly went in all directions." He nodded his head toward the wagon, "We weren't the only ones it affected. It knocked the horses out. They just woke up about five minutes ago." He held up his hand so Holliday could see his wristwatch. "We were out about twenty minutes."

"I never even heard it," said Holliday.

"I told you you wouldn't."

"So there's no way you can use it?"

"It's too dangerous. Remember: this was just the miniature model. Hell, the big one would probably knock out every man and animal for half a mile in every direction."

"So we're down to three weapons."

"Three *prototypes*," said Edison. "They're as powerful as anything that exists anywhere in the world, and they operate on principles that will be alien to Hook Nose. But we won't know until we try them on the station if they'll work."

"Maybe we're looking at this all wrong," said Holliday.

"Oh?"

"Maybe we ought to be trying them on Hook Nose."

Edison shook his head. "It won't work."

"Why not?" asked Holliday.

"First, you don't know where to look for him. He could be protecting that station from hundreds of miles away. Second, if he was an easy target, Geronimo wouldn't be asking for your help. And third, you have to figure that he's at least as well protected as the station, since he's the one supplying the protection."

"All right," said Holliday. "It was just a thought."

"We'll take the train back to Lincoln in the morning," said Edison. "And it would be better if the Kid didn't know about it. It's going to be hard enough to dismantle the station without his lending his gun to the other side."

Especially since shooting him if he shows up won't do any good, thought Holliday. He pulled his flask out of his pocket and took a long swallow. *This may not be all bad*, he concluded. *If we can figure out how to destroy the station, the same thing should work on the Kid.*

And then, somehow, through some means he couldn't fathom, he seemed to see Hook Nose peering into his thoughts.

And laughing.

19.

THE TRAIN RIDE BACK to New Mexico was uneventful.

Holliday drank himself to sleep while Edison and Buntline went over their notes, discussed which devices to try and in which order, and generally planned their attack on the station and its surroundings. They elected not to get off at the station, but to go into Lincoln, return to their rooms at their hotel, assemble their weaponry, and head back to the station the next day.

When the train screeched to a stop in Lincoln, Holliday awoke, grabbed his suitcase, and made arrangements to meet his companions the next morning. He climbed down from the train, signaled a surrey driver, and was driven to the Grand Hotel, where he went directly to his room, emptied his suitcase, checked to see if there were any birds-that-weren't-birds perched on his windowsill, and then went downstairs to the desk.

"Welcome back, Doc," said the clerk. "Anything I can do for you?"

"The lady I arrived with," said Holliday. "Charlotte. I don't know her last name. Is she still staying here?"

"You mean Mrs. Branson?"

"Yeah, Branson—that's right."

"Yes, she is."

"Do you know if she's in?"

"I believe so."

"Good. I'm looking for a dinner companion. Give me her room number, please."

"It's against our policy," said the clerk. "But what the hell, since you're friends . . ."

A moment later Holliday was knocking at Charlotte's door.

"Why, Doc!" she said happily. "I thought you'd left town, someone said for Tombstone."

"Been there and came back. If you don't have any plans for dinner, I'd be honored if you'd agree to be my guest."

"I'll be happy to," she said. "When do you propose to go?"

"Right now, if you're hungry."

"It's a little early." Suddenly she smiled. "That just means the restaurant won't be crowded. Just wait while I get my hat."

She joined him in the corridor a moment later.

"How have you been?" asked Holliday, as they began walking.

"Fine," she replied. "Though I must confess it's not the most exciting town in the world."

"It's a little less exciting now than a few days ago, with Billy the Kid in Tombstone."

"You saw him?" asked Charlotte.

Holliday nodded. "I saw him, I shared some drinks with him, I even shared a meal with him." He smiled at her. "You'll be better company."

"What's he like? Everybody's talking about him, but it's very hard to separate fact from fiction."

"He's a young guy, maybe twenty. Seems nice enough, especially for someone who's killed twenty or more men. He's as good with a gun as any man I've ever seen."

"You saw him shoot someone?" asked Charlotte as they left the hotel and began walking on the raised wooden sidewalk.

Holliday shook his head. "No, I just saw a little exhibition of speed and marksmanship." He found the sunlight uncomfortable and tried to remain out of it, but that was almost impossible, as none of the stores had overhangs or awnings. The sidewalk was nearly devoid of people, but he had to keep stepping around chairs and benches that local shop owners had put out front, either to attract customers or for the owners to use when their stores got too warm and stuffy in the New Mexico sun.

"You lead an exciting life," said Charlotte.

"I could do with a little less excitement and a little more health," answered Holliday.

"I would have thought this climate would do you a world of good."

"It's good for asthmatics, not consumptives."

"I'm sorry."

"Not your fault I've got it, not your fault I can't cure it," said Holliday, as they reached the closest restaurant. "This good enough?" he asked. "You've had more meals in this town than I have, so I'll be guided by your judgment."

"It's all right," she said. "But the one across the street is better."

Holliday looked where she had indicated and read the sign above the door. "Mabel Grimsley's."

"She's the owner and the cook," said Charlotte. "I gather her husband died during Pickett's Charge, and since she was in her early twenties she wasn't ready to lock herself away from the world in widow's weeds, so she went to work for a restaurant over on the next street, and when she'd saved enough money she left it and started her own."

"Then let's give it a try," said Holliday, starting across the street with her.

They reached the restaurant, a small room with six wooden tables and an unused fireplace in the corner. There were gas lamps along the walls, but with the sun pouring in through the window there was no need for them to be lit. They seated themselves, the only customers at that moment. After they had read the limited menu, Holliday looked across the table at her.

"You look like you want to ask me something, Doc," said Charlotte.

"If it's not too personal, just what are you doing in Lincoln? You never said a word about it on the trip here, or during the brief times we've been together since then. It's unusual for a married woman to be traveling alone out here, and even more unusual to stay in a town where she has no family. Or do you have some here?"

"None alive," she answered. "My brother died in the Lincoln County War. He may even have been killed by Billy the Kid. I have no idea, and I haven't found any eyewitnesses. He'd been a reasonably successful rancher, and I've been putting his affairs in order." She made a face. "It's taken longer than I anticipated. He kept no records, and while this is an exaggeration it feels like half the town owed him money and he owed an almost equal amount to the other half."

"My friend Tom Edison says someday there'll be machines to keep track of all your business," offered Holliday.

"Thomas *Alva* Edison?" she said, clearly impressed. "Is *he* here?"

"He came here to do me a favor."

"You know him that well?"

"Pretty well," answered Holliday.

"I'm impressed," said Charlotte.

Holliday allowed himself the luxury of a small chuckle, hoping it wouldn't bring on a coughing seizure. "I survived the O.K. Corral, and I survived Johnny Ringo, and I had breakfast with Billy the Kid two or three days ago, but what impressed you is that I know Tom Edison."

"No one's ever going to remember gunfights and killers," she said.

"That's a minority opinion," he noted.

"Perhaps, but they'll remember Thomas Alva Edison. Why, in ten or twelve years, people won't be able to remember how they lived before he invented the electric light."

"You could be right," answered Holliday. "Personally, I'd rather be forgotten than remembered for killing a couple of men in a gunfight next to a corral."

The waiter approached and they made their selections. A moment later a middle-aged blonde woman came out of the kitchen and approached their table. She stopped a few feet away and stared at Holliday.

"Doc?" she said at last. "Doc Holliday?"

"At your service," replied Holliday.

"Damn! My waiter told me it was you!" She took a step toward him and extended her hand. "I'm Mabel Grimsley. This here's my place."

"I'm pleased to meet you, Mrs. Grimsley," said Holliday, taking her hand and trying to ignore how vigorously she shook it.

"I've got a proposition for you, Doc," said Mabel. "There's no charge for the meals if I can post a sign saying you ate here."

"I accept your kind offer," replied Holliday. "But do you really think advertising that I ate here will bring in any extra business?"

"Sure will!" she said happily. "Maybe not right away, but when the Kid gets back to town and he learns you've been here, he'll come looking for you, either to team up or to kill you, meaning no disrespect—and either way, people will line up to see it. Only I won't allow any lines in my establishment, so they'll have to sit down and order their dinners." She paused for a moment, then added: "If you could postpone killing him or getting killed for a few meals, I could pay this place off."

"I shall endeavor not to get killed," Holliday promised her.

"That's good enough for me," said Mabel. "When Jasper—he's your waiter—brings you your check, just tear it up."

"I'll remember."

"And if he doesn't," Charlotte chimed in, "I'll remind him."

"Deal!" said Mabel, grabbing Holliday's hand and shaking it vigorously, then heading back into the kitchen.

"I'll bet you get offers like that all the time," said Charlotte.

"It's flattering, but it also tells your enemies where to find you," replied Holliday.

"I've not asked, but I assume your being here has something to do with Billy the Kid?" said Charlotte.

"Why should you think so?"

"Because for the life of me I can't imagine what other business you have in Lincoln. I know you're not gambling, and you just mentioned that you had breakfast with him in Tombstone."

"Interesting conclusion based on absolutely minimal evidence," commented Holliday noncommittally.

"What I can't figure out is what Thomas Edison has to do with it. You said he was here as a favor to you."

"Then clearly you're wrong about the Kid."

"But you'd say that whether I was wrong or not," she persisted.

"Why?" asked Holliday, as Jasper arrived with their food.

"Because if you're here to kill him, it makes sense to deny it so that word never gets to him. And if you're here to do business with him, you don't want Sheriff Garrett or any other lawmen to know about it, so that you're not suspected as being an accessory to any of his crimes."

"Charlotte, I think you missed your calling."

"You don't even know what I do, Doc."

"I know what you *don't* do," he replied with a smile. "You don't write complex puzzle stories like Mr. Poe back East."

She laughed. "All right, Doc. I'm all through prying. I hope I haven't offended you."

He shook his head. "On the contrary, you're the first person who wasn't a lawman, an outlaw, or a medicine man to show an interest in me in a very long time. Your curiosity is flattering."

"Now you're going to make me blush."

"Good. Red is one of my favorite colors." *When it's not wearing buckskins and feathers, anyway.*

They began eating their meals and decided that Mabel Grimsley was as good a cook as Charlotte had thought. Holliday, who usually had to force himself to eat a small main course and nothing else, actually ordered a piece of her pie. They finished their coffee as Jasper was nailing up a sign to the effect that this was the famous Doc Holliday's favorite restaurant in all of New Mexico. Finally they got up, Holliday left some coins on the table, and they walked out into the hot New Mexico day.

Charlotte window-shopped her way back to the hotel, admiring some dresses imported from "back East," which probably meant Dallas or St. Louis. A leather goods store was displaying a line of slim, lightweight suitcases made of buffalo hides, and Holliday made a mental note to pick one up to replace his old, scarred bag before he returned to Leadville.

When they reached the Grand Hotel, Charlotte turned to him.

"Thank you, Doc, for a very pleasant meal."

"My pleasure," he said with a gentlemanly bow. "Your husband is a very lucky man."

"He would have appreciated that," said Charlotte.

"Would have?"

"He died last year."

"I'm sorry to hear that," said Holliday.

They stood in awkward silence for almost a minute. Then she shook his hand, bade him good-night, and went off to her room.

Holliday, who was used to gambling until dawn, still hadn't adjusted to his new hours, and decided to stop at the hotel's bar for a drink. He sat at a table by himself, staring off into space and comparing Charlotte Branson to Kate Elder, who could swear like a cowboy, hit like a prizefighter, had a temper like an enraged bull, and a moral code that made shootists look like saints. He'd enjoyed some of his time with her, hated some of it, and actually feared for his life on occasion.

Then he thought of Charlotte, and found himself mouthing the words: "Maybe, just maybe . . ."

20.

HOLLIDAY AWOKE IN THE MORNING and got painfully to his feet. He climbed into his clothes, rinsed his face off, donned his holster and gun, walked down the hallway to the privy, returned to the room, put on his hat, and pulled his flask out of his pocket. He cursed when he realized it was empty, replaced it, and walked down the stairs to the main floor.

There was a new clerk at the desk, but he'd evidently been told who Holliday was, because he was positively obsequious in his greeting.

Holliday handed him the flask. "Get this thing filled up, please."

"It'll be waiting for you this afternoon, sir."

"I didn't say anything about the afternoon," replied Holliday coldly, as Buntline joined him.

"Yes, sir," said the clerk. "It'll just be a minute, sir. I'll be right back, Dr. Holliday, sir."

Buntline smiled as the clerk raced off to get some whiskey. "I never knew your name was 'sir.'"

"It's early in the day," said Holliday hoarsely. "Spare me your attempts at humor." He looked around. "Where's Edison?"

"He'll be along."

"Damned well better be. It must be seven o'clock in the morning. There are days I don't get in from playing cards until seven."

Holliday fell silent, and Buntline decided not to disturb him. The clerk returned about three minutes later and handed Holliday his flask. Holliday instantly opened it and took a swallow, then screwed the top on and tossed a nickel to the clerk.

"Okay," he said, turning to Buntline. "I'm human again."

"Shall we get some breakfast while we're waiting for Tom?" suggested Buntline.

"I just had mine. You go ahead if you're hungry."

Buntline shook his head. "I packed some meat and a loaf of bread in a basket. One of the lads is loading it into the buckboard as we speak. We can eat as we travel. And this time I rented an extra horse, too. Three in a buckboard is too damned uncomfortable."

"I hope you don't think *I'm* riding the damned horse," said Holliday.

"I'll take turns with Tom."

"Where the hell *is* he?" asked Holliday, looking up the staircase.

"He's not in his room," replied Buntline. "He's out back with the buckboard, making sure everything's in order. This means a lot to him, even more than it means to you. If we can destroy the station, whichever of the devices does it might also work on the medicine men."

"You're going to turn one of those things on Geronimo?" asked Holliday with a smile. "He'll just vanish and show up fifty miles away a second later."

"We have to start somewhere," said Edison's voice, and Holliday turned to see the inventor entering the lobby. "Are we all ready to proceed?"

Holliday grunted an affirmative, Buntline nodded, and the three of them went out the back entrance where a wagon drawn by two horses was awaiting them, as was a saddled gelding. Holliday winced at the sunlight, tried to ignore the dust that was blowing in his face from a gentle breeze, and climbed painfully up to the top of the wagon. Edison followed him, while Buntline mounted the gelding.

"All right," said Edison. "Let's go. If we're lucky, we'll make it there by nightfall."

"Why don't we just take the goddamned train?" growled Holliday, as the wagon shook and bounced over the uneven street.

"Because if we're successful," answered Edison, "and we have to assume we'll be or why go out there at all, we'd have to walk all the way back to Lincoln."

"I hadn't thought of that," admitted Holliday. "I just pull teeth and play cards." *And shoot people who need it every now and then*, he added mentally.

They passed a row of wooden buildings that had been bleached almost white by the sun, reached the outskirts of town in a few minutes, and then began following the railroad tracks to their destination. They rested the horses every two hours, stopping at a series of shaded water holes, some natural, some created by the construction crews that had laid the tracks, all of them welcome in the blazing New Mexico sun.

"It's so hot I actually prefer water to whiskey," remarked Holliday, leaning up against a small, twisted tree during a late afternoon rest stop.

"That's enough to give a man religion," said Buntline with a chuckle.

"You really think any of these gadgets will work on the station?" Holliday asked Edison.

"We'll know tomorrow," answered the inventor.

"Got a question," said Holliday.

"What is it?"

"What you're doing tomorrow—or hoping to do—is to destroy a station, a physical object, that's protected by a medicine man, maybe Hook Nose, maybe someone else, but definitely by someone using magic. Let's suppose you succeed."

"I'm happy to suppose that," said Edison. "What's your question?"

"How the hell does that help you combat the magic Geronimo and Hook Nose are using to keep the United States from expanding across the Mississippi? There are no stations, no physical barriers. So how does destroying the station help you lift their magic at the river?"

"No one's found a way to combat their magic yet, Doc," answered Edison. "If we can do it here, at least we'll have proof that it *can* be done, that science can successfully combat magic. I'll analyze what worked, what principles we applied, and we'll go from there with the certain knowledge that we can hold our own against the supernatural as practiced by the medicine men."

"I hope you're right," said Holliday.

Edison smiled. "I hope so too."

"We've already made some progress," added Buntline. "They've attacked my brass coaches dozens of times with arrows and bullets, and we've yet to lose a passenger."

Edison shook his head in disagreement. "That's a function of the super-hardened brass, Ned, not of our ability to combat magic. The Apaches and Southern Cheyenne never attacked one of your coaches with magic."

"How do we know that?" Buntline shot back.

Edison shrugged. "Point taken," he said, deciding not to argue.

They stayed in the scant shade for another few minutes, then climbed back onto the wagon and the horse—Edison rode it this time—and continued following the tracks to the west, coming to the edge of the valley that held the Apaches' sacred burial ground just before sunset.

"No sense floundering around in the dark," announced Edison. "We'll go to work at sunrise."

They pulled out their sleeping gear, started a fire, cooked their very simple dinner, and soon all three were asleep.

Holliday felt like he'd only been sleeping for five or six minutes when the toe of Edison's boot gently nudged him.

"What is it?" he rasped, sitting up promptly, drawing his gun, and looking around.

"Calm down, Doc," said Edison. "It's time to get up."

Holliday blinked his eyes furiously for a few seconds, finally remembered where he was and what he was doing there, and got stiffly to his feet. He took a swig from his flask, then a swallow of water from a canteen that Buntline offered him. "Damn!" he muttered. "It's even brighter and hotter than yesterday. And I don't remember that many dust devils," he added, indicated the swirling cloud of dust sweeping across the barren valley floor.

"Well, what's our first step?" asked Holliday, wiping his mouth with a handkerchief.

"We could start right here," said Edison. "The tracks are protected once they start descending into the valley. But I think it makes more sense to start at the station."

"Why?"

"Because if any of these devices work, we could wreck a fully loaded train if we begin on the rails. If we make any headway on the station, we can evacuate it before anyone gets hurt, then warn off the trains from both directions before going back to work on the rails."

"Okay, it makes sense," agreed Holliday. "Besides, I'm just here for moral support. I wouldn't know which end of those damned things to point at the station."

They proceeded down the slope to the floor of the valley, then approached the station.

"Well, at least it's empty," said Buntline.

"Except for the attendant."

"We'll move him out when the time comes," said Edison. He turned to Holliday, "We'll probably need more from you than moral support, Doc. I'm sure the attendant doesn't want us to destroy his place of business."

"Leave it to me," said Holliday.

They reached the station, moved the wagon around to the side, and soon all three men were on the ground.

"Give me a minute," said Holliday, walking to the front of the building and entering it.

"Good morning, sir," said the attendant, a different one from the last time. "May I help you?"

"You certainly may," said Holliday. "Have you got a deck of cards?"

The attendant frowned. "I'm afraid not, sir."

"Well, come out from behind there and let's get acquainted," said Holliday. He displayed his flask. "I might even be persuaded to share some of this with you."

"I'm afraid I'm not allowed to interact with the customers, sir," said the attendant. "Nor am I permitted to imbibe while on duty."

"I won't tell anyone if you don't."

"I'm sorry, sir."

Holliday casually drew his gun and pointed it at the man. "You can be sorry and alive, or sorry and dead. It's entirely up to you."

The man raised his hands well above his head. "Please don't shoot me, sir," he said. "I have a wife and two daughters."

"I think that's charming," said Holliday. "Come sit over here and tell me about them."

The man walked out from behind the counter, hands still reaching for the ceiling, and sat down next to Holliday.

"You can put your hands down now," said Holliday.

The man obeyed.

"And here, have a sip," continued Holliday, handing him the flask.

"Thank you, sir," said the man. He took a swallow and returned it. "I assume you want my money, sir?"

Holliday shook his head. "If you've got a wife and two daughters, you need it more than I do. What's your name?"

"Raymond, sir."

"Well, Raymond, very shortly you're going to see and hear a couple of men working around the station. It's perfectly all right. They're friends of mine, and they mean you no harm."

"I find that difficult to believe, sir," said Raymond, eyeing Holliday's gun.

"You mean *this*?" asked Holliday, indicating the gun. "Don't worry about it. I haven't shot anyone since sun-up."

Buntline opened the station door and peered in. "Everything okay, Doc?"

"Just fine. My friend Raymond and I are having a pleasant visit."

"All right, Doc. Just wanted to alert you that we'll be going to work now, in case you hear anything strange."

Buntline went back outside, and Raymond turned to Holliday, "He called you Doc," he said.

"A lot of people do," replied Holliday.

"Are you *him*?" he asked. "Are you Doc Holliday?"

"At your service."

Raymond clasped his hands together and began whispering a prayer.

"Relax, Raymond. No one's going to hurt you."

"But you're Doc Holliday, and you're pointing your gun at me!"

"I've got to point it *some*where," replied Holliday. "Now try to calm down. Tell me about your daughters. What are their names?"

"You're not going to kill them too, are you?" asked Raymond in tremulous tones.

"I'm not going to kill anyone unless you keep irritating me!" snapped Holliday.

"I'm sorry, Mister Doc, sir. It's just that I'm very nervous, talking about my family with such a notorious killer, meaning no offense, sir."

Holliday shook his head in disgust. "You should never have left Boston."

Raymond's eyes widened. "How did you know?"

"A shot in the dark," said Holliday. Raymond looked blank. "Your accent," he added. "Well, we've got to talk about something, and clearly you don't want to talk about your family. Tell me about Billy the Kid."

"I've never seen him, sir."

"Tell me what you've heard."

"He's a ruthless killer," said Raymond. "Some people say he's only thirteen years old, but I find that difficult to believe."

"Why?" asked Holliday.

"He would have had to start killing when he was five."

"Probably he's a bit older than thirteen, then," suggested Holliday.

"I agree, sir. Sixteen at least."

Holliday resisted the urge to smile at the notion of an eight-year-old desperado. He was about to comment when they heard a loud buzzing sound from the corner of the building.

"Any luck?" he yelled when the buzzing stopped.

"No," Buntline yelled back. "Thought we had something for a minute there, but we didn't."

"What are you using?"

"The Imploder, but it's not getting anywhere. I think we'll be trying the Deconstructor next."

"What are they doing?" asked Raymond.

"Nothing to worry about," said Holliday. "They're just trying to destroy the building."

Raymond jumped to his feet. "Destroy the building?" he repeated, panic in his voice.

"Just a piece at a time," said Holliday. "They'll give us plenty of warning if we have to evacuate."

"But—"

"You sure you don't have a deck of cards?"

"Why do they want to destroy this station?"

"That requires a very complicated answer for this early in the day," replied Holliday. "Just relax and try not to think about it."

During the next half-hour they heard explosions, whining, buzzing, and thudding. Each time Holliday would call out and ask if his companions had made any progress, and each time the answer was an increasingly frustrated negative.

Buntline appeared once more. "Just two more to try," he announced.

"Do you get the feeling that this damned station will be here to the end of Time?" asked Holliday.

"Give us fifteen minutes and ask again," responded Buntline grimly.

"And you haven't even made a dent in it?"

Buntline sighed, shook his head, and went back to join Edison.

"Can I ask a question, Doc, sir?" said Raymond with a puzzled expression on his face.

"Go ahead," said Holliday.

"Your friends are trying to blow up the station, right?"

"No," said Holliday. "They just want to destroy it. They don't much care if they blow it up, burn it down, melt it with electricity, or use some other method."

Raymond frowned. "And they've been trying for almost an hour, and haven't made a dent?"

"That's what they say."

"I don't want to offend you, Doc, sir," said Raymond, "but just what kind of fools are you associating with? This is a wooden building, and they not only can't burn it, but in a full hour they haven't even made a mark on it."

"Puzzling, isn't it?"

"What are they doing running around loose?"

"Maybe I'll lock them back up when they're done here," said Holliday.

"I don't understand any of it."

Holliday reached inside his shirt and withdrew the knife that hung around his neck on a very fine string. One tug and the string broke.

"Here, Raymond," he said, handing the knife to the surprised attendant. "Carve your initials on a wall."

Raymond took the knife, aware that Holliday's gun was still trained on him, walked to a wall, and tried without success to make a mark.

"It doesn't work," he said, surprised.

"Try another spot."

Raymond walked ten feet to his left and tried again with the same results, then turned to Holliday, frowning in confusion. "It's like it's petrified," he said at last.

"Try the counter," said Holliday. "It's clearly a different kind of wood."

Raymond did as he was instructed. All that happened was that the blade broke.

"I won't even charge you for ruining my knife," said Holliday.

"I don't understand any of this," said Raymond. "You see over here, where the counter was coming loose from the wall? I nailed it back in place not ten weeks ago."

"When did the railroad come through the valley here?" asked Holliday.

"You mean what time yesterday?"

Holliday shook his head. "No. When was the track laid and the station built?"

Raymond shrugged. "Six months ago."

"Makes sense."

"Not to me, it doesn't," said the attendant.

"This isn't Geronimo's home territory," said Holliday. "He probably didn't learn about it until a month or two ago—and *that's* when it became protected. You could drive a nail in before that, but even he couldn't get rid of it afterward."

"Geronimo?" repeated Raymond. "What's he got to do with anything?"

"It's complicated," said Holliday. Before he could say anything further, there was a sudden explosion at the side of the station, followed by a bellowed curse from Buntline. A moment later he and Edison both entered the building.

"I'm about ready to concede defeat," said Edison unhappily. "I used almost everything we tested at the *Silver Spoon*, and as far as I can tell we haven't made so much as a scratch on the damned wall."

"Well," said Holliday, getting to his feet, "I thank you for your hospitality, Raymond."

"It's hard to believe this really happened," said Raymond.

"You know what's harder to believe?" said Holliday. "All the time I was pointing *this* at you"—he held up his gun—"you were never in any danger."

Raymond just stared at him.

"I know it's going to be hard to believe," said Holliday, "but you're as impregnable as the station."

"Don't be silly," said Raymond. "I'm flesh and blood, like everyone else."

"In this valley, you're flesh and blood like no one else," said Holliday. "When that knife broke you should have cut your thumb off, but you didn't break the skin or even leave a mark. You can't be hurt until you leave the valley."

"I don't believe it," said Raymond.

"You want proof?" Holliday fired two shots into Raymond's chest. The force knocked him back a few feet, but nothing broke the skin. "There's proof."

"It's a miracle!" exclaimed Raymond.

"It's magic, anyway," said Holliday. "I should warn you, Raymond, that the likelihood is that we are just as invulnerable in this valley as you are, so if you've got a shotgun hidden behind the counter, I'd think very carefully about using it on us, because sooner or later you have to go home, and once you're out of the valley you *are* just flesh and blood again."

"I don't have a gun," said Raymond. "I wouldn't know how to use it if I did."

"So much the better for you," said Holliday. He tipped his hat. "It's been nice meeting you." He turned to Buntline and Edison, "Gentlemen, let's take our leave of this place."

The three of them walked to the wagon.

"Not a mark?" said Holliday.

"See for yourself," said Edison.

"About the only thing we accomplished was to attract a hawk," said Buntline, indicating a large raptor that stood on the roof of the station, staring at them.

"It's an eagle," said Holliday.

"Hawk, eagle, what's the difference?" said Buntline. "It's a spectator."

"No need to worry about him," said Holliday. "Eagles don't eat people."

"He makes me nervous, the way he keeps staring at me as if he'd like to break his diet and bite off a piece of me," said Buntline.

"Can't be done," noted Holliday. "Not while you're in this valley." He pulled out his gun. "Still, if he bothers you . . ."

"You can't kill *him* in the valley either," said Edison.

"No, but I can urge him to go away," said Holliday, taking aim and firing the gun.

The eagle shuddered as the bullets bounced off it, then flew to the wagon and perched on the seat, staring at him.

"All right, we can't hurt him," said Edison, "but maybe we can annoy him enough to get him off our wagon."

He walked to the back of the wagon and pulled out a small, pointed device.

"What's that?" asked Holliday.

"Just a whistle," answered Edison. "Well, not *just* a whistle. It's at a far higher frequency than even a dog whistle. I didn't use it on the station because it seemed so, well, *puny* after our more powerful devices failed—but it just might drive the eagle away."

"Do you blow into it?"

Edison smiled and shook his head. "I just push this button here . . . like this."

And as he pushed it, suddenly, instead of an eagle, an aging Indian screamed once and fell off the wagon into the dirt, dead.

"What the hell . . . ?" said Buntline.

Holliday walked over to the body and rolled it onto its back with a toe. "He's not Hook Nose," he said. "He's not wearing any of the Southern Cheyenne totem."

"He is Isa-tai," said a familiar voice, and they turned to find themselves facing Geronimo. "The White Eyes know him as White Eagle, a medicine man of the Comanche." He turned to Holliday. "You can now keep the rest of your bargain, and when the last of the station and the tracks are gone from the valley, I will keep mine."

"So he wasn't Hook Nose after all," said Holliday, as he, Edison, and Buntline looked down at the dead White Eagle. He turned back to where Geronimo had been standing, but there was only empty air.

"Was Geronimo ever really here at all, I wonder?" mused Buntline.

"Those aren't imaginary moccasin prints," said Edison, pointing to Geronimo's tracks.

"Well," said Holliday, "time to go back to work."

"Agreed," said Edison.

"Hey, Raymond!" yelled Holliday.

The attendant stuck his head through the doorway.

"Get out of there," said Holliday. "You're about to lose your station."

"I thought you couldn't make a scratch in it."

"That was then. This is now."

Raymond frowned. "What's changed?"

Holliday pointed to White Eagle's corpse. "It lost its armor."

Raymond exited the station, and with one more exposure to the Deconstructor, two minutes later the station was a pile of rubble.

"I can melt the tracks, but I think Geronimo won't consider them *gone* if they're just misshapen," said Edison. "When we get back to town we'll hire a crew to pull up all the tracks and re-route them outside the valley."

"How long do you think it will take?" asked Holliday.

"I'll send for two crews—one to construct the new route around the valley, and one to clean up the mess here. They're pretty fast once they get on the job," answered Edison. "The valley should pass Geronimo's inspecting in perhaps two or three days, four at the outside. It all depends on when they get here. And since it involves my overcoming magic, the government will pay for it."

Edison wired for the crews when they got back to town late that evening, and Holliday returned to the Grand Hotel, counting the minutes until the Kid was a normal—and vulnerable—man again.

21.

HOLLIDAY CLIMBED OUT OF BED with his usual lack of enthusiasm, got dressed, and walked down the stairs and through the lobby. He wandered out into the sunlight, winced at the brightness of the world, and decided to get some breakfast. He checked his wallet to see how his money was holding out, realized that he had nothing smaller than a ten-dollar bill, and walked over to the bank to break a bill so he'd have meal, barber, and tip money.

"Welcome, Dr. Holliday," said the bearded teller as he entered the bank. "Isn't it a beautiful day?"

"Except for the sunlight and the fresh air," replied Holliday.

The teller laughed. "What can I do for you, sir?"

Holliday handed a bill to the teller. "Change this into nickels, dimes, quarters, and gold dollar pieces."

"What quantities would you like?"

"Whatever's convenient. Otherwise I might have to let Charlotte leave the tip for dinner tonight."

"Charlotte, sir?"

"Mrs. Branson."

The teller shook his head. "I'm not familiar with the lady, sir."

"You must have dealt with her," said Holliday. "She's in town to settle her brother's estate."

"I'm sorry, sir, but we've never dealt with a Mr. Branson."

Holliday grimaced. "Of course not. She's a married woman. I have no idea what her maiden name was." He described her in detail for the teller.

"No, sir. I'm sure I'd have remembered her. We don't get that many women doing business in here."

"Is there another bank? Maybe her brother kept his money there."

The teller nodded. "Go out the front door, turn left for a block, and it's across the street, right next to the dry goods store." He pulled out a small booklet. "I can give you the name of my opposite number there if you'd like."

Holliday shook his head. "No, I was just making conversation." He gathered his coins and put them in a pocket. "Thanks for your help."

"It's my job, sir."

Holliday smiled grimly. "You have no idea how little that means to a lot of people."

He walked out of the bank, and turned left to hunt for a restaurant. He walked along the raised wooden sidewalk, past a casino, a brothel, a butcher shop, a trio of other stores, and finally, after coming to the corner and proceeding to the next block, he came to a restaurant that was open and doing a brisk business. He was about to enter it when he looked across the street and found himself facing the other bank.

He debated with himself for a moment, then walked across the unpaved street and entered the bank.

"Yes, sir," said a clerk. "May I help you?"

"I was wondering if Mrs. Branson has been in today," said Holliday.

"Mrs. Branson? I don't think I know the woman, sir."

"Charlotte Branson," said Holliday. "She's settling her brother's estate."

"I'm not acquainted with the lady."

"My mistake," said Holliday, turning to leave. "I'm sorry to have bothered you."

"No bother at all," the clerk called after him.

Holliday, frowning, crossed the street and entered the restaurant, trying to assimilate what he'd heard. Maybe he'd heard her wrong; he wasn't really listening that carefully. Maybe she *hadn't* gone to any bank to clear up the estate.

He shook his head. That was ridiculous. If the brother owed money, if he was owed money, of course she'd be working with a bank. *But probably*, he decided, *she'd see the manager and not a lowly clerk.* That *would be why the tellers didn't remember her.*

He ordered coffee and some eggs. He'd have preferred whiskey, but he wanted a clear head to work this out. After all, he'd only spent a little time with her, hadn't touched any part of her except her arm. If she were here visiting a lover and she had lied to him, it was better to know it now before he got involved.

He finished his breakfast in silence, then started making the rounds of the places Charlotte would have had to visit to settle any estate. No one at the assay office knew her. The small clapboard building that served as the city hall had no record of any farm, ranch, or mining claim changing hands in the past seven months. He stopped in at the newspaper office and checked the obituaries for the past year. Seventeen men had died, including three farmers. None listed her as a surviving family member.

It *had* to be a lover. He could find out the man's name just by checking the various hotels in town. There were only six besides the

Grand, and he was certain no clerk would deny the notorious Doc Holliday what he wanted. But then what would he do with the information? Shoot her lover? Tell her never to see him again?

He sighed deeply. He didn't have that long to live anyway. He could put up with Kate Elder for another year or two. There was no way he thought he would last any longer than that. The fights, the screaming matches, at least they kept him on his toes, and she had never denied her bed to him. They'd split up three times in the past—no, make it four—and they always got back together. They didn't even have to make apologies any more. One or the other would show up, there'd be no recriminations, and they'd be back together again as if nothing had happened.

Still, he resented Charlotte's lying to him. If she'd just said that she was visiting a friend, he's have instantly figured out what she meant and he wouldn't feel somehow duped or betrayed.

He decided he wanted a drink after all, and went over to the nearest saloon, walking through the swinging doors and approaching the already-crowded bar. There was a piano in the corner, but no one was playing it. A huge mirror hung behind it, perhaps twenty feet long, allowing him a perfect view of the entrance. He didn't think he had any enemies in Lincoln, but one never knew, and it was good to be able to see who came and went.

"Bottle and a glass," he said, walking past a number of men until he found a space at the bar.

"Mind if I join you?" said a voice, and he turned to find himself facing a tall, well-built man with dark hair, a large mustache, and piercing gray eyes. He wore a shining star on his vest, and a gun on each hip.

"Be my guest," replied Holliday.

"Thanks," said the man. He extended a hand. "Garrett. Pat Garrett."

"The sheriff," said Holliday. "I've heard about you. And I'm—"

"Doc Holliday, I know," said Garrett. "I've been hearing about you for years. Especially that shootout at the O.K. Corral in Tombstone. Was it everything they say it was?"

"Probably not," said Holliday.

"I hear you were there again last week," continued Garrett. "And that you might have met someone I know."

"It's possible," said Holliday. "Who do you know?"

"Let's not play games, Doc. At long as he's in Tombstone, he safe. Well, safe from *me*, anyway. But if he comes back to New Mexico Territory, it's my job to bring him in or kill him."

"Why are you telling me all this?" asked Holliday.

"Because you're Doc Holliday," said Garrett. "There can only be one reason you're here. I just want you to know: if he's anywhere in Lincoln County, he's *mine*."

"Have you ever heard anything—a rumor, an eyewitness account, even a tall tale—about me being a bounty hunter?"

"If you're not here to kill him, you're here to join him, in which case I'll have to kill you too."

"I'm in a bad mood this morning," said Holliday irritably. "Threaten me some other time. You'll live longer."

"I'm not threatening," said Garrett. "I'm just suggesting that this might be a good time for you to go back to Tombstone or wherever you're from these days."

"That's good to know," said Holliday, staring into Garrett's eyes. "Because I've been threatened by experts. Two or three of them are probably still alive. Crippled, to be sure, but alive. Now shut up, drink your drink, and let's preserve at least the illusion of civility."

Garrett returned his stare. "I don't rattle, Doc."

"Then you won't make any noise when you hit the floor," said

Holliday. "I suggest you concentrate on the illustrious Mr. Bonney, and leave an honest dentist to his own devices."

"Just remember," said Garrett, "don't get between him and me. And if you're here to join him, you're a dead man."

Holliday stood away from the bar and gathered his coat behind him with his left hand.

"Enough threats," he said coldly. "Either try to back them up, or walk out of here."

Garrett glared at Holliday, saw something in his eyes that made him rethink his position, forced an insincere laugh, then turned on his heel and stalked out.

"Is one of you gone?" said the bartender's voice.

"One of us is," said Holliday, and the bartender stood up from where he'd been crouching behind the bar. Other customers who'd hit the floor began climbing back onto their chairs.

"Thank goodness!" said the bartender. "That mirror cost more than three hundred dollars. One bullet could destroy it."

"That's a lot of money to pay for a mirror," noted Holliday.

"We had to do something to make us different from the other bars. It was this, or import Lily Langtry. This was cheaper."

Holliday smiled. "Not as entertaining, though."

"Still," continued the bartender, "it's a shame you didn't follow him outside and kill him. You would have put this place on the map."

"I doubt it," said Holliday. "No one will ever remember Pat Garrett."

"Probably not," agreed the bartender thoughtfully. "Hell, if you don't kill him this week, the Kid'll kill him next week or next month."

"Is the Kid in town?" asked Holliday, trying not to appear too interested.

The bartender shrugged. "Who the hell knows? He comes and goes pretty much as he pleases."

"And no one's tried to claim the reward?"

The bartender smiled. "Usually he'll toss a coin in the air, then draw and put a hole through it before it lands. Most people are content to leave him alone after that."

"Including Garrett?" asked Holliday.

"Pat used to ride with him. Quite the pair of desperados they were. But Pat, he stopped short of shooting any lawmen. He saw enough friends killed that he decided to change sides, and went to work as a sheriff. He and Billy don't like each other much these days. I know Billy doesn't hate him enough to hunt him down, but he wouldn't think twice about shooting him if they find themselves face to face."

"And he'd win?"

"He'd win. Garrett is good, don't get me wrong—but the Kid is, well, the Kid." The bartender stared at him. "Don't take it wrong, Doc, but I think even you couldn't beat him."

"Your confidence is appreciated," said Holliday dryly.

"Doc, I didn't mean no offense," said the bartender nervously.

"None taken," said Holliday. "Fortunately I'm just a dentist and a card player."

The bartender chuckled, though he was clearly still nervous. "So if he walks in here today or tomorrow, I shouldn't tell him you're looking for him?"

"I wouldn't want Billy the Kid mad at me," said Holliday. He placed a couple of coins on the bar. "If he does stop by, buy him a drink for me."

He left the bar, wandered around aimlessly for a few minutes until the heat of the day began to affect him, and finally returned to the Grand Hotel. He'd never used the bar there; if someone was hunting for him, that would be the first place they'd look.

It was just off the lobby, a little more elegant than the bars he usually frequented. There were curtains on the windows, leather cushions on the chairs, and the long bar had been polished to the point where one could almost see his face in it. Holliday ordered a bottle and a glass, seated himself across from a painting of George Armstrong Custer, and filled his glass.

Edison was coming back from wherever he'd spent the morning, spotted Holliday as he walked through the lobby, and joined him.

"Have a drink," said Holliday, pushing the bottle over to him.

"Too early in the day for me," replied Edison. He stared at it for a minute, then sighed and took a swallow. "I'll be honest, Doc," he said. "I was just about ready to give up. If none of those things worked on the station, how the devil could I stop Geronimo and the others from containing the United States on the east side of the Mississippi? But now I'm on to something. I don't know *why* that ultrasound, or so I call it, killed White Eagle but didn't seem to bother Geronimo at all. I don't know if it'll affect Hook Nose, either—but that's the first positive result I've had in two years. It means they *can* be stopped, and I'm going back to my experiments with renewed enthusiasm."

"If anyone can do it, you're the man," said Holliday sincerely.

"Thanks, Doc," said Edison. "It's easy to get discouraged when you're so long between successes, especially when I know my country's depending on me. I appreciate your support."

"You want discouragement?" asked Holliday. "Watch the Kid in action. Now, *that's* discouraging. He doesn't *need* magic." He paused. "How's the clean-up coming?"

"Well, they'll reach the valley tonight or tomorrow morning. I'll be getting daily reports," said Edison. "As for the Kid, I've never seen him in action—but I've seen *you*. I don't think you have much to worry about, once I find a way to neutralize Hook Nose's magic."

As they were drinking and talking, Charlotte entered the hotel.

She was heading toward the stairs when she saw them and entered the bar.

"Hello, Doc," she said with a friendly smile.

"Hello, Charlotte," said Holliday. "I've been meaning to introduce you to Tom Edison. Tom, say hello to Charlotte Branson."

"I'm honored, Ma'am," said Edison.

"Not as honored as I am," she said. "Imagine meeting the greatest genius in the world!"

"I'm flattered that you should think so," replied Edison.

"Would you care to join us?" asked Holliday.

"I'd like to, but I still have all kinds of things to do," said Charlotte. "I'm due at the lawyer's office in just a few minutes. I've just got time to get out of these dusty clothes."

"Dinner, perhaps?"

"I'd enjoy that."

"Six o'clock?" asked Holliday.

"I'll be in the lobby then," she replied, turning and leaving the bar, then climbing the stairs up to her room.

Holliday got up and walked over to the bar. "How many lawyers are there in town?" he asked softly.

The man shrugged. "I don't know. Ten, twelve. Maybe a few less, maybe a few more."

"Thanks." He returned to the table.

"I heard what you asked," said Edison. "Why should you care?"

"Just curious."

"Well, I can stay here all afternoon and get drunk, or I can go back to my room and work on some of my ideas."

"I'll see you later."

Edison left the bar and went through the lobby to the staircase. A moment later Holliday finished his drink and walked out into the street. He considered following Charlotte when she emerged from the hotel, but he couldn't do it without being spotted, and he didn't want her to think he was suspicious of her.

He was still troubled, not by the thought of her visiting a lover, but by the fact that she felt the need to lie about it. He had no claim on her, none whatsoever, so why these lies, why this secrecy? It was *that* that made him want to follow her, to find out what was really going on.

But he knew he wouldn't follow her when she emerged. He didn't like being deceived by someone he admired, but he was honest enough to admit that she was under no obligation to tell him the truth. They'd shared a coach ride and a few dinners, nothing more. *In fact*, he thought, *I'd better get out of sight before she comes out, or she might feel obligated to lead me on a two-hour wild goose chase.*

He ducked into a store and stood there, watching the hotel until Charlotte emerged a few minutes later. She turned right to the corner, then right again, and he lost sight of her.

Almost against his will, Holliday asked the shopkeeper where he could find a lawyer.

"I'm no expert on which ones are any good, but just about every lawyer in town is two or three blocks down on the left, mostly on this side of the street, but one or two are across the street."

"Thanks," said Holliday.

He went back to the hotel, spent another hour in the bar, climbed the stairs to his room, rinsed the sweat off his face, felt restless, killed another hour in the bar, and then decided to go over to the sheriff's office to see if the reward on the Kid had gotten any larger.

The building was the only all-brick structure on the block, and he could see the bars of a trio of cells facing the alley between the building and the neighboring bootmaker's shop. His experience told him that this was a stupid way to build a jail; you never wanted a window where a prisoner's confederates could work at removing the bars.

"Good afternoon," he said, entering the office and tipping his hat to the deputy who sat behind a battered desk.

"Hi," said the deputy. "You're Doc Holliday, ain't you?"

"That I am."

"Garrett said you might be stopping by one of these days. He said you'd talk about a bunch of other things, but you'd really want to know about the reward." The deputy smiled. "It's still ten grand."

"I take it Mr. Garrett isn't in town?"

"No. He got word that the Kid was seen about forty miles west of here, so off he went." The deputy leaned forward, "Best thing could happen is for him not to find him."

"You get no argument from me," agreed Holliday. "By the way, how did you know I was me—I mean, that I'm Holliday?"

"He said you made a skeleton look fat. Fits you top to bottom." The deputy stared at him for a moment, then opened a drawer. "Care for a chaw?" he asked, offering him some tobacco.

Holliday shook his head. "That's one of the very few vices that has eluded me."

"I could offer you a drink, but I got word that you've been drinking all over town and it's only early afternoon."

"Drinking's my hobby," said Holliday wryly. "I assume Garrett's keeping a watch on me?"

"Well, you *have* killed fifty-six or fifty-seven men."

Holliday smiled at the way the number kept growing. "I'll accept your kind offer."

The deputy opened another drawer, pulled out a bottle, uncorked it, took a swallow, and handed it to Holliday, who did the same.

"I hope you'll keep this between us, Doc," said the deputy. "I could get fired for drinking when I'm on duty."

"My lips are sealed," said Holliday. Suddenly he smiled. "Except when I do *this*," he added, taking another swallow.

"Tell me about the gunfight," said the deputy.

"Which gunfight was that?" asked Holliday.

"Aw, come on, Doc, you know what I mean."

For the next few minutes Holliday recounted the Gunfight at the O.K. Corral. He had just finished when he saw the deputy suddenly looking past him, out the front window.

"Here comes another one," the deputy announced, getting to his feet.

Two burly men, one of them a Mexican, carried a body wrapped in blankets into the office.

"Third cell," said the deputy. "The door's open."

"What's this?" asked Holliday. "I thought Garrett was out of town."

"He is. Gonna have to pay a bounty on this one." He rifled through a stack of warrants and posters. "Charlie Sanford, four hundred dollars, dead or alive. Nice afternoon's work."

"How do you know which one to pay?"

"*They're* not bounty hunters," said the deputy. "They've just been paid to tote the body over here. In fact, there's only one bounty hunter in town at the moment, unless you've joined the ranks," said the deputy. "Damned good one. This is the third this week."

"I'm impressed," said Holliday. "If I were the Kid, I'd be on my guard." The two men walked out through the office into the street. "I was going to ask where I could meet this guy, but hell, I've probably run into him already in one of the bars."

"I sure as hell doubt it," said the deputy.

"Why do you say that?"

"Because here she comes now."

The door opened and Charlotte Branson walked in.

"Hello, Doc," she said, unperturbed. "What a surprise meeting you here."

"You're not half as surprised as I am," replied Holliday.

The deputy unlocked a drawer, counted out eight fifty-dollar bills, and handed them over to her.

"Are we still on for dinner?" she asked. Suddenly she smiled and held up the money. "It'll be my treat."

22.

"I HAD NO IDEA WE WERE RIVALS," said Charlotte, as the waiter brought their dinners to the table on a silver serving dish and then left them alone in a corner of the restaurant.

"I'm only after one bounty," replied Holliday.

"I thought I was, too," she said.

Holliday looked around to make sure no one could overhear them. There were some fifteen tables with tablecloths and dishes that would not have impressed at the better restaurants back East but were the height of elegance in Lincoln. Only the three farthest were occupied; clearly none of the respectable citizenry that frequented the restaurant had any urge to sit near the notorious Holliday.

"You'll forgive me if I point out that you are far from the typical bounty hunter," said Holliday.

"I find that it works to my advantage."

"How so?" he asked curiously.

"I come and go without attracting any attention. There must be a lot of hot-blooded empty-headed young men who want to call you out on the street and draw against you. After all, you're Doc Holliday, and anyone who kills you will find his reputation is immediately enhanced." She smiled. "But who wants to prove his manhood against an overweight middle-aged woman whose hair is starting to turn gray."

"Eventually someone must draw against you," replied Holliday. "I mean, eventually you have to go to work."

"I don't wear a holster, Doc," said Charlotte. "I don't shoot it out with the men I'm after. They're *killers*. They've got to be wanted dead or alive. I'm not capable of bring them in alive, so I only go after the ones with a price on their heads even if they're dead. And I don't believe in giving wanted killers an even chance. *You* might invite the Kid or Clay Allison out into the street to have it out, but there's no need to. They're outlaws, the law wants them dead or alive, and I'm not required to enter into a shootout with them."

"So what do you do?" asked Holliday.

"I wait until they're alone, or perhaps playing poker or faro, and then I walk up behind them and put a bullet in their ear. Most of them never know what happened."

Holliday stared at her. "How many men have you killed?"

"A few."

"How many?" he repeated.

"Counting today, seven."

He shook his head in wonderment. "And I've never heard of you."

"If you had, I'd be totally ineffective," she responded with a smile. "If any of these men *knew* who and what I was, I wouldn't stand a chance."

"Well, I'm impressed as all hell," said Holliday.

"Thank you, I think," said Charlotte. "Now eat your dinner. It's getting cold."

"Yes, ma'am," he replied. "I sure wouldn't want to get a deadly killer like yourself mad at me." He began cutting his steak with exaggerated motions.

She laughed at his efforts. He kept them up for a few more seconds, then stopped and had a swallow of his whiskey.

"What got you started?" he asked.

"The same man you're after," she said.

"The Kid?"

"He killed my husband."

"I'm sorry to hear that," said Holliday.

"Dwayne wasn't even involved in the Lincoln County War. He was just riding through, after his mine over in Cochise County had played out. The Kid thought he was on the other side and never gave him a chance to explain. He just shot him down in cold blood." She paused, her face reflecting her emotions. "I was teaching school a couple of hundred miles north of here. When I heard about it I made up my mind to kill him." She stopped again when she realized she had picked up her steak knife and was holding like a dagger. She placed it down on the table and continued.

"I bought a gun and spent months practicing with it. I knew I could not beat the Kid in anything remotely resembling a shootout, but I was and am quite prepared to trade my life for his."

"Whether you shoot him from six inches or sixty feet, you'd better make your first shot count," said Holliday, "because you'll never get a second."

"When I was ready to take my revenge," Charlotte continued, "he'd either left Lincoln County or gone into hiding. I knew he'd come back, and in the meantime, there was a wanted bandit taking up residence in my little town. I went to the sheriff's office, found that he was worth five hundred dollars dead or alive, and asked why the sheriff hadn't killed or jailed him. He explained to me that law officers can't collect rewards, and that he wasn't willing to risk his life for the small salary they were paying him."

"Can't say that I blame him," agreed Holliday with a smile.

"Well, *I* blame him," she said. "What's the point of having law officers if they won't go after these villains? At least Pat Garrett wants the Kid as badly as I do." She took a sip of her tea, decided it had grown too cold, signaled to the waiter, and asked for a fresh cup. "Anyway, I knew if I was going to travel to New Mexico to hunt for the Kid, I'd need money. So one day I saw Jonah sitting on a rocking chair outside the general store—"

"Jonah?" interrupted Holliday.

"Jonah Stone," she replied. "The outlaw. I walked toward the store, and he paid no attention to me. So when I passed behind him I pulled my gun out of my purse, held it an inch from the back of his head, and pulled the trigger."

"I'll bet *that* woke everyone up," said Holliday in amused tones.

"Everybody but Jonah," she agreed. "The sheriff came up, identified him, told the people that I had every right to shoot him, and invited me to return to his office with him, where I signed some official documents and he wired for my money. It arrived the next day, I quit the school as soon as they found another teacher, and I began my new career." She smiled. "I killed three more men up north, then heard that the Kid had shown up in Lincoln County again, and decided to come down here to find him. That was when I met you."

"I gather you haven't been exactly sedate and inactive since you got here," said Holliday.

"Not exactly," she agreed, still smiling.

"If you kill the Kid, is that the end of it? Do you retire to a nice little home, or maybe go back to teaching school?"

She shook her head. "I made more today than I'd make in three years of teaching, and I've made sure one desperado will never kill again. I think I've found my metier."

Holliday stared at her. "You're making a serious mistake."

"I don't think so."

"I admire your courage, but it's born of ignorance," said Holliday. "No one knows who you are yet, and you've somehow managed to kill seven men. Maybe you can protect your identity a little longer, maybe you can't—but if you kill the Kid, you're a marked woman, and the smartest thing you can do is take a new name and go live in Chicago or Baltimore or some other city east of the Mississippi." He pushed his mostly uneaten meal aside and leaned forward. "Don't you understand that you're not a bystander anymore? The second you became a bounty hunter, you became the enemy to a couple of hundred deadly killers. The only reason you're alive today, the only reason they're not taking aim at you through the door and windows right now, is because they don't know what you are or who you are."

"And I plan to keep it that way," said Charlotte.

"It's too late," persisted Holliday. "The deputy knows you're a bounty hunter. I know it. Probably Garrett knows it. The lawmen up north who paid you know it."

"They're officers of the law," she pointed out.

"You think they'll protect your identity when a desperate killer points a gun between their eyes and demands to know who some bounty was paid to?"

"I'll have to think about it, Doc," said Charlotte. Then: "Would *you* give them my name?"

Holliday shook his head, "No. But I'm half-dead already, and I don't have any family."

"I'll consider it," she said again. "But I've really gotten very good at what I do." Suddenly she smiled again. "Would you like dessert?"

"No, thanks."

"Neither would I," she said, getting to her feet. "Come with me. I want to show you something."

She left a gold piece on the table and walked to the door. Holliday fell into step beside her.

"Where are we going?" he asked.

"At least a mile out of town. Are you up to walking?" She stared at his frail frame. "No, I think not. We'll ride."

They walked to a stable on the next block, and she rented a horse and surrey. They got aboard, she grabbed the reins and clucked to the horse, and a few minutes later they were a mile and a half beyond the city limits. She pulled the horse to a halt, Holliday climbed down to the ground, and then helped her down.

"All right," he said. "We've only got an hour of daylight left. What did you want to show me?"

"Now I show you why I'm not that worried."

She walked about fifty feet away, picked up half a dozen stones, and laid them out in a line, each a foot from the previous one.

Then she returned to where Holliday was standing, pulled her pistol out of her purse, handed the purse to Holliday, took aim while holding the weapon in both hands, and fired six shots at two-second intervals. Five stones flew apart; the dirt right next to the sixth seemed to explode as the bullet buried itself there.

She turned to him, an excited smile on her flushed face. "Well?" she said.

"They weren't shooting back," replied Holliday.

"I shot them before they had a chance to," she said.

"Easy to say. How accurate are you when you're ducking for cover?"

"Damn it, Doc! I took you out here to show you that you don't have to worry about me."

"I'm pretty good," he said as she reloaded her pistol, "and when it comes to gunfighting, I worry about *me*."

"Somehow I don't believe that," said Charlotte.

"Well, if I don't, it's because I'm mostly dead already."

He paused. "That was an interesting experiment. May we try another?"

She stared at him suspiciously. "Yes," she said at last.

"Don't worry," he said. "Nothing will be shooting back at you."

He pulled his gun, surveyed the area with an expert eye, then fired into the ground next to a scrubby bush. A terrified rabbit darted out.

"Shoot him," said Holliday.

She tried to take aim, but the rabbit was changing direction every two jumps and she couldn't keep up with him. Finally she lowered the gun.

"I didn't want to kill him," she said lamely.

"Would the result have been any different if you wanted to?" he asked her.

"I'm not after rabbits who are running away, but men who are stationary targets."

"Just remember," said Holliday. "If the Kid wasn't suspicious of everyone, if he was ever a stationery target, he wouldn't still be around, not with that price on his head. If he winds up killing one hundred men before he's done, you have to figure that seventy-five or eighty will be bounty hunters."

She stared at him for a long moment. "Are you sure you're not just trying to scare me off so you can get to him first?"

He sighed deeply, then forced a smile. "I admire your spunk, Charlotte. I truly do."

Not your brains, alas. Or your sense of self-preservation. But you do *have spunk, little good will it do you against Billy the Kid.*

23.

HOLLIDAY WAS SITTING AT A TABLE in the Blue Peacock, one of the larger taverns in town, a bottle and a glass in front of him, as usual.

There were some thirty tables in the place, all of them filled, some hosting games of poker, others just where friends gathered to drink and visit. He missed the action of the gaming tables, but he simply didn't have enough money to buy into any of the better poker or faro games, and so he was playing solitaire to amuse himself, and to enjoy the feel of a deck of cards in his hands.

He'd been there since sundown. He had no reason to stay, but on the other hand, unless Edison needed him for something, he had no reason to leave. He'd already checked with Edison to see if work had begun in the valley. It had, but they were still a couple of days from finishing it.

"Black nine on the red ten," said a familiar voice.

"Welcome back," said Holliday without looking up. "Have you disposed of the illustrious Mr. Garrett yet?"

"Soon," said the Kid. "You gonna invite me to sit down?"

"Be my guest," said Holliday. "No reason not to be friendly," he added with a smile. "We couldn't hurt each other if we wanted to."

The Kid chuckled at that, and pulled up a chair. "How have you been, Doc?"

"Fine, thank you," said Holliday. "I'm touched that you care."

"Don't make fun of me, Doc," said the Kid, not in a threatening manner. "You're damned near the only friend I've got in this county."

"From what I hear, your friends don't tend to live to ripe old ages," said Holliday. He saw the Kid tense, and continued: "Not that you kill them. Just that you lead a very dangerous existence, and those who don't handle a gun as well as Billy the Kid but ride with you tend not to live very long,"

The Kid relaxed noticeably. "I never set out to be an outlaw or a killer, you know," he said. "Things just happened. And sooner or later you do what you're good at."

"How did you get to be so good with a gun?"

The Kid shrugged. "I honestly don't know. I never played with toy guns back in New York or Kansas, never dreamed of being a gunslinger, never practiced much with a gun once I got one. I just strapped on a holster one day, and pulled and fired my gun, and hit what I was aiming at every damned time. It's like pointing my finger."

"I would say that you're what they call a natural," said Holliday. "Most men can't hit what they point at with their finger."

"You think so?" asked the Kid. "Coming from you, that sounds right complimentary."

"Of course, being protected by Hook Nose doesn't hurt either," added Holliday.

"Who says I'm protected?" demanded the Kid.

"Geronimo."

"I've heard of him. Never met him, though."

"Consider yourself lucky," said Holliday. "Have you actually met Hook Nose?"

The Kid nodded. "Yes. But he calls himself something else."

"Woo-Ka-Nay?"

"That's it. I wonder why he'd tote around a name like that."

"Not everyone speaks English," said Holliday. "Geronimo calls himself Goyathlay."

"You keep mentioning Geronimo," said the Kid. "Ain't he supposed to be back south of Tombstone?"

Holliday smiled. "Now, that's kind of difficult to say. He's pretty much wherever he wants to be, much like Hook Nose."

"I thought all white men were the Apaches' enemies, but you sound like you've actually talked to Geronimo."

"I have—just like you've talked to Hook Nose."

"What does Geronimo want from you?"

"He's already got it," answered Holliday.

"Didn't know you were a gun for hire," said the Kid. "Who'd you shoot for him?"

"No one."

The Kid frowned. "I'm not following this. He asked for a favor. What did you do for him, and what did he pay you for it?"

"You know that train station where we first met?" asked Holliday. "About a day's ride west of here?"

"Yeah." The Kid grinned. "I sure had you fooled, didn't I?"

"You sure did," agreed Holliday.

"So what about the station?"

"It's not there any more."

The Kid laughed. "He paid you to burn down a train station? Why didn't he do it himself?"

"I didn't exactly burn it," said Holliday. "And he couldn't do it because it had a magical protector, a Comanche named White Eagle."

"I can't tell you how sick I get of all this magic crap!" said the Kid. "Geronimo's a warrior. Why can't he do his own killing and station burning?"

"He's a warrior *too*," answered Holliday. "But first and foremost he's a medicine man. If he could have destroyed the station on his own, he would have. But he couldn't, so he asked me to do it for him."

"And you agreed, just like that?" asked the Kid, snapping his fingers.

Holliday shook his head. "No, we made a trade. I did him a favor, and he's doing one for me."

"What's he doing for you?"

Holliday stared at the Kid. "I couldn't kill you before. Now there's a chance that I can in another couple of days."

The Kid tensed. "You want to step outside and try it right now?"

Holliday shook his head. "The same thing would happen that happened in that whorehouse in Tombstone." He paused. "But in the meantime, *I've* got a trade to make with *you*."

The Kid stared coldly at him. "I'm listening."

"There's a woman of my acquaintance who's staying at my hotel," said Holliday. "Her name is Charlotte Branson."

"Never heard of her," said the Kid.

"I'll introduce you as soon as I get the chance," continued Holliday. "I'll want you to take a good look and remember her."

"And what else?"

"Don't kill her."

"You think I just go around killing women as the mood suits me?" demanded the Kid.

"No, I know you don't. All I'm saying is if you see her, keep out of sight. That's not asking too much, is it?"

"I don't know."

"That's my proposition," said Holliday. "You promise not to kill her, and I promise that you and I will never have to find out who's the better shootist."

"You got a soft spot for this lady?" asked the Kid, suddenly amused. "I hear Big-Nose Kate can be pretty formidable when she's jealous."

"She's hundreds of miles away," said Holliday. "Let *me* worry about her. Do we have a deal?"

"First I want to know why I would ever see this Branson woman."

"She has a grudge against you."

"Oh?"

"You killed her husband," said Holliday.

"Branson, Branson," repeated the Kid, frowning. "I don't know any Branson."

"He got caught in the middle in the Lincoln County War."

"Then he should have kept his head down, or ridden around us."

"I admire your sense of compassion," said Holliday.

"People were shooting at me. Ain't my fault if he got in the way."

"Nobody's blaming you," said Holliday. "I just want to know: Have we got an agreement?"

The Kid frowned as he considered his options. "Let me just make sure I understand this. If I don't kill this woman, who I've never seen and won't recognize if you don't point her out to me, you'll be my friend?"

"I'm already your friend," said Holliday. "It won't stop me from hunting you down if you kill her."

"Let me say it another way, then," replied the Kid. "If I don't kill her, you and I will never have to draw on one another?"

"That's a promise," said Holliday.

The Kid reached his hand across the table. "Shake on it."

Holliday extended his hand gingerly as a cheer arose at a neighboring table when someone won a large pot. The Kid ignored the cheer, took Holliday's hand, gripped it tightly, and shook it vigorously. Holliday found himself in agony, but refused to complain. Finally the Kid released him, and he tried to rub a little life into his fingers.

"You ain't got much of a grip there, Doc," noted the younger man.

"I'm told it was a fine firm grip when I was fourteen," said Holliday. "Of course, they probably lied."

The Kid laughed. "I *like* you, Doc! I've liked you from the start." He reached across the table for the bottle.

"I'll signal for a glass," said Holliday.

"No need," said the Kid, lifting the bottle to his lips. He took a deep swallow. "Good stuff. What is it?"

"Just Kentucky whisky. Probably fertilized by Aristides or Hindoo."

The Kid looked amused. "Who the hell are they?"

"Bat Masterson could tell you a lot more about them that I can," replied Holliday. "In fact, I heard it all from him. Aristides won the first Kentucky Derby, a race they started six or seven years ago. Hindoo's supposed to be the fastest horse ever to look through a bridle since the American Eclipse."

"The *American* Eclipse?"

"There was an Eclipse in England, too. That's how you know which one people are talking about."

"Why would Masterson know all this?" asked the Kid.

"He was a sportswriter first and a lawman second," answered Holliday.

"You were friends?"

"From time to time."

"That sounds kinda flighty," said the Kid disapprovingly.

"We were never close, but we got along, and found ourselves on the same side most of the time."

"I saw a baseball game back in Kansas," offered the Kid. Then: "Silly sport."

Holliday, who had been playing solitaire all through the conversation, finished his game, scooped up the cards, shuffled them, and began dealing another game.

"How about you and me playing a little blackjack?" offered the Kid.

Holliday shook his head. "I'm short of funds."

"The great Doc Holliday? I don't believe it."

"Believe what you want, but if you win, I'll have to kill you for the reward so I can pay off my losses."

The Kid threw back his head and roared with laughter.

"And I'll send off for the money five minutes later," said a voice, and both men turned to see Garrett's deputy standing near the doorway.

"Hi, Doc," said the deputy.

"Good evening . . ." began Holliday. "You know, I never did catch your name."

"Nate," said the deputy. "Nate Crosley."

"Good evening, Nate," said Holliday.

"Leave us alone," said the Kid. "We ain't bothering anybody."

"I never said you were," answered Crosley. "I just said I'd send for the reward five minutes after Doc kills you."

"And if I kill *him*?" demanded the Kid.

"Then I'll send for it after his ladyfriend kills you. Hell, for all I know, she's better with a gun anyway."

The Kid looked sharply at Holliday. "The woman we made the deal about—she's a bounty hunter?"

"On occasion," answered Holliday.

"And she's here for *me*?"

"I've seen her," said Holliday. "She's not in your class. Just steer clear of her. You won't enhance your reputation by killing a middle-aged widow."

"Well, what the hell," said Crosley, "we can just wait for Garrett to kill him and save the taxpayers ten thousand dollars."

"I've had enough of what passes for your sense of humor!" said the Kid angrily. "You think being a lawman's something special? Hell, I've been a lawman!"

"You have?" asked Holliday.

"You bet your ass," said the Kid, still hot under the collar. "Back in March of '78 I was one of the Regulators. We were the toughest lawmen you ever saw."

"I heard about them," said Holliday.

"They were great lawmen," said Crosley sarcastically. "The first thing they did was go out and kill Sheriff Bill Brady and his deputy, a guy named Hindman."

"Killing deputies could get to be a habit!" growled the Kid.

"You won't talk that tough when Garrett gets back," said Crosley. "He told me how he used to tan your hide."

"He lied!" roared the Kid, leaping to his feet as the men at the closest tables scattered or ducked.

"Then kill *him* and leave this nice gentleman alone," said Holliday.

"I don't let anyone rag me," growled the Kid.

"Why don't you walk down the street and hit some other drinking hole, Nate?" suggested Holliday.

"When I'm ready to," replied Crosley. "I've got as much right to this space as anyone."

"Good!" snapped the Kid. "Then *keep* it!"

His gun was out and firing before Crosley even realized he was in trouble. Two, three, four shots tore into his chest, and he was dead before he hit the floor. It took the smoke from his gun a good fifteen seconds to dissipate, and the smell of cordite filled the air. The room was deathly silent.

"Anyone else got anything to say?" yelled the Kid to the room at large.

No one said a word.

He turned to Holliday. "What about you?"

Holliday held his hands above the table. "We have a deal. He wasn't part of it."

"Good," said the Kid, still in a fury. "You get to live another day."

He stalked out of the tavern, and some men rushed over to Crosley to see if there were any signs of life.

Holliday stood up, brushed himself off, put his deck in his pocket, left the tavern, and began walking slowly back to the Grand Hotel, wondering if he'd have had a chance to stop the Kid if they were done working in the valley, and if he'd have risked his life to do so. He was just honest enough to admit to himself that he didn't know.

JSG

24.

"I REALLY THINK I'M MAKING PROGRESS," said Edison.

He was sitting on a leather sofa in the lobby of the Grand Hotel with Holliday and Buntline, who were seated opposite him on overstuffed chairs.

"The problem is, there are only two people we can test it out on," added Buntline, lighting a thin cigar.

"One," Edison corrected him.

"Two," insisted Buntline. "Hook Nose and Geronimo."

"One," said Edison. "If it works, we don't want to disable Doc's protector before the crew's done cleaning the valley and we know that the spell's been lifted from both of them—or at least from the Kid." He turned to Holliday. "That'll be at least another day, maybe two."

"Why just one or two?" asked Holliday. "Every tribe has at least one medicine man."

"True," said Edison. "But only one of them is watching over you at the moment, and only one's protecting the Kid. The others are doubtless adding their powers to keeping the United States from expanding, but I see no reason to think they have any interest in either of you."

"How soon do you think this thing, whatever it is, will be ready?" asked Holliday, unscrewing the top of his flask and taking a sip.

Edison shrugged. "I don't know. Hell, for all I know it's ready now. But I need to try it out to be sure." A look of excitement crossed his face. "I'll tell you this much: if it *does* work, if the principle is valid, then I truly believe the United States will extend from the Atlantic to the Pacific during my lifetime."

"If this thing takes care of Hook Nose, then all you have to do is turn it on Geronimo and your job is done," said Holliday.

Edison shook his head. "I doubt it. Hook Nose and Geronimo are the two most powerful medicine men, but they're not the only ones. Just about every tribe has one. Alone they're not much, but if they're pooling their power . . ."

"*Are* they?" asked Holliday.

"I don't know," admitted Edison. "But it makes sense."

"There's only one way to find out," said Buntline. "If we eliminate these two—Hook Nose and Geronimo—either we can start spreading across the Mississippi in our millions, or we can't."

"So what's this principle?" asked Holliday. "Sound or electricity?"

"They're not mutually exclusive," said Edison. "I need an incredibly strong current to power the ultrasonic device."

"And that's just for Hook Nose and Geronimo or their surrogates, who are close enough to be watching things," added Buntline. "If Tom's right about how many medicine men are involved, think of the power we need for the silent sound to reach medicine men in Colorado and Montana, or on the Pacific Coast."

"So this is just a test?"

"Right," said Buntline. "And if it works, it's a deadly one."

"I wish you luck," said Holliday, who could read the enthusiasm on Edison's face and was afraid he was about to be subjected to a two-hour lecture on how to convert invisible electricity into unheard sound. He was almost happy for the distraction when Pat Garrett entered the hotel and walked right up to him.

"I need an official statement from you, Doc," said Garrett.

"I'm pleased to see you too," answered Holliday.

"Damn it, Doc! Billy murdered Nate Crosley and you didn't lift a finger to stop it!"

"It's not as if they agreed to go out in the street and face off," replied Holliday. "The Kid drew and killed him before he or anyone else knew what was happening, including me."

"Why didn't you try to stop it?"

"I did. I told your deputy to shut up and stop encouraging him."

"Goddamn it!" yelled Garrett. "You're the only man in the whole territory besides me who might have stopped the Kid, and you didn't do a damned thing!"

Holliday held his lapel out. "You see a badge?"

"When did you ever need a badge to kill anyone?" growled Garrett.

"I know it's escaped all the dime novelists, but I was wearing a badge at the O.K. Corral." Holliday smiled. "I'm told you *weren't* wearing one back then. In fact, I'm told you rode with a desperado known as Billy the Kid."

Garrett tensed, glared at him, muttered "Be at my office in half an hour!" turned on his heel, and walked back out into the street.

"I'd heard a deputy was killed yesterday," said Buntline. "I didn't know you were there."

"I can't spend *all* my time drinking in the hotel," replied Holliday easily.

"And the Kid gunned him down?"

Holliday nodded. "He's got a temper, and the deputy was too stupid to realize it."

"You make it sound like the deputy's fault," noted Buntline.

"If you taunt a mountain lion and the lion attacks, whose fault is it?" asked Holliday.

"Does the lion know right from wrong?" interjected Edison.

"I doubt it," said Holliday.

"Then he needs to be put down before he can harm anyone else."

"I think that's the purpose of this exercise," said Holliday with a grim smile.

"It's surprising," said Edison. "This is the third time I've been in the same town with him, and I've yet to lay eyes on him."

"He's not all that much to look at," said Holliday. "Just an ordinary-looking young man with an uncommon skill."

Edison stared at him. "Do you like him, Doc?"

"I've liked my share of killers over the years," answered Holliday. "I get along with him, but it's hard to like a man who might try to kill you at any minute on a whim."

"But he can't."

"That doesn't make him any more likeable," said Holliday with a smile.

"He's also a little young and a little uneducated from what I hear," suggested Buntline.

"With Johnny Ringo dead and John Wesley Hardin in jail, I'm the only educated shootist still walking around free, so that doesn't count against him any more than it counts against anyone else," said Holliday. "As for being young, hell, I'm the oldest shootist I know, and I'm only thirty-two. It's not a profession that leads to a long life."

"Well, eventually I suppose I'll meet him," said Edison.

Holliday nodded. "If someone doesn't kill him first."

"You think someone will?" asked Buntline. "Someone besides you, I mean?"

Holliday shrugged. "The Kid's only bulletproof for another day or two, and he's got the biggest price on his head that anyone ever saw. All he has to do is turn his back on the wrong man. It doesn't have to be a shootist, just someone who's hungry enough to try for the reward or the fame, and good enough to hit a standing target at maybe twenty feet."

"I wonder why it hasn't happened yet?"

"Because they only raised the price on him a month ago, and because he's got good instincts. And for the last few months or maybe even longer, he's been invulnerable." Holliday got to his feet. "And now I'd better get over to the sheriff's office before he comes after me with guns blazing."

"He wouldn't do that!" scoffed Buntline.

"A year or two back he was riding with Billy the Kid," replied Holliday. "He became sheriff because he's just bright enough to know that sooner or later everyone who rides with the Kid is going to die, shot down either by the law or by the Kid himself." Holliday paused thoughtfully. "I've never shot a sheriff before, though I'd have been happy to kill Johnny Behan back in Tombstone. I'm not real anxious to kill one here, when I've come for other business. So it's best that I go before he comes back here."

He walked out of the bar and through the lobby, then out into the stifling New Mexico heat. He tipped his hat to a pair of women who passed him, nodded to a saloonkeeper he recognized, and then presented himself at Garrett's office.

"There it is," said Garrett, indicating a sheet of paper on his desk. "I assume you can read and write?"

Holliday simply stared at him.

"Okay, you're a dentist, of course you can," continued Garrett. "Write down what happened and sign your name. Then I'll have something for the court in case someone slits your ugly throat or they run you out of town."

Holliday walked to the desk and looked at the paper. "I'll need a pen, an inkwell, and a chair."

"Here's the pen and ink," said Garrett, pushing them across the desk. "Pull up a chair yourself."

Holliday brought a chair over and began writing. He finished in less than three minutes, signed it with a flourish, then pushed the paper back to Garrett's side of the desk.

"You don't like me very much, do you?" said Garrett.

"Not very," said Holliday.

"I hope you're not dumb enough to side with the Kid."

"I like him a lot better than I like you, but no."

"Good," said Garrett. "I might have a little trouble taking you both at once."

Holliday stared coldly at him. "You couldn't take either of us on the best day you ever had, and you know it. Now just keep playing at being a fearless sheriff, and sooner or later someone will kill the Kid for you."

"You've never seen me in action."

Holliday got to his feet.

"And if you're lucky, I never will," he said. "I've given you my statement. Now I'm going back to the bar to continue drinking, unless you want me to see you in action right now. I warn you up front that I am not a merciful man, and I do not shoot to wound or disarm."

The two men stared at each other for a tense minute. Then Holliday turned and walked back out into the street.

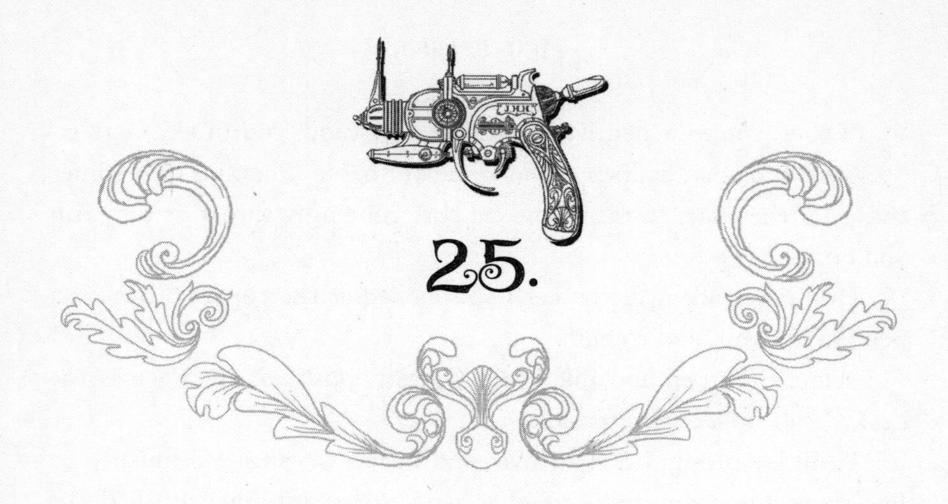

25.

EDISON POUNDED ON HOLLIDAY'S DOOR with the news: the crew had worked solidly for two days and two nights, and the valley was clear of both the tracks and the debris from the station.

"I just hope to hell Geronimo knows it," muttered Holliday.

"He knows," said a voice from the window. Holliday walked over to it just in time to see a bird flying away.

"Thanks, Tom," said Holliday. He started getting dressed as Edison left. He'd had a bad coughing fit during the night, so bad that he knew no amount of laundering could ever get the bloodstains off his handkerchief and he'd thrown it out before leaving the hotel, replacing it with a brand-new one.

For some reason the coughing hadn't killed his appetite as it usually did. He went over to Mabel Grimsley's, was shown to his usual table, and ordered three eggs, toast, and coffee. While he was waiting, Charlotte Branson entered and walked over to his table.

"Do you mind if I join you?"

"Happy to have you," said Holliday. "You'll forgive me if I don't stand up, but I had a hard night."

"The consumption?"

"Yes."

"There must be *some* way to cure it!" said Charlotte.

"Tom Edison assures me that there will be," replied Holliday. He smiled wryly. "But not until some years after I'm pushing up daisies."

"Don't talk like that!" she said severely.

He shrugged. "Okay, marigolds."

"Doc, please!"

"You've chosen a business where death is the desired result," said Holliday. "You shouldn't let the thought of it distress you so much."

"It's the thought of *your* death," said Charlotte. She leaned forward confidentially. "I found out where Billy the Kid is staying. After breakfast I aim to ride out there and see to *his* death."

"Forget it," said Holliday. "I've see what you each can do. You haven't got a chance."

She smiled. "I'm not going to call him out in the street and draw against him, Doc."

"What *are* you going to do?"

"I thought I'd present myself as a tax assessor," she replied. "I won't be asking for money, just appraising, so whoever owns the place shouldn't object to my presence."

"And then what?"

"Then, when he's relaxed and I'm so close I can't miss, I'll blow the back of his head off."

"Do you know for a fact that he's alone?" asked Holliday.

"It's almost certain that he's not," she said. "After all, it's a working ranch."

Holliday was momentarily silent as Mabel herself brought his breakfast, and Charlotte ordered from the short menu. Then, when he was sure they couldn't be overheard by Mabel or any of the diners, he spoke again.

"I'm coming with you," he said.

"I thought we were friends," said Charlotte, half hurt, half angry. "He's *mine*."

"I'm just riding shotgun," said Holliday. "For all you know he's got half a dozen cowboys who won't let you anywhere near him."

"Doc, if you come along, there's bound to be a lot of shooting," she said. "If I go alone, there'll be just a single shot, and it'll be over."

Holliday shook his head. "Your courage does you no credit," he told her. "It's a result of ignorance."

"Damn it, Doc!" she said angrily. "I've brought in seven men who were wanted dead or alive, and I've never been in so much as an instant's danger."

"He's not *any* wanted man," said Holliday. "I've only seen a couple of men who were in a class with him as shootists."

"Bill Hickok and who?"

"Not Hickok. Johnny Ringo, who's dead, and John Wesley Hardin, who's rotting in a Texas jail. And me."

"You don't suffer from false modesty, do you?"

"I don't know that any of the three of us could beat him. I just know that no other shootist I've ever seen would have a chance, current company included."

"I keep explaining, Doc: I'm not going to draw on him. I'll wait until he's relaxed and his guard is down, and then I'll retire the notorious Mr. Bonney."

"His guard is never down."

"If the opportunity doesn't present itself, I'll explain that I have to check some facts in the County Assessor's office and that I'll be back in a day or two." She frowned. "Except that I hate to do that. There's no guarantee that he'll still be there, or even in New Mexico Territory, two days from now."

Holliday nodded his head. "It sounds very reasonable."

Mabel Grimsley brought Charlotte's tea and biscuits, and took Holliday's empty plate away.

"Then I've convinced you?" said Charlotte when Mabel had retreated to the kitchen.

"That you're going about it the safest and most careful way possible? Absolutely."

"Fine! At least that's settled. How do you plan to spend your day?

"Riding out there with you," said Holliday.

"Doc!"

"Doing it the safest possible way doesn't mean it isn't a damnfool thing to do when you can't hit a rabbit on the run at ten paces."

"I keep explaining: he'll be standing still."

"Then you won't need any backup, and I won't have to draw my gun."

She sighed deeply. "You insist?"

He smiled a grim smile. "I insist."

"I suppose the only way to stop you is to shoot you." Suddenly she smiled back at him. "Too bad there's not a price on *your* head." She sighed. "I guess we're riding out there together. Just remember: he's *mine.*"

"Have I said otherwise?" replied Holliday.

"And you don't mind?"

"He's not mine unless and until he kills you, and I don't mean to let that happen."

"Actually," she said, buttering a biscuit and taking a bite of it, "I find that comforting. If I'm going to have someone protecting my back, who better than Doc Holliday?" She took a sip of her tea. "Needs sugar."

Holliday signaled to Mabel, ordered sugar, and went back to sipping his coffee.

"If you kill him, do you retire and go back home?" he asked.

"That was my initial plan," she admitted. "But if I can kill Billy the Kid, why should I quit?"

"Because you're about fifteen years older than most of the men you'll be hunting," replied Holliday. "Doesn't that imply something to you?" He waited for an answer that was not forthcoming. "Charlotte, no one who makes a living, legal or illegal, with a gun lives to a ripe old age. Only a very few make it to early middle age, lawmen as well as desperados."

"Your friend Wyatt Earp is well on his way to middle age," she pointed out.

"He has competent friends."

She was silent for a moment. "Doc, I really haven't decided. Let me think about it after I take the Kid."

Holliday shrugged. "It's your life."

"I'm glad you acknowledge it."

"Just seems a shame to end it twenty or thirty years early."

"Can we drop the subject, please?" said Charlotte.

"All right," said Holliday. "Hell, the next argument I win with a woman will be the first." He finished his coffee. "When did you want to head out to wherever the hell we're going?"

"Right away."

"Can you wait maybe half an hour?"

She looked concerned. "You said you had a bad night. Are you going to be sick again?"

"No, I'm going to get well," he said, getting to his feet. "I'll meet you back here. Do you have a wagon?"

"I rented a surrey. I don't like riding atop a horse."

"We have that in common," said Holliday. "I'll be back soon."

He walked out and headed over to the shuttered storefront where Edison and Buntline had temporarily set up shop. Even shuttered, the frame building looked unique, with an electric light over the front door and an electronic bell—and, he was sure, three or four security devices. He was about to knock on the door when it opened and he found himself facing Buntline.

"Good morning, Doc. A bit early for you, isn't it?"

"Good morning, Ned. I need your help for a few minutes, yours or Tom's."

"Happy to. Come on in."

Buntline escorted him to the interior of the building, which was filled with wires, batteries, and machines that made very little sense to Holliday. Edison was bent over a desk, scribbling some figures in one of his ever-present notebooks, when he noticed Holliday.

"Hello, Doc," he said. "What can I do for you?"

"You still got that brass armor you and Ned made up for me before the O.K. Corral?" asked Holliday.

"Yes," said Edison. "But it's just a prototype. Give us a week and we'll have something much better."

"I haven't got a week. Charlotte's going after him this morning."

"Charlotte?" said Buntline. "You mean Mrs. Branson?"

"Right," said Holliday.

"Why in the world . . . ?" mused Buntline. Suddenly he grinned. "Don't tell me she's a bounty hunter!"

"Okay, I won't tell you."

"But that's *wonderful*!" continued Buntline. "Who'd ever suspect her? She can probably stand out there on the sidewalk and shoot her prey as he walks by, and he'll never know what hit him!"

"I think she'd enjoy chatting with you," said Holliday wryly.

"So if the Kid's coming to town, why bother with the armor? Let her kill him when he's sitting down to have a drink."

"Doc's after the bounty, remember?" Edison chimed in.

"Damn!" said Buntline. "I forgot for a minute."

"If she wants him, she can have him," said Holliday. "I'll find some other way to make the money I need. Problem is, she's not waiting for him to come to town. She found out where he's staying—some ranch outside of town—and she's going out there after him."

"She's crazy!" said Buntline. "You'll face him, of course."

"She's got first shot at him. I'm just along for the ride."

"Bring her over," said Buntline. "I've still got some armor left over from Morgan Earp. I'll bet I can adjust it to fit her in an hour or two."

"You start measuring her legs or her chest and she just might shoot you first," said Holliday, only half-kidding. "When she sees it on me, she can make up her mind then."

"All right," said Buntline. "Let's start putting it on you."

"Just the legs and the left shoulder," said Holliday. "It's hot as hell out, this stuff is heavy, and for all I know we're an hour or more away from the ranch. I have enough trouble breathing without that stuff wrapped around my chest, and I want my right hand and arm free."

"You're the boss," said Buntline, sorting through a pile of trunks and boxes. Finally he found the trunk he wanted, opened it, and pulled out the still shining brass.

"I wish I had a weapon for you, Doc," said Edison, walking over and helping Buntline attach the armor. "But the Buntline Special was built to work against an animated corpse. It killed Johnny Ringo, but it won't do a thing against a living man."

"I understand," said Holliday. He spread his legs as they attached the brass shin and thigh plates, then stood still while Buntline adjusted the armor on his shoulder.

"I asked you back in Tombstone," said Buntline. "Are you sure you don't want a brass skullcap? It'll fit right under your hat."

Holliday shook his head. "You're not talking to a healthy man. If I have to look right or left in a hurry, I don't want any weight on my head."

"Then," said Buntline, stepping back and inspecting him, "you're as ready as I can make you."

Holliday walked to the door, turned to shut it behind him only to find it had closed by itself, and made his way back to Mabel Grimsley's restaurant, where Charlotte was waiting for him.

"What *is* all that?" she asked, looking at his brass armor.

"The latest fashion from New York," he answered. "Would you care for the ladies' version?"

She considered it for a moment, then shook her head. "No, it'd be a giveaway. What county assessor wears armor?"

"Then shall we go?"

Each insisted that the other ride in the surrey's compartment, and they settled for both sitting up top on the wide driver's seat under the canopy. Within three minutes they were out of town and on their way to confront Billy the Kid.

26.

HOLLIDAY COULDN'T HELP BUT NOTICE a certain sameness in the landscape, a sameness that extended all the way to Tombstone hundreds of miles to the west. You couldn't travel by horseback, by stagecoach, by wagon, even by foot, without raising clouds of dust. If you passed a plant, it would most likely be a cactus or a sagebrush. If you passed a tree, it was rarely much higher than ten feet at the top. And if you passed a water hole, there was at least a fifty–fifty chance that it had gone dry. There was the occasional rabbit, the infrequent bird, the rare coyote, and for the life of him Holliday couldn't figure out how this arid landscape was able to support enough cattle to feed the inhabitants.

He pulled out a handkerchief, not to cough into it for a change, but to wipe the sweat from his face. He considered taking a drink from his flask, but instead decided to take a swallow from the canteen that someone at the stable had thoughtfully left just beneath the driver's seat.

He wished that Buntline's automated stagecoach line had established a branch in Lincoln so that he could ride inside it, on a comfortable cushion, but he wouldn't leave Charlotte alone to drive the surrey, so he sat up top, trying to ignore the heat, the dust, and the occasional flies.

"Are you ready to tell me where we're going?" he said after they'd gone three miles.

"Josh Brady's ranch," answered Charlotte. "From all I've been able to gather, he's been a horse thief ever since he moved out here."

"Horses?" said Holliday, frowning. "I thought the Kid rustled cattle when he needed money."

"Six of one, half a dozen of the other," she said. "I don't understand why he doesn't rob a bank."

Holliday smiled. "If he steals cattle or horses from Mexico, he's got one ranch coming after him, and even if they find him, he can probably get enough help to kill them or chase them back over the border. But if he robs the Lincoln bank, or any other bank, he's got every citizen in the town and probably most of the ranch owners gunning for him. Even the Kid can't face odds like that."

"I hadn't thought of that," Charlotte admitted. "That does seem to explain it, doesn't it?"

"If you're going to hunt down criminals, you have to learn to think like them," replied Holliday.

"So how did *you* learn?" she asked.

"Don't believe everything you read in the dime novels," said Holliday. "I've never been convicted of a crime, and I've worn a badge more than once."

"Didn't I hear that Kate Elder broke you out of jail?" said Charlotte.

"Yes, she did."

"Well?"

"I'd been arrested, and was awaiting trial." He smiled. "Obviously we never had the trial, so I was never convicted."

She chuckled. "I think you're embroidering the situation just a bit."

He shrugged. "Perhaps."

"The history books may see it differently."

"Nothing you or I do will ever be recorded in any history books," said Holliday. "We're just the flotsam and jetsam of the history of the frontier."

"Who do *you* think will be remembered?" she asked.

"On this side of the Mississippi? For starters, the governor of this territory."

"Lew Wallace?" she said, surprised. "What's he ever done, besides bribe the Kid with his freedom in exchange for testifying against all his gang members."

"He wrote a novel called *Ben-Hur* a couple of years ago that figures to outlast all of us. And just before I came south I met an Englishman, a bit of a dandy, named Oscar Wilde, who has it in him to be a fine writer—though he probably doesn't count, since he's just here on tour. And there's John Clum, who has written some damned fine articles and editorials for the *Tombstone Epitaph*."

"Why, John Henry Holliday," she said with a smile, "I do believe you're a closet elitist!"

"I'm a dying man with a gun," he replied. "That allows me the luxury of being honest."

"I wish you wouldn't talk that way."

"I don't mean to upset you," said Holliday. "We celebrate birth as a miracle, and we forget dying's just an extension of the same process. It's nothing special."

"Do you really believe that?"

"Don't you?" he responded.

"No."

"That's curious," said Holliday. "When you've meted out death as often as I have—and I would have thought as often as you have, too—I don't know how you can look at it any other way."

"I just figure they're bad men, and the world is safer and better off without them," said Charlotte.

"I think maybe the difference between us is that I knew most of the men I've killed, and you've known none of them."

"Still, you'd never kill a friend."

Holliday thought back to an animated corpse in Tombstone. "I killed one of the best friends I ever had."

"I'm sorry," said Charlotte.

"I'm not," said Holliday. "He needed killing, and he *wanted* killing—a *permanent* death. But it hurt just the same."

"Was that Johnny Ringo?"

Holliday nodded. A dust devil—a whirling cloud of sand—suddenly blew into their faces, and they were blinded for almost a minute. The horse kept walking, and when the wind died down and they were finally able to see the landscape, they saw a ranch house in the distance, with a trio of corrals off to the left.

"Is this it?" asked Holliday.

"Horses in the corral," said Charlotte. "And this is where they told me I'd find it. I'd say we're here." She stared at him, frowned, and pulled the horse to a stop. "How am I going to explain your presence away? I hadn't thought about it."

"He should know I'm not here to kill him. I've had too many opportunities here and in Tombstone." Suddenly he smiled. "Hell, he probably thinks we still *can't* kill each other."

"Can't?" she repeated.

"Don't worry about it," said Holliday. "He bleeds, just like you and I."

"I still need a reason why you're with me."

"I heard you were coming out to the farm, someone told me the Kid might be there, and I came along to have a drink with him and warn him that Garrett's back in town and looking for him."

"He'll never buy it if you're wearing that armor."

"You have a point," he said, starting to unstrap it. "Hell, I never could stand the way this stuff feels anyway." He laid the armor down beneath the seat. "*Now* he'll buy it."

"You're sure?" asked Charlotte.

"Why not?" responded Holliday. "It's true. Garrett *is* looking for him, someone—you—told me he might be here." He paused. "I figure the safest way for you to kill him is while I'm drinking with him and he's concentrating on me."

Charlotte considered his answer, then nodded her head.

She clucked to the horse, and it began moving forward again.

A lone bird flew high overhead, riding the warm thermals. *There was a time when I would have looked and thought, "There's a bird,"* thought Holliday. *Now I wonder if it's Hook Nose or Geronimo.*

As they drew closer they could see that two men were feeding hay to the horses, while a third stood on the ranch house's porch, leaning against a post that supported the overhang, staring at the surrey.

"Be careful," said Holliday softly. "I've seen this one on wanted posters."

"What's his name?" asked Charlotte.

"I never paid any attention. I'm not a bounty hunter." *Well, except for the man I don't see here.*

The man on the porch held his hand up, signaling them to stop.

"That's far enough," he said. "What's your business here?"

"Are you Mr. Brady?" asked Charlotte.

"He's not here. My name's Luke Beckett. What can I do for you?"

"Beckett—that was his name," whispered Holliday. "Watch out for him."

"I'm from the County Assessor's office," said Charlotte without missing a beat. "We heard that Mr. Brady had made some improvements, and I'm here to inspect and evaluate them."

Beckett issued a harsh laugh. "This house look improved to you, lady?"

"Our records say you only have two corrals on the property," she replied, lying on the spot, "yet I can see three from here."

"So what?"

"I'm just doing my job, sir," said Charlotte. "If that's the only improvement I find, I doubt that there will be any increase whatsoever in Mr. Brady's property taxes."

"He doesn't pay property taxes."

"If that's so, I'm sure someone else from our office will be out to discuss that with him. My job is simply to appraise the property."

"You always travel with a famous killer?" asked Beckett, indicating Holliday.

"I don't like riding horses," replied Holliday. "The Kid and I are friends. I heard he was out here, and this lady, Mrs.—I've forgotten her last name—was kind enough to offer me a ride."

"He ain't here either," replied Beckett. "He's off taking care of business with Brady."

"Do you mind if I get out of the sun while this lady is going about her business?"

Beckett considered the suggestion, then shrugged. "Yeah, go ahead. But leave Josh's whiskey alone. He don't like no one touching it without his okay."

"It's still morning," said Holliday. "Why would I sample his whiskey before noon?"

"You got a reputation," said Beckett. "Go inside if you want, but keep your hands off the booze."

"You have my word as a gentleman," said Holliday, clambering down from his perch and then helping Charlotte down. As he did so he looked for her pistol, but couldn't spot it. He hoped she wasn't carrying it in her purse; she'd never have time to get it out.

"Any idea when the Kid is due back?" asked Holliday as Charlotte was brushing the accumulated dust from her dress,

"Day or two, maybe three," answered Beckett.

"Ah, well, tell him I'll catch up with him in town when he returns," said Holliday, walking toward the house.

He was almost there when he heard the single shot. He whirled around and saw Charlotte standing over Beckett's body as blood trickled out from the hole in the back of his head.

"I hope you were right about the reward," she said, tucking the tiny revolver back into her sleeve as he approached her.

"Go into the house *now*!" said Holliday harshly.

"What are you—?"

"*NOW!*" he repeated.

"If you think you're going to claim the reward for yourself . . ." she began.

"Shut up and move!" he snapped, turning toward the corral, where the two men were approaching on the run.

"I'm sorry, Doc!" she said. "I didn't mean—"

"Just go. I can't face them and watch you at the same time."

"I can help you."

"I'm going to try to talk to them. Now move, damn it!"

She reluctantly backed away toward the ranch house while Holliday stood next to Beckett's body.

"Goddamn it!" snarled one of the men. "What did you want to do that for?"

"There's a price on his head," said Holliday.

"Hell, there's a price on *all* our heads!" said the other. "So what?"

"You're gonna pay for what you did!" roared the first.

"Take a good hard look at me and see if you know who I am," said Holliday.

Both men squinted at him in the bright sunlight, shading their eyes.

"Damn! You're Doc Holliday!"

"That's right," said Holliday. "I have no business with you and no grudge against you. Are you sure you want to go up against me?"

"You can't just come out here shooting people!"

"Of course I can. There are prices on all your heads. Now, do you want to walk away whole, or do you want me to cart your corpses into town?"

"Why should we bother? When the Kid comes back, he'll kill you."

"A sage decision," said Holliday. "Now lift your guns out *very* slowly and toss them on the ground."

The two men moved their hands carefully to their guns. Then the one on Holliday's left tried to draw and fire it, and got a bullet lodged between his eyes before the weapon cleared its holster. The other probably had been planning on obeying his instructions, but instinctively pulled and tried to fire his gun when he heard the report from Holliday's gun, and was dead an instant later, falling across the body of his companion.

"I'm certainly glad I don't have to go after *you*!" said Charlotte admiringly, walking back to stand at Holliday's side as he surveyed the carnage.

"The Kid's as good, maybe better," said Holliday. "You haven't got a chance against him."

"We'll see."

"Damn it, Charlotte! You didn't have the brains or the experience to kill Beckett when he was alone. How are you going to go up against the Kid?"

"He was as alone as he was going to be," she replied defensively.

"Did you think the other two would just keep feeding the horses?" continued Holliday.

"I thought if they didn't, you and I could each handle one."

"And I thought your specialty was shooting unsuspecting men when their backs were turned. That little toy of yours isn't accurate at much more than ten paces. What did you plan to do if they fired from where they tried to fire at me?"

She suddenly looked uneasy. "I confess that I never thought of that."

"You've killed eight men," said Holliday. "You've been damned lucky. I suggest you quit now, while you're still alive and unharmed."

"I didn't get into this for the money," she replied. "That's just been a pleasant windfall. I got into it to kill the man who murdered my husband."

Holliday realized he wasn't going to convince her while they were standing out there in the sun next to three corpses, but he made up his mind to try again later. He took the horse by the harness and led it over to Beckett's body, found he wasn't strong enough to lift it into the surrey without her help, and when that was done they loaded the other two.

"By the way," she said as they drove back into town, "*you* killed the other two. If there really were prices on them, I insist that the money go to you."

"I wasn't bounty hunting," said Holliday. "I was just protecting a friend."

"It comes to the same thing," she said. "They're dead. Either you accept the money, or the government can keep it."

"Under those conditions . . ." he said.

It was when he delivered the three bodies to Pat Garrett's office that he found out that they were worth a thousand dollars apiece.

That night he hit the faro table in the back of the Blue Peacock and ran his two thousand up to eighty-seven hundred before the sun came up and the game ended, and he realized, as he counted his winnings, that he had a big enough bankroll that he wouldn't have to face Billy the Kid after all.

27.

"YOU SPOKE TO ME VERY HARSHLY YESTERDAY," said Charlotte as they ate their breakfast as Mabel Grimsley's.

"You were in a dangerous situation, and you didn't believe me," answered Holliday.

"I just want to tell you that I understand, and you were right to do so."

"As long as you're admitting I was right about one thing, perhaps you'll agree that I'm right about another—that it's time to retire from the business, or at least to steer clear of the Kid."

"That's more than business, Doc," she said seriously. "It's vengeance."

"Leave it to the Lord," said Holliday.

"Did *you* ever?"

"No," he admitted. "But I'm headed for hell anyway. You might not be."

"I owe it to Dwayne."

"Your husband?" asked Holliday, and she nodded. "Have you considered that you owe it to him to stay alive?"

"I plan to stay alive," she told him.

Something in her expression said that further arguing, at least at this time, would be useless, so he sighed and began eating his toast.

Mabel Grimsley stopped by with a hot pot of coffee and refilled their cups.

"I want to thank you again, Doc," she said. "Business has doubled since I started advertising that you eat here." She smiled. "If you could just get your friend Wyatt Earp to pay you a visit . . ."

"He's a married man, making his fortune up north," replied Holliday.

"Of course, if you could get the Kid to stop by, that would be even better."

"I'll mention it the next time I see him."

"Thanks, Doc."

"As long as you're here, what do I owe you?"

"Your money's no good here, Doc."

"Then I thank you again."

She performed an awkward curtsy, picked up the coffee pot, and retreated to the kitchen.

"I hear you got very lucky last night," said Charlotte, adding sugar to her coffee and stirring it.

"I prefer to think of it as my skill dominating all the lesser talents," he said with a smile. "But yes, I had a lucky night."

"Be sure not to lose it tonight," she said, returning his smile.

"I won't be playing again," replied Holliday. "I needed a certain amount of money to pay for the sanitarium where I plan to spend my final months. This will just about cover it. I had this much once before, and I was very foolish with it. I won't be again."

"Then will you be going back to Leadville?"

"Eventually," he said.

"Eventually?" she repeated, frowning.

"As soon as Tom and Ned go back."

"Ah, you're just waiting for your friends!" she said. "I never mentioned it, but there was a time when I thought you were here to do me out of the reward for Billy the Kid, to kill him before I could."

"Now why would I want to kill him?" said Holliday. "We're both notorious killers, cut from the same cloth."

"Damn it, Doc," complained Charlotte, "why do you say things like that?"

"Like what?"

"That you're a villain, and you're dying tomorrow, and you're going straight to hell. Don't you know how it upsets people?"

"Not most of the people I associate with," he replied. "And I suppose I say it because if I don't they will. I apologize if I've upset you."

She sighed deeply. "What are you doing out here, Doc? With your education and good manners, you should be repairing teeth back in Georgia." Suddenly she smiled. "If you enjoy causing pain, what better profession than a dentist?"

Holliday couldn't help laughing. "You've got me pegged, Mrs. Branson, ma'am."

"Seriously, was it the consumption?"

He nodded. "You'd be surprised how quickly your clientele vanishes when you keep coughing blood on them."

"And no one minds it at a poker table?" she continued.

"When there's a few hundred dollars in the middle," he replied with a smile, "no one much cares if it's got blood on it or not."

"No, I suppose not."

"Let's change the subject. I shouldn't be talking about blood and disease when a lady's eating."

"Actually, I just finished," said Charlotte. "But I agree: let's change the subject."

"Shall we talk about longevity?" suggested Holliday.

She stared at him curiously. "What about it?"

"I think if you want to practice it, you'll go back to the Grand and stay in it for a few days."

"Why?"

"Because the last man you brought in wasn't connected to the Kid, but yesterday we cashed in on three of his friends. Anyone who was around saw us unload them from the surrey and carry them into Garrett's office."

"Why just a few days? Why not a month, or a year?" she said. "I can't hide forever, nor do I wish to."

"He may come into town to find out who killed them, but he's in a profession where his friends and confederates get killed all the time. He won't spend more than a day looking for you, and he won't know one woman from another. If no one can point you out to him, he'll get tired of looking and go back to wherever he stays when he's in the area, probably some other ranch out of town."

She considered what he said. "Four days, no more," she announced.

"Four should do it, though a week would be better."

"Four," she insisted. "I came here to kill him, not hide from him."

"All right," said Holliday. "Four it is."

He finished his coffee, then helped her to her feet and walked her back to the Grand Hotel. They stopped along the raised wooden sidewalk while she admired some recently arrived Eastern fashions in a dress store, bought a book and some magazines at the general store ("If I'm to be a shut-in for four days, I am *not* going to just sit there staring at a wall."), and finally arrived in the lobby twenty minutes after leaving Mabel Grimsley's.

As she climbed the stairs to the second floor, Edison was coming down. He greeted her, stood aside to let her pass, and then continued down on to the lobby.

"Good morning, Doc."

"Hello, Tom."

"I heard you were doing well at the Blue Peacock last night," said Edison. "I hope your luck didn't change."

"It held."

"Good."

"We can all go back to Leadville," continued Holliday. "I've got enough for the sanitarium. Well, almost enough, and I'll stay sober at the tables long enough to make up the rest of it." A quick smile. "Or else I'll just die a little sooner."

"Well, you can go back, of course, but Ned and I will be staying here awhile longer. Or if not here, at our lab and factory in Tombstone."

"Why?" asked Holliday. "You came here to help me. Well, I've got enough money now, almost enough anyway, and even if I didn't I don't need your help against the Kid any longer."

"Doc, we came here to try to break a spell that Hook Nose had cast," said Edison. "In case you've forgotten, that's what the United States government is paying me to do—counteract the medicine men's magic. I just had my first success in the two years I've been out here. Geronimo and Hook Nose are in the area, or at least have made their presence manifest here, so it makes sense that this is where I should combat them. The ultrasonic device worked on White Eagle, but he was just one medicine man, and not the most powerful of them. I have to stay here and keep working."

"Well, maybe I'll stick around for a couple of weeks," said Holliday. "They've got some mighty poor faro players here, and you never know when you might need someone to protect your back."

"With all due respect to your unquestioned skill, I don't think a gun is going to be very effective against the men I'm here to neutralize."

"Well, I'll stay a little longer anyway." *Long enough to talk Charlotte into getting into a stagecoach and going back north before she gets her head blown off.*

"Up to you," said Edison. He turned and headed to the front door. "I'm off to the post office to see if some of the equipment I ordered has arrived yet."

"See you later," said Holliday. He walked up to the desk. "Got a safe?"

"Yes."

He pulled the previous night's winnings out of a pocket, counted off eighty-five hundred dollars, and handed it to the clerk.

"I want a receipt for it."

"Of course, Doc," said the clerk, counting it again and then scribbling down a receipt.

"And if it goes missing, you are going to find out just how slowly I can kill a man."

"There's no need to say that, Doc," said the clerk in hurt—and mildly terrified—tones.

"There's every need to say it," replied Holliday. "Just see to it that there's no need to demonstrate it."

He put the receipt in a pocket and walked out into the hot New Mexican sun. He stood motionless for a moment, making up his mind which of the many watering holes to go to, and finally decided on the Blue Peacock, feeling it was only fair to spend his money there since he'd won so much of their other patrons' the previous night.

He walked across the dry, dusty street, stepping back as a team of horses trotted past him, pulling a stagecoach behind them. He tipped his hat to a trio of local women who were walking down the wooden sidewalk, pretended to shoot a small boy with his finger and clutched at his chest as the boy fired an imaginary bullet into it, and finally reached the Blue Peacock. It was only about a third full, since it was still early in the day, and the bartender was serving sandwiches as well as whiskey and beer.

He'd barely sat down when a voice behind him said, "I been looking for you."

"And now you've found me," said Holliday. "Sit down and have a drink."

"I'm mad as hell!" growled the Kid, sitting down opposite Holliday.

"I'm desolate to hear it," said Holliday, then realized that the Kid had probably never heard the word "desolate," and amended his statement: "I'm sorry to hear it."

"You killed three of my friends!"

"They probably weren't real friends," said Holliday with a shrug.

"What the hell were you doing out there in the first place?" demanded the Kid.

Holliday filled a glass, pushed it across the table to the Kid, and signaled for another.

"I went out there to talk to you," replied Holliday.

"What about?"

"Nothing in particular. I'm not employed, and I only know three or four people in town."

"Why did you kill them?" demanded the Kid. "I know it had to be you. No one else could have done it. Those men were *good*."

You had *to deduce it*, Holliday realized. *You couldn't very well walk up to Garrett and ask who claimed the bounties. You two aren't exactly on speaking terms. And that means you don't know about Charlotte.*

"I'll be honest," lied Holliday. "They didn't recognize me. They were sure I'd come out to collect the bounties on them when you weren't around to weigh in on their side, and they drew on me before I could set them straight. What else could I do?"

The Kid stared long and hard at him, then finally nodded his head. "Makes sense."

"Then we're friends again?"

"At least we ain't enemies."

"I hope your excursion with the estimable Mr. Brady was successful?"

"Do you use them words just to show off?" said the Kid with a frown. "I know you been to school back East."

"I'll try to express myself more simply," replied Holliday. "I hope you and Brady got whatever you were after."

"Mostly. We'd heard where there were thirty head of cattle. Turns out there were only eighteen." The Kid sipped his drink as the bartender arrived with a glass for Holliday. "But we took 'em anyway."

"It's so dry and barren out here," said Holliday. "Back where I grew up, fifteen acres could support fifteen head of cattle. Here it barely supports one, and he'll look skinny as hell."

"Makes you wonder why the Indians keep it or the United States wants it," agreed the Kid.

"You ever think of going back across the Mississippi?"

The Kid shook his head. "I used to think of it all the time. Then I killed a man who was bullying me when I was fifteen, and a few more at sixteen, and suddenly I wasn't Henry McCarty or Henry Antrim any more, I was Billy the Kid, and too damned many people were out to kill me. So I figured there are less people out here than back East, so I'm less likely to be backshot here."

"I take it you don't worry about being frontshot, to coin a word?" asked Holliday. The Kid just stared at him. "No, I guess not." Holliday paused long enough to fill his glass and take a drink from it, "How'd you come to be Billy Bonney?"

"It sounds nice, kind of like a song or a poem. So I use it. Or I did, until everyone started calling me the Kid." Suddenly he smiled. "I reckon I'll be thirty by the time they stop."

"Could be," agreed Holliday. "It's a pretty famous name."

"I don't read too good, but I love reading about myself in all the dime novels. I even saw one where you and me teamed up."

"Anything's possible."

"I saw another where we shot it out in the street."

"Amazing," said Holliday with a smile. "Bill Hickok has one shootout in the main street of the town he's in, and suddenly every damned writer, most of whom have never been on this side of the Mississippi, assumes every gunfight takes place in the street."

"You didn't ask me who won," said the Kid.

"Okay, who won?"

"I did."

"Saves us the trouble of finding out who's better," said Holliday, smiling again.

"Didn't you ever wonder about it?"

"About the story?" said Holliday. "I never read it."

"About who was better."

Holliday shook his head. "I've always gone on the assumption that every man walking around with a gun is undefeated. I'd rather not find out who was better until I have to."

The Kid laughed. "Makes sense the way you put it."

"I'll drink to that," said Holliday, holding up his glass.

"Damn! I said it back in Tombstone, I *like* you, Doc!"

"Makes me feel better—and safer," said Holliday with a smile.

"Don't worry about those three out at the ranch. Serves 'em right for drawing on Doc Holliday."

"I'm glad we're in agreement on that," said Holliday.

"You know," said the Kid, "reading that dime novel got me to thinking."

"About shooting it out with me?"

The Kid smiled. "No. About us teaming up."

"Interesting idea."

"You want to talk about it?"

Holliday shook his head. "No."

"Is there something wrong with me?" asked the Kid, suddenly pugnacious.

"No," said Holliday. "There's something wrong with me."

"The consumption?" asked the Kid, the pugnacity instantly gone.

Holliday nodded. "I've only got a couple of years left. Three if I'm lucky. I even know where I'm going to die. I've picked it out and reserved a room with a nice view."

"Wouldn't you rather go fast, guns blazing, taking some men you hate with you?" said the Kid. "I sure as hell would."

"I'd rather not go at all," said Holliday. "You can't always choose."

"Sure you can," said the Kid. "There's this bank I've heard about in San Diego. I ain't ever robbed a bank before. But think about it, Doc. If we win, we're richer than kings, and if we lose, we go down in a hail of bullets, we never spend a day in jail, and they write about us and sing songs about us for a hundred years."

"That's probably what John Wesley Hardin thought," replied Holliday. "He's been in prison close to five years now, and he's not getting out anytime soon."

"Maybe they caught *him*, but they'll never catch *me*," said the Kid.

Holliday smiled. "The reward for him was four thousand dollars when they finally caught him. There's two and a half times more reason for people to come looking for you."

"Damn!" said the Kid, his face suddenly flushed with pride. "You think anyone's ever had a bigger price on his head?"

"Not out here," said Holliday. "Maybe John Wilkes Booth, the guy who shot President Lincoln, but no desperado on this side of the Mississippi."

"Do me a favor, Doc."

"What?"

"You're book-learned," said the Kid. "Find out how much they were offering for that Booth feller."

"All right."

"I got some business back at Brady's ranch for the next few days—we got a buyer for those cattle, and another one for some horses—but why don't we meet here at noon a week from now, and you can tell me what you found out. Maybe I can top Booth before I'm done."

"It's a deal," said Holliday.

"Damn! We should have teamed up back when you were healthy!"

"You were about three years old the last time I was healthy," said Holliday.

"Don't seem fair, that an asshole like Garrett is healthy as a horse and you're a lunger."

"Nothing I can do about it."

"Well, there's something *I* can do about it," said the Kid. "Not for your consumption, but about Garrett's good health."

"I have no problem with that," said Holliday. "I don't like him much."

"Son of a bitch rode with me for a couple of years, then turned around and swore to see me hang." The Kid emptied his glass, then stood up. "I got to get back out to Brady's place. You'll have that information for me when I get back to town?"

"If it's available."

"And be thinking about the pair us going down with guns blazing instead of slowly choking to death in some hospital."

As the Kid walked out of the Blue Peacock, Holliday took another swallow of his drink and had to admit that going out in a blaze of glory was looking like a very acceptable alternative to the future he was facing.

28.

HOLLIDAY HAD JUST AWAKENED and, cane in hand, was making his way to Mabel Grimsley's when a Bunt Line coach pulled up. The door opened and Edison, sitting inside, beckoned to him.

"When did this thing arrive?" asked Holliday, indicating the self-propelled coach.

"I telegraphed Tombstone and had Henry Wiggins send it over," answered Edison. "I'm going to be going out into the countryside almost every day testing various things, so why should I keep renting a horse and buggy?"

"That's a good, reasonable answer," said Holliday. Suddenly he grinned. "Now how about the truth? The government is paying you, so surely they were paying for the buggy too."

"All right," said Edison with a guilty smile. "It gets so damned *hot* up there holding the reins. This thing hasn't got any reins, because it doesn't have any horse pulling it, and I don't even have to steer it. Henry supplied a driver," he pointed to the top of the carriage where the driver sat. "And it *is* essential that I get out into the country. In fact, why don't you come along? I want to test something out on you."

Holliday looked at him suspiciously. "You've got a driver. Why not test it on *him*?"

"I can't."

"Tom, I need a better answer than that," said Holliday. "The only one that comes to mind is that if you kill him you don't know how to drive the coach and you won't want to walk all the way back."

Edison chuckled and shook his head. "I can't test it on him because he's deaf."

"I couldn't hear what you used on White Eagle," said Holliday. "You already know it works."

"What I'm testing today is infinitely more powerful, and has a far broader range."

Holliday frowned. "Are you sure you're on the right track? It may have worked on the Comanche, but it didn't seem to bother Geronimo at all."

"I've added some new twists," answered Edison. "Either climb in or don't, but I'm anxious to test it. I can't stay here talking."

"All right," said Holliday, climbing into the coach. "Let's see what it can do."

"Loan me your cane," said Edison.

Holliday handed it over.

"I'm glad you have it with you today." He poked the top of the coach just above Holliday's head three times, and suddenly it began rolling down the street. "That's the problem with a deaf driver," said Edison, handing back the cane. "He can't hear when I yell at him to stop and start."

"I can see where that would be a problem," said Holliday.

"I hear you had another good night at the tables."

Holliday nodded. "The cards are running my way. I've worked my bankroll up to thirteen thousand, more or less. I'll stick around another week or so, and then make my way back up to Leadville." He paused. "Probably."

"Probably?" repeated Edison, arching an eyebrow.

"I had a business proposition yesterday that I'm considering."

"Long term or short term?"

"Short term, most likely."

"Care to tell me about it?"

Holliday shook his head. "No, I'm still thinking about it."

"I've seen the way you look and act when Mrs. Branson's around," said Edison. "You might give a thought to getting married."

"Who'd want to marry a man who's dying of consumption?" asked Holliday.

"I've seen the way she looks and acts around you, too," replied Edison with a smile. "A few good years are better than none at all. Seriously, you might consider it."

Holliday shook his head. "No, if I don't accept the proposition, I'll be going back to Leadville and spending my last few years fighting with Kate."

Edison shrugged, "If that's what you want."

"I'll tell you what I *don't* want," replied Holliday. "I don't want to marry a woman and have her turn into my nurse less than a year later."

"Won't Kate be your nurse if you go back to Leadville?"

"Kate's had a few good years with me; Charlotte hasn't," said Holliday. "Besides, if I go back to Leadville, I'll pay for my own nurses. That's what the hell I came down here for in the first place—to put enough money together to pay for the sanitarium when I have to go there."

"Okay," said Edison. "Your life is your own. I have no business making suggestions."

"Thank you."

"For what?"

Holliday smiled. "For saying that, so I won't have to."

Edison returned the smile. "I'm sorry. It comes from all these long days of working alone. I think I'd beg Ned to stick around, even if I didn't need his super-hard brass and his manufacturing skill."

"He doesn't seem like he's in a hurry to leave Lincoln."

"Oh, he will, sooner or later," said Edison. "Hopefully later. Do you know what he *really* wants to do?"

"I've no idea," said Holliday.

"He wants to be a publisher and a producer."

"A producer?" asked Holliday, frowning.

"The man who puts on a show, like a rodeo or a play," said Edison. "Can you imagine it? A genius like him, and he wants to do that. Hell, the next thing you know he'll be talking you and Annie Oakley into going to New York to put on a sharpshooting exhibition."

"Ned?" said Holliday disbelievingly.

"We all have our dreams," said Edison. "That's his." He turned to Holliday, "What's yours?"

"Mine's a lot simpler," said Holliday with a grim smile. "To cough up phlegm instead of blood. How about you?"

"To find a way to combat the medicine men's magic."

Holliday shook his head. "That's your *job*. What's your dream?"

"Same thing," said Edison. "An entire nation is depending on me to open up half a continent to westward expansion. My dream is that I'm not remembered as the man whose failure kept the United States forever east of the Mississippi."

Holliday stared at him. "I once faced eight Mexicans who were out to kill me after a card game south of the border. I scared off maybe twenty men when they had Wyatt Earp cornered in Dodge. But I wouldn't have your burden for anything. I couldn't stand up under it. I wonder if anyone else could."

"If you had to, you could," said Edison. "If you were the only man who could do it, you'd find a way. And so will I."

Holliday continued staring at him, and finally spoke, "I haven't called many men friend in my life, but I'm proud to call you my friend."

"Thank you, Doc. That means a lot to me."

"Good," said Holliday, suddenly uncomfortable by what he considered a display of emotion. "Now let's go out and see how the hell to kill Hook Nose and Geronimo."

Edison shook his head. "We're not interested in killing them, Doc. If we do, tomorrow there'll be two more medicine men, probably just about as powerful. What we have to do is neutralize their magic."

"How do you fight something you can't see?"

"I lit all of Tombstone with something you couldn't see," replied Edison. "Can you see the electricity that's powering the motor that's running this coach?"

"Okay," said Holliday with a shrug of defeat. "I'm just along for the ride anyway."

"And that ride should be ending soon," said Edison, looking out a window.

The coach went another five hundred yards, and then Edison borrowed Holliday's cane and knocked on the ceiling twice. There was no response. He waited a moment and did it again, and this time the coach came to a stop.

"Probably we were driving over a bumpy patch the first time and he didn't feel it, or interpret the feeling correctly," said Edison, returning the cane.

"You didn't have a cane when you picked me up," said Holliday. "How did you get him to stop?"

Edison smiled. "When we started, I wrote a note that told him to stop if he saw you or Ned on the street." He laughed and tapped his head with a forefinger, "Genius. No doubt about it."

Holliday joined in the laughter, then began coughing, and Edison climbed out and left him to finish on his own, which he did a minute later.

"Where are your weapons?" asked Holliday, looking back into the empty coach after he'd climbed down to the ground.

"I prefer to think of them as devices," said Edison. He reached in, lifted a cushioned seat, and pulled out a large box. He opened it, removed some padding, and withdrew a small metal object that he could hold comfortably in one hand. It looked somewhat like a pistol to Holliday, but there was no trigger, nothing with which to aim or sight it, and not much of a handle.

Edison bent over the box and withdrew one end of an electric wire, which he inserted into the metal device. It immediately emitted a low humming sound.

"If that's as loud as it gets, we've made the trip for nothing," remarked Holliday.

"No, it's a totally silent device. The humming just alerts me to the fact that it's receiving power from the battery it's attached to. It'll stop in a minute, when it's fully powered."

As Edison had said, the device did indeed fall silent in another sixty seconds, after which he removed the wire and placed it back in the box.

"All right," said Holliday. "What does this thing do?"

"That's what we have to find out," answered Edison.

"How?"

Edison smiled. "First we spot Geronimo or Hook Nose. One or both will be watching us."

Holliday scanned the barren landscape. "My eyes are as good as anybody's, but I don't see Geronimo, and while I've never met Hook Nose I'm sure I could spot an Indian out here."

"Think back, Doc," said Edison, starting to walk toward a small stand of trees a quarter mile away. "How did Geronimo first contact you back in Tombstone? Didn't you tell me you were in an alley and were confronted by a snake that turned into a warrior?"

"Son of a bitch!" said Holliday. "And Geronimo himself visited me as a bird on my windowsill at the Grand. That was when he offered to take the Kid's protection away if I'd destroy the station." He looked around with renewed interest. "I see two lizards off to the left, and there's a rabbit about fifty yards on the other side of the coach."

Edison shook his head. "No, that's not him."

"How do you know?" demanded Holliday.

Edison smiled. "Because I've spotted him."

"Where?"

"Do you see that large bird perched at the top of the very last tree there?"

"Yes."

"That's him."

"I repeat: how do you know?"

"That's a Great Gray Owl."

"Okay, it's a Great Gray Owl," said Holliday. "So what?"

"They live in the northeastern United States and up in Canada," said Edison.

"So he flew south. Birds do that."

"Not this far south, and not this far west."

"That's mighty thin reasoning," said Holliday.

"There's more," said Edison. He checked his wristwatch. "It's past eleven in the morning. The sun is almost directly overhead."

"You say that as if it should mean something."

"The Great Gray Owl is nocturnal, Doc. If that were a *real* owl, he couldn't see a damned thing in this sunlight."

Holliday stared at the owl, which stared back. "Okay, that makes sense," he said. "Which of the two do you suppose it is?"

"I don't know," answered Edison. "I don't know if it's either of them, or a surrogate warrior, or if it's actually a bird they somehow control and use to spy on us. The nice part is that it makes no difference for this experiment. It's clearly operating on magical principles, and all I want to know is if what I've brought along will disrupt the magic."

"Just a minute," said Holliday. "How the hell did you know *anything* would be out here watching you?"

"I proved I could kill White Eagle," answered Edison. "Wouldn't you keep an eye on me if you were Geronimo or Hook Nose?"

"What if they attack you?"

"If nothing I have with me harms them, why bother?" asked Edison. "And if I *can* hurt them, then how much more damage might I do if they attack?"

"There's a difference between harming and killing," Holliday pointed out.

"Damn it, Doc," said Edison in exasperation, "I can't just make notes and spout theories. I have to put them into practice sooner or later." He paused. "I'm sorry. I didn't mean to snap at you."

"It's all right," answered Holliday. "Sometimes I forget what kind of pressure you're under." He looked at the device in Edison's hand. "What do we do now?"

Edison suddenly stared at Holliday's pistol for a moment, then off at the owl. He didn't say a word, but Holliday could see that the man was *thinking*, his jaw clenched, his gaze darting—and suddenly he snapped his fingers. "I've got it!" he exclaimed. "Bringing you along was a stroke of genius!"

Holliday studied the inventor's face, which seemed more elated than he'd ever see it before. It did not translate into elation on Holliday's part. "Am I going to want to hear this?"

For a moment Edison seemed too preoccupied to answer him. Then he suddenly became himself again. "There was one problem, Doc," he explained. "I could use this"—he held up the device—"and annoy or disable or even kill the owl. Or I could have no effect on it. And it would *imply* things, but it wouldn't *prove* a thing. After all, the Great Gray Owl *does* exist. The odds are hundreds to one that the one we're looking at didn't migrate across half a continent to a climate it's not suited for, and thousands to one that it wouldn't try to observe *anything* with a cloudless sky and the sun directly overhead—but while those odds may be incredibly unlikely, they're not impossible. That's where you come in."

"How?"

"Get close enough to the owl so you can't miss, and then shoot it." Holliday merely stared at him without saying a word, and Edison continued. "If you kill it, we know it was just a misplaced and unlucky bird. But if I'm right, bullets won't have any effect on it at all. That's what I'm counting on."

Holliday frowned. "You're hoping I *can't* hurt it?"

"Right," said Edison. "Because if you can't, then we know it's part of Hook Nose's or Geronimo's magic—or maybe both of theirs together. And if I can then harm, or kill, or somehow disrupt it with this device, we'll know it's effective against magic."

"What if it only harms it, but doesn't kill it?"

"Makes no difference," answered Edison. "It'll mean I've got the right principle, and I simply have to find ways to strengthen and refine it."

"Am I going to need ear plugs?"

Edison shook his head. "This noiseless sound will be beyond the ability of any man, any dog, any living thing at all, to hear. It doesn't harm people or animals; if it works, what it does is disrupt magic."

Holliday shrugged. "I hope you're right. I suppose we might as well start right now."

Edison nodded his assent, and Holliday began walking toward the stand of trees. The owl watched him approach, but made no effort to fly away. Holliday walked around the stand to the far side of it, where he had a better view of the owl. He felt uncomfortable shooting at something that might be, and probably was, magical. He had an urge to pull his gun, fire off three or four quick shots, and then back away, but he knew he had to be sure he hit it. So when he was about twenty paces from the tree he slowly withdrew his gun, took careful aim, and squeezed off a shot. He heard the *thunk!* as the bullet hit, and saw some feathers fly off, but the owl never moved, never gave any indication that it had been shot. He fired twice more with the same effect, or lack of effect, and finally he holstered his gun and walked back toward Edison.

"You're sure you hit him?" asked the inventor.

"I'm sure."

"Then let's see if I'm on the right track, or if I've wasted a week."

Edison pointed the device at the bird.

"Don't you want to get closer?" asked Holliday.

"This will affect everything for miles," said Edison. "In theory, anyway."

His thumb moved to a small switch that Holliday hadn't seen. There was no noise, not even a low humming, nothing glowed, nothing sprang forth from the end of the device—but the owl screeched, began flying off, and suddenly burst into a fireball and vanished as a handful of ashes swirled down to the ground.

"Well, I'll be damned!" said Holliday.

"But maybe the United States won't be," said Edison, a satisfied smile on his face.

"That wasn't either of them, was it?"

"I doubt it," answered Edison. "They knew what I did to White Eagle. They'd have known what we were doing when you fired your gun at them, and would have fled. No, he or they—make it *they*, I'm sure they were both watching, even if only one wove the bird from a spell—just wanted to see how far I've gotten."

"Have you figured out that makes you a marked man?" said Holliday.

"In a way," replied Edison. "But they don't know what this can do to them personally, and they don't know what else I've got that might do even more damage. I think I'm reasonably safe for the moment."

"I think you're an optimist."

"Perhaps," said Edison. "But just to put this into historical perspective, this is the first time since the war between science and magic began that science has won a skirmish."

"White Eagle would disagree with that if he were here," said Holliday with a grim smile.

"All right, the second time."

Edison, using overdone gestures, finally got the driver to understand that he was to take them back to town. They climbed back into the coach, and Holliday pulled out his flask and offered Edison a drink.

"No, thanks. I've got to make notes of this, and I'll need a clear head."

Holliday took a drink, capped the flask, and put it back in a coat pocket. "I was just wondering, Tom . . ."

"Yes?"

"Do you think maybe the bird *was* Geronimo or Hook Nose?"

Edison looked out the window and smiled. "Not a chance," he said firmly.

"You sound very certain."

Edison pointed to a tree, "See that white bird?"

"Yes."

"It's a Snowy Owl. It has even less business being in New Mexico, and watching us at high noon, than the Great Gray Owl."

Holliday raised his hand from his lap and waved at the owl. Later he would doubt it, but at that moment he could have sworn that the owl lifted a wing and waved back.

29.

HOLLIDAY LOST THREE HUNDRED DOLLARS at poker that night, won fifty back at the faro table, and decided to quit before he got too drunk and had a repeat of the fiasco at the Monarch the night Oscar Wilde came to watch him gamble.

He was up at ten the next morning. There was a bird perched on his window. He spoke to it, but all it did was chirp and fly off as he approached it.

He looked around the lobby for Charlotte, in case she was having a late breakfast, couldn't spot her, and went out the front door. He ran a hand over his cheek, decided he needed a shave, and stopped in at the barber shop.

"You could use a haircut too," noted the barber as he lathered Holliday's face.

Holliday was about to tell him to forget it. Then he looked in a mirror, decided that he *was* getting a little shaggy, and concluded that Charlotte might appreciate a clean-cut dining partner, and okayed it.

"Your friend Mr. Buntline was in earlier," said the barber as he began clipping away at Holliday's hair. "Tried to sell me a brass razor." The barber chuckled. "Can you imagine that? A brass razor!"

"I'd buy it if I were you," said Holliday.

"Actually, he tried to sell me two dozen of them. Swears they'll never get dull."

"Believe it or not, he's right."

The barber grinned. "How many hands have I got? If they never get dull, what do I need with twenty-four of them?"

Holliday smiled. "I think he just invented himself out of the market."

"He wasn't bullshitting, though?" persisted the barber. "They really work?"

"If he says so, I'd believe him."

"You're his friend, Doc. Tell him if he'll sell me just four, I'll buy."

"I'll mention it next time I see him," replied Holliday.

"Okay, hold still now, and I'll take this stubble off your cheeks with a *real* razor."

It was over in three minutes, Holliday flipped him a dime, and walked out into the street. After spending two years in Tombstone and Leadville, cities Edison had virtually re-made, he found it difficult to adjust to horses tied to hitching posts, to the piles of horse manure as he walked across the street, and to the gaslights that illuminated the interiors of the darker buildings in the daytime.

He made his way to Mabel Grimsley's and sat at his usual table. Mabel came out of the kitchen with a cup in one hand and a pot of coffee in the other and approached him.

"Ah!" she said. "My favorite customer!"

"Your most notorious, anyway," replied Holliday.

"Same thing," she said with a smile. "You stay notorious and you'll stay my favorite."

"Has Charlotte been in here this morning?"

"Two or three hours ago. She said she had things to do, and figured you'd been playing cards and would be sleeping 'til noon."

"She was half right," said Holliday with a wry smile. "I was losing at cards, and I slept 'til ten."

Mabel laughed. "I heard you won a few thousand the other night. You can't win every time."

"No," agreed Holliday. "But you can wish you could."

"What'll it be, Doc? Same as usual?"

He'd been about to order toast and a scrambled egg when it occurred to him that he was *hungry*, and decided it came from not drinking as much as usual the night before.

"I'll take a small steak."

"Funny," said Mabel, smiling. "I could have sworn you were Doc Holliday."

She went off to the kitchen, and Holliday pulled a book out of his pocket. He was still reading it when she returned with his breakfast.

"What have you got there?" she asked, indicating the book.

"A biography of President Lincoln," answered Holliday. "I picked it up in the general store." He closed the book and put it in a pocket. "How big a reward do you think they offered for John Wilkes Booth?"

"Who was he?" asked Mabel.

"The man who kill Mr. Lincoln."

She frowned as she considered it. "What are they offering for Billy these days?"

"Ten thousand."

"Okay, fifteen."

Holliday smiled. "One hundred thousand."

"For one man?" she said. "Hell, even Geronimo's not worth much more than twenty." She shrugged. "That's what comes of reading books. You learn all kinds of useless things."

"I'll give it to you when I'm through with it," said Holliday. "In fact, you can have it now if you like. I've found want I wanted to know."

She shook her head. "No offense, Doc, but I limit my reading to the Good Book. Ten chapters every morning before I come over here."

"Sometimes ten chapters barely comes to half a page," noted Holliday.

"It ain't how long they are," she replied. "It's how important."

"True enough."

"Do you ever read the Bible, Doc?"

He shook his head. "Not anymore."

She nodded her head. "I suppose it'd be a hindrance in your profession."

"My profession is dentistry."

"If all you were was a dentist, you wouldn't be getting all these free meals."

Holliday grinned. "Touché."

"Whatever *that* means," she said. "Well, don't just sit there talking about rewards and bibles. Dig in before it gets cold."

Holliday did as she told him, and decided that the steak tasted even better than it smelled. When he was done he asked for a second cup of coffee, wished his weakened lungs would let him light up a cigar, and pulled the book out once again.

"If your pal Tom Edison would stick his electric lights in here," said Mabel, cleaning up a table near him, "you could read that a little easier."

"He's a little busy these days," said Holliday, "but I'll tell him to come by and look the place over so he can tell you what he'd need to do and how much it would cost."

"I could make a deal with him, too," said Mabel. "Free meals for lights."

"I'll let him know."

"Thanks."

Holliday got up, walked out the door, and headed back to the Grand. He stopped by the desk and asked if Charlotte had returned yet.

"No she hasn't, Doc," said the clerk. "I ain't seen her since she went out maybe three, three and a half hours ago,"

"Did she say where she was going?"

The clerk shook his head. "Nope. Can't imagine why she'd tell me anyway."

"Got a pen and a piece of paper?" asked Holliday.

"Sure," said the clerk, reaching behind the desk and withdrawing them. "Here you are, Doc."

Holliday penned a four-word note—*Dinner at six? Doc*—and handed it to the clerk. "See that she gets this when she comes in, would you please?"

"Sure. She should be back any time. She didn't take her luggage with her."

"What are you talking about?" demanded Holliday, suddenly alert.

"That surrey you two rented a couple of days ago," said the clerk. "She rented it again."

"When?"

"I don't know. Maybe eight o'clock, maybe eight-fifteen. She was sitting right over there. I figured she was waiting for you to wake up so you could walk over to Miz Grimsley's for breakfast like you often do. Then some guy came in and said something to her, and she gave him some money and sent him off, and he was back a couple of minutes later with the surrey."

"Did he go with her?"

The clerk shook his head. "No, she went alone. Didn't say where." He studied Holliday's face and suddenly felt very uneasy and more than a little bit afraid. "Is something wrong, Doc?"

Holliday shook his head. "Just a little restless."

"You probably ain't used to seeing the sun in the eastern half of the sky," suggested the clerk.

"I think I've been up before noon more often in New Mexico than at any time since I was a dentist."

"I wonder," said the clerk, rubbing his chin thoughtfully. "Why do you suppose most men do their drinking and their gambling at night?"

"I don't know. It's a way to relax."

"That's probably why there ain't a line at any of the bawdy houses at noontime," agreed the clerk. Suddenly he stared out the front door. "There he is!"

"There *who* is?"

"The guy who was talking to Mrs. Branson this morning."

Holliday was out the door instantly and approaching the man, who was dressed pretty much like a ranch hand: blue jeans, Stetson, worn boots, a plain shirt, and a bandana around his neck.

"Excuse me," said Holliday, walking up to him. "May I speak to you for a minute?"

"Sure," said the cowboy. "You're Doc Holliday, ain't you?"

"Yes, I am. You said something to Mrs. Branson this morning, and then went and got a surrey for her. What exactly did you say?"

"Just that Billy the Kid and Josh Brady were back at Brady's place. She'd paid me a gold dollar a couple of days ago to let her know anytime the Kid was in the area."

"And that's when she asked you to get her the surrey?" said Holliday.

"Right."

"Did you actually see him, or did you just hear he was back?"

"I seen him with my own eyes, just after daybreak. So I saddled up and came to town to tell her. I figured that was the least I could do for my gold piece."

"Thanks," said Holliday.

"Nice meeting you," said the cowboy, starting to walk off. "Now if I ever have any kids, I can tell 'em that I've met Billy the Kid, Cole Younger, and Doc Holliday."

Holliday began walking toward the stable to rent a buggy, a surrey, a horse and saddle, *anything*, to take him out to Brady's ranch. He was within fifty paces of it when a horse-pulled wagon that was going down the street stopped as it came abreast of him.

"You're Doc Holliday, right?" said the driver.

"Yes."

"I thought so. Come on over to the undertaker's. I got a body for you to identify."

"I'll do it right here," said Holliday with a sick feeling in the pit of his stomach.

"It's in the back."

Holliday walked around to the back of the wagon. A body was wrapped in a pair of blankets. He unfolded them and found himself looking at Charlotte Branson. She had one bullet hole through her right eye, and two more in her chest, just below her heart.

Holliday stared at her, the muscles in his jaw clenching and unclenching, saying nothing. After a couple of minutes the driver climbed down, walked over to Holliday, and stared down at the corpse.

"Is she who I think she is?" he said. "The lady I seen you eating with a couple of times?"

Holliday nodded. "Charlotte Branson."

"I'll tell the undertaker and Sheriff Garrett, but they may want official identification from you."

"I'll stop by the undertaker's in a few minutes," said Holliday emotionlessly.

"And Garrett?"

"I'm on my way," said Holliday, turning and walking briskly toward the sheriff's office.

He opened the door, walked in, and stood in front of Garrett's desk.

"What is it?" demanded Garrett, making no attempt to hide his dislike for the man facing him.

"In a few minutes, you're going to be told officially that the Kid killed a woman named Charlotte Branson," said Holliday. "Her body has just been delivered to the undertaker."

"*Shit!*" growled Garrett, getting to his feet. "He's gone too far this time. He's never killed a woman before!"

"Stay where you are," said Holliday in a low voice. "I'll handle this."

"What the hell are you talking about?" demanded Garrett. "*I'm* the sheriff!"

"I know there's no love lost between us," said Holliday. "And I really don't want to kill you, but I will if I have to. If you want to live, just sit back down and relax."

Garrett looked into Holliday's eyes and didn't like what he saw. He sat down.

"You want to tell me why you're preventing me from doing my duty?" said Garrett.

"He's *mine!*" said Holliday so softly Garrett could barely hear the words.

30.

HOLLIDAY WAS HEADING TO THE STABLE to rent a horse to take him out to Brady's ranch when Ned Buntline caught up with him.

"Hello, Doc!" he said breathlessly.

"Go away," growled Holliday. "I'm busy."

"You're going out to Josh Brady's, right?"

Holliday looked surprised. "How did you know?"

"I was in the lobby when someone told the clerk that Mrs. Branson wouldn't be using her room anymore, that the Kid had killed her."

"He's going to find out what it means to break his word to Doc Holliday."

"What are you talking about?"

"We made a deal," said Holliday. "His end of it was not to kill Charlotte."

"And now you're going off to face him?" said Buntline.

"That's right."

"If you want to live through it, you'd better come with me."

Holliday stared at him curiously.

"I'm not kidding, Doc. Come with me to Tom's room."

"I've got business elsewhere."

"What can it cost you—ten minutes?" said Buntline. "Twelve? He'll still be there."

"Leave me alone," said Holliday.

"Damn it, Doc—it's important!" yelled Buntline.

Holliday stopped walking. "It damned well better be."

"Come with me," said Buntline, turning and heading off toward the Grand.

They reached the lobby in less than a minute, and were at Edison's door in another forty seconds.

"Come in, Doc," said Edison as Holliday opened the door without knocking. "You too, Ned. I may need your help." He reached out a hand and laid it on Holliday's shoulder. "I'm sorry about Charlotte, Doc."

"Someone else is going to be even sorrier," said Holliday grimly as he entered the most cluttered room he had ever seen: part bedroom, part laboratory, part storage room. And, like his offices in Tombstone and Leadville, there were books and notebooks piled everywhere.

"That's why you're here."

"I don't need any brass armor," said Holliday. "*He* doesn't wear it; *I'm* not wearing it." He withdrew his gun from its holster and held it up. "This is all I need."

"You're wrong, Doc," said Edison.

Holliday turned to him. "What do you know that I don't know?" he said sharply.

"When Ned and I got back from breakfast—we ate at Ben Tanner's two streets over—we found our rooms had been plundered. When we went downstairs to report it, a couple of residents said they'd seen the

Kid and Josh Brady walking out the back way, and the Kid had a bag slung over his shoulder." He paused and grimaced. "So we did an inventory, and what he stole was a pair of brand new prototypes of an electric gun."

Holliday frowned. "You mean it's powered by electricity? It won't do him any good. I can pull a trigger faster than he can flip a switch."

Edison shook his head. "It's not that simple. These guns aren't only powered by electricity, but electricity is what they fire instead of bullets."

"Explain," said Holliday.

"You know that electricity can be extremely powerful," said Edison. "It can light a whole city. You also know that you have to be very careful around it to avoid getting a shock."

"I've seen you get shocks in your labs back in Tombstone and Colorado," said Holliday. "You cuss like a cowboy for a minute, rub wherever you got the shock, and go right back to work."

"That's because I know better than to work with incredibly strong electrical currents, and I'm always grounded," answered Edison. "But the Kid's guns will shoot out a bolt of electrical energy—kind of like a controlled, aimed lightning bolt. If he figures out how to use the latest thing I've added to them, he'll be able to set up a field that will repulse any bullet that you shoot at him."

"So you're saying he can burn me to cinders with one shot, and I can't hit him even if I shoot from five feet away?"

"As things stand now. But if you'll give me half an hour, I believe I can even the odds."

"He's got Hook Nose, I've got Geronimo, he's got an electric gun and an invisible shield, I've got whatever you're about to give me. This world would be a whole lot easier to understand if all you guys would just let the two of us shoot it out on our own."

"I'm just trying to make it an even fight," said Edison.

"Why did you even create those damned guns the Kid's got?" asked Holliday.

"I did it before I conceived of the ultrasonic device," answered Edison. "At the time, I thought possibly a severe electrical shock would neutralize whoever was protecting the station and the tracks."

"All right," said Holliday. "What have you got for me?"

"Let me outfit you with your defense first," said Edison, pulling out a dresser drawer and withdrawing what looked like a pair of leather wristlets. "Take off your coat and put these on, Doc."

"What the hell do I need them for?" asked Holliday with a frown. "They're just for stopping my shirtsleeves from flapping in the wind."

"They were once. Put them on."

Holliday did as he was told, slipping his hands through the wristlets, and noticed a series of small, almost hidden, wires on the backs of them.

"What the hell are these?" he asked.

"You'll see. Now turn around while Ned and I wire you up." Edison and Buntline attached a set of metal wires to his shoulders, hips, and arms, all leading down to the wristlets. "The battery, Ned?"

Buntline handed a battery to Edison, who strapped it to the small of Holliday's back.

"Move your arms," ordered Edison.

Holliday reached up, then forward, then whirled them in a circle.

"Looks good," said Buntline from behind them. "Everything's still attached."

"Okay," said Edison. "Now bring that switch around to his belt buckle."

Buntline walked around Holliday, tucking a thin wire from the battery under his belt until he reached the buckle, then hooking a small switch onto it.

"All right," said Edison. "Turn the switch on." Holliday did so. "Any pain, anything at all?"

"No."

"Good, Now you can turn it off."

"Since I'm the one who has to use it, suppose you tell me what it is and what it does," said Holliday.

"Turning on the switch activates a defensive electronic field," said Edison. "It won't stop a bullet or a knife, but we have to assume that's not what he'll be using. This will negate the electric charges he'll be firing at you." He looked around the room, walked to a corner, and picked up what Holliday had thought was a small, thick walking stick from where it leaned against the wall.

"What the hell is *that*?" asked Holliday, arching an eyebrow. "A gun or a rifle, or maybe a cannon?"

"It's a gun," answered Edison, holding up the thirty-inch-long weapon.

"They sure as hell don't make a holster for it," observed Holliday. "And even if they did, no one could draw it in less than ten seconds."

"You won't have to draw it," said Edison, as Buntline began tacking a strip of material to Holliday's pants leg with needle and thread. "There are very small magnets on that strip of cloth, and they'll hold the gun in place."

"Then how the hell do I use it?" demanded Holliday irritably. "Point my leg?"

Edison laughed. "It's an interesting thought, but no, you won't have to do that." He pointed to a small button just above the trigger mechanism. "You see this? When you want the gun, just press it, and it'll change the polarity of the magnetic field."

"What the hell does that mean?"

"It means that instead of the gun being attracted to those magnets, it will now be repelled by them. When you want to bond it back to your leg, just press the button again." He looked at Holliday's leg. "Ned, that strip's too long. Cut it off higher or he'll never be able to bend his knee once the gun's attached."

As Buntline was shortening the strip, Holliday took the gun from Edison and examined it.

"What does *it* shoot?" he asked. "Electricity?"

"Bullets," said Edison. "Well, sort of."

"It sort of shoots them?" asked Holliday, frowning.

Edison smiled. "Oh, it shoots them, all right. I meant that they're sort of bullets."

"What else are they?" asked Holliday, who was getting frustrated with Edison's explanations.

"Negatively charged pellets made of a silver alloy," said the inventor. "The negative charge will allow them to get past the Kid's defensive field."

"You're sure?"

"It works that way on paper," answered Edison. "I haven't field-tested your weapons and defenses—*or* his—yet."

"All right," said Holliday. He pressed the button and bonded the gun to his left leg.

"I thought you were right-handed," said Buntline.

"I am," replied Holliday. "And I'm keeping *this*," he patted his own gun, "right where I can reach it. I know *it* works." He took a few steps to get used to the feel of the long gun against his leg. "Okay, let me go over it once more. I hit this switch to activate the defensive field, and this button to release the gun?"

"Right."

"I assume the trigger works like any other trigger?"

"Better," said Edison. "There are a hundred pellets in the chamber. It fires ten a second for as long as you hold the trigger down."

"All right," said Holliday, walking to the door. "I'm ready to go."

"One more thing, Doc," said Edison. He slipped a metal vest around Holliday's neck and shoulders. "Just in case."

"I thought this stuff worked."

"It does," said Edison, "but that defense field takes so much energy that the battery is only good for about three minutes, four at the outside. So don't activate it until you have to."

"Got it," said Holliday, walking out the door.

Much as he hated riding atop a horse, he knew it would get him to the ranch faster than a buckboard or a surrey, so he rented a horse at the stable and headed toward Brady's ranch.

He was within a quarter mile of it when a familiar voice spoke out.

"You have no idea what awaits you at this Place of Death," it said.

31.

HOLLIDAY LOOKED TO HIS LEFT, then down. A large, savage-looking wolf stood next to his horse, its glowing eyes staring up at him.

"Who or what the hell are you?" demanded Holliday.

"You know who I am."

"Geronimo?" There was no answer, which he took for an affirmative. "Well, that explains why my horse didn't shy. He knows you're not a wolf. Besides," he added, "there probably hasn't been a wolf in these parts in twenty years."

"McCarty who is called the Kid will not have the usual weapons," said the wolf. "Are you prepared?"

"I'm ready." Holliday looked down at the wolf, frowning. "Why are you here? I thought you neutralized Hook Nose."

"Woo-Ka-Nay has grown in power. I cannot hold him at bay from a distance. I must be here with you."

"You can do whatever you want to him, but the Kid is mine."

"I have no interest in McCarty who is called the Kid."

"Fine," said Holliday. "I have no interest in Hook Nose."

"Then you are a fool," said the wolf.

"I've been called worse," said Holliday, urging his horse forward.

"Are you prepared to defend yourself from the weapons he stole from the man Edison?"

"I'm prepared."

"Then go forward. I cannot see Woo-Ka-Nay, but I sense his presence. I will seek him out and make certain that he does not interfere."

"Thanks." Holliday rode to the top of a ridge that looked down at the ranch.

"I do not do it for you, Holliday," said the wolf. "I do it only because we made a trade and I always keep my word."

"I'll give you this," said Holliday. "You're honorable men who honor your deals—some of you, anyway. I told you about Que-Su-La."

"He who lifted *my* curse on the man Masterson."

"I forgot that for a minute. Yeah, he's the one."

"He acted in good faith, and you avenged his son. I bear him no malice."

"I can't say that I think favorably of Hook Nose," said Holliday. "Still, like I said, some of you are honorable men, just as some of us are. And I'm not here to kill an Indian, just a white man."

"Possibly two," said the wolf, and vanished. Holliday looked toward the small, dilapidated ranch house, where a burly, balding man had just emerged. Holliday let his horse walk slowly down from the ridge toward the flat, barren spot where he had so recently killed two men.

"What's your business here?" demanded the man.

"Are you Brady?" asked Holliday.

"I am, and you're on my property."

"I have nothing against you," said Holliday. "You tell that son of a bitch you work with that I'm here to blow him straight to hell."

"No one talks like that on my ranch but me!" snarled Brady.

"If you want to live to bellow another day, you'll go find the Kid and keep clear of this."

"Climb down off that horse and say that!"

Holliday dismounted, and suddenly the wolf appeared at his side again.

Brady pulled his pistol and fired three quick shots into the wolf's body, to no effect. The horses in the corral began prancing and nickering nervously.

"He's my pet," said Holliday, amused at Brady's reaction when the wolf didn't even flinch. "Now get Mr. McCarty Antrim Bonney, and keep your ugly nose out of this."

Brady uttered an obscenity and aimed his gun at Holliday.

"Big mistake," said Holliday as he drew and fired before Brady could squeeze the trigger. He flew backward, and Holliday put another bullet into his chest before he hit the ground.

"I was right to bring my own gun along," said Holliday, nodding his head in satisfaction. "And no one's going to miss one more cattle thief. I wonder if there was paper on him?"

"He was just an ant," said the wolf. "You want the spider."

"He'll be along," replied Holliday. "He won't like anyone messing with his web."

And as the words left his mouth, the Kid opened the door of the ranch house and stepped out onto the flat, dry ground. Holliday studied him and saw that he was armed with the weapons he'd stolen from Edison: two wicked-looking pistols, each connected to electrical wires that led to the large battery that stretched across his back and actually stuck out a few inches on each side. Suddenly Holliday remembered to switch on his own protective field.

"You killed my partner," said the Kid, brushing a few flies away from his face with a hand.

"I'll kill anyone who gets between us," replied Holliday.

"Why?"

"We had an agreement. You broke it."

"Her?" said the Kid with a contemptuous laugh. "She was an ugly old woman. What the hell do you care?"

"You promised not to kill her," said Holliday coldly. "You lied."

"Well, damn it, Doc, she came out here to kill me!" snapped the Kid.

The horses in the corral, which were merely nervous when the shots were fired, were near to panicking now, terrified by the vitriol in the two men's voices.

"*Could* she have killed you?"

"Not on the best day she ever had."

"Then why the hell didn't you just put a bullet in her arm, or shoot the gun out of her hand. You're good enough to have done either."

"She was two feet away."

"Then you could have slapped it away."

The Kid considered Holliday's remark, and nodded. "Maybe I could have. So what? She was a fucking bounty hunter."

"She was my friend and we had a deal—and you lied to me," said Holliday. "And now you're going to die for it."

"For killing her or lying to you?" asked the Kid with a smile.

"Take your choice."

"I see you've got a wolf with you," noted the Kid. "Nice pet."

"He won't interfere with this."

"*Mine* will," said the Kid with a grin. He stepped aside, and Holliday found himself facing a puma with the same glowing eyes that the wolf had. "Looks like the gang's all here," he said as he threw back his head and laughed.

"I can't wait much longer," said Holliday, lowering his voice so only the wolf could hear it. "Have you got my back?"

"Woo-Ka-Nay will not hinder you or help him," answered the wolf.

"You'd better know what you're talking about," said Holliday.

The two men faced each other, suddenly oblivious to the animals. Holliday pressed the button that released Edison's gun from the magnetic strip on his leg and fired it, just as the Kid pulled the twin pistols from his holster and squeezed the triggers.

And nothing happened. Holliday's pellets were absorbed into the Kid's protective field, and the Kid's lightning bolts dissipated as they reached Holliday's invisible shield.

"Shit!" snapped Holliday.

"It is not Woo-Ka-Nay's doing," said the wolf.

Holliday fired again. There was still no effect.

"Thanks a lot for not testing it, Tom!" he muttered.

The Kid was still firing electrical charges at him to no effect.

Use your brain, Doc, thought Holliday. *You're smarter than he is—and you've only got maybe two minutes left before you're helpless.*

Then he looked at the Kid. *I wonder how long* his *battery is good for.*

Holliday shifted the huge gun to his left hand, drew his own Colt with his right, and aimed just to the right of the Kid's shoulder, burying a pair of bullets into the battery that extended past the trunk of the Kid's body. He put another bullet into the left end of it, just for insurance.

The Kid staggered from the force of the bullets, but quickly regained his balance and fired again—and this time there was no lightning bolt, no discharge of any kind.

Holliday fired a bullet at the Kid's head, but it never got there. *Damn! He's still immune to bullets! Then what did the battery control? Just his guns?*

Holliday pointed the long, electrically charged weapon at the Kid, who'd thrown away Edison's guns and was pulling his own out of his belt.

I can't have a minute left. This had better work!

Holliday fired the weapon, and this time the Kid grunted in surprise as the pellets tore into him. Holliday fired again, holding his finger down on the trigger for almost two seconds, and the Kid reacted like a puppet being jerked on a string before he fell to the ground.

Holliday turned and aimed the weapon at the puma.

"Another day," promised the puma, and faded into nothingness.

As Holliday approached the Kid's body, he felt a sudden weight on his shoulder, and two claws digging in.

"And now we are even," said the coal-black eagle that had just perched on him. He looked around, and the wolf was gone. Or transmogrified.

Holliday walked uncomfortably the rest of the way, for the eagle was heavy and despite his skills his body was frail. He stared at the Kid, who lay there with his eyes open, his torso perforated—there was no other word for it—and blood started to trickle out of his mouth.

"I didn't have to do this," said Holliday grimly. "I had enough money. I didn't need the bounty any longer."

"It was a debt of honor," said the eagle. "He betrayed you, as Woo-Ka-Nay betrayed me. Now I must do to him what you did to McCarty who was called the Kid, or he shall kill me."

"For what it's worth, I hope you win," said Holliday. "As for me, I'll take my money back to Colorado and spend my last year or two there."

"I do not think so," said the bird, and vanished.

JSG

32.

HOLLIDAY FOUND TO HIS SURPRISE that he didn't have the strength to sling the Kid's body over his horse to carry it back to town. He couldn't even drag it back into the house, so he went inside, found a couple of blankets, carried them out to where the Kid and Brady lay on the ground, and wrapped the bodies in the blankets to keep scavengers away.

Then he rode back to Lincoln, dismounted in front of Garrett's office, tied his horse to the hitching post out front, and entered.

Garrett sat at his desk, doing paperwork. He looked up, saw who was confronting him, and pushed the pile of paper aside.

"Well?" he said. "Did you find him?

"I found him."

Garrett looked out the door. "Is that your horse?"

"For a few more hours," said Holliday.

"Then where's the body?"

"Back at Brady's ranch."

"That was a stupid thing to do," said Garrett. "Anyone could come along and claim it."

"They won't. I left it less that fifteen minutes ago. Besides, who has any business at Brady's ranch?"

"Mostly horse thieves and cattle rustlers," admitted Garrett. "Well, if the Kid's there, what are you doing here? I can't send for the reward until I certify he's dead."

"*That's* what I'm doing here," answered Holliday. "Telling you to come out and identify the body." He paused briefly. "Is there any warrant for Brady?"

"You killed him too?"

"In self-defense."

"I wonder if there's been a killing this century that wasn't done in self-defense," said Garrett sardonically.

"My question?" persisted Holliday.

"Yeah, there's five hundred for him."

"Dead or alive?"

"Dead or alive," confirmed Garrett.

"Let's get a wagon and bring them both in."

Garrett nodded and got to his feet. "Return your horse. The sheriff's office will pay for the wagon."

They got Holliday's horse, walked it to the stable, and were soon riding out of town atop a buckboard that had seen better days. They rode in silence until the ranch came into view. Garrett urged the horses on, pulled them to a stop by the blanket-covered bodies, checked to make sure one of them was the Kid, loaded him onto the back of the buckboard, then lifted Brady's body and tossed it next to the Kid.

"Any others?" he asked.

"Aren't they enough?"

"This one alone's enough for a lifetime," said Garrett, patting the blanket-covered body. He looked around. "Nothing else to see here.

Might as well head back to town."

They rode in silence again for the first mile, but Holliday sensed that Garrett had something to say, and finally the sheriff spoke.

"What are you going to do with the money?" asked Garrett, closing his eyes as a breeze blew dust into their faces.

"I'm not sure," answered Holliday. "I came down here because I was broke, and I needed money to pay for the sanitarium I plan to die in. But I got hot at the tables with the bounties from the two men I killed a few days ago." He shrugged. "I'll probably just use this bounty to drink and gamble until it's time to move to the sanitarium."

"You'll never make it that long," said Garrett. "Every punk this side of the Mississippi who wants to make a reputation will be after the man who killed Billy the Kid."

"Not much I can do about it," said Holliday.

"Well, actually there is," said Garrett.

Holliday turned and stared at him. "Do I detect the hint of a proposition?"

"You don't like me much, Doc," said Garrett. "And believe me, I like you even less. But you're a man of your word, and I'm a man of mine. If we make a deal, we'll keep it, and that's vital in this case."

"Tell me about 'this case,'" said Holliday, "and I'll tell you what I think."

Garrett pulled the horse to a stop, and turned to face Holliday. "You said you had enough money to buy into your sanitarium before you shot the Kid. Howsabout if I send for your five hundred, and turn over Mrs. Branson's thousand to you as well?"

"And?"

"And you take the money and go back to Colorado, and maybe you'll live long enough to get to that sanitarium before some hotshot newcomer guns down the man who killed Billy the Kid."

"What do *you* get out of it?" said Holliday. "You're a lawman. You can't collect a reward for doing your job."

"I won't have to," said Garrett.

"Explain."

"I've been offered a lot of money for a book on the life and death of Billy the Kid," said Garrett. He grimaced. "There's just one catch. They'll only buy it if I'm the man who's responsible for killing him." He paused. "What do you say, Doc? You never tell anyone I didn't kill the Kid, and I never tell anyone you did."

"Let me think about it," said Holliday.

They rode the rest of the way in total silence.

As Garrett pulled the horse to a halt in front of the undertaker's, he turned to Holliday. "Well, Doc?"

Holliday nodded his agreement. "And if I find out that you collected any part of that bounty, I'll come back and kill you."

"Fair enough," said Garrett. "And if you ever contradict a word of my book, I'll hunt you down and kill you."

33.

TWO DAYS LATER Holliday was atop a buckboard again, sitting outside the Grand Hotel while he waited for Edison and Buntline to emerge. Charlotte Branson's casket was in the back.

He pulled out his flask, took a quick drink, and was tucking it back into his pocket when Edison walked out the front door, a large suitcase in his hand.

"I didn't know you had to pack a change of clothes to go up to Boot Hill," observed Holliday cynically, as Buntline came out with another piece of luggage.

"We don't," replied Edison. "But the last time we left the hotel for more than an hour, the Kid and Brady broke into our room and stole those prototype pistols. I've got all the ultrasonic equipment in these cases, and I'll be damned if anyone's going to steal them."

"Makes sense," agreed Holliday. "Well, stick 'em in the back and we'll be on our way."

"There's not room for three up there," said Buntline as Edison climbed up to share the driver's seat with Holliday.

"If you don't mind sitting in the wagon, it'll save you the bother of renting a horse," noted Holliday.

"Yeah, why not?" said Buntline, pulling himself up to the wagon, sitting at the back, and letting his legs dangle down. "It's only about half a mile out of town, right?"

"Right," said Holliday, urging the horses forward.

"Did you arrange for a preacher?" asked Edison.

Holliday shook his head. "I don't know what religion she belonged to, but I don't think she was much of a believer. We'll just bury her, plant the headstone, and leave."

"Headstone?"

"I had one made up," said Holliday. "It'll be better than Julia Bulette's, anyway."

"I don't believe I've heard of her," said Edison.

"She was a madam in Virginia City, up in Nevada," said Holliday. "Gave a goodly percentage of her take to the local police and fire departments, and when there was a cholera outbreak she turned her whorehouse into a free hospital. Got killed by a drunken customer a few years back, at which point the local ladies, who wouldn't say a word against her when she was alive, decided she wasn't fit to be buried in the local cemetery, and insisted they plant her in Boot Hill. Her only marker was the brass headboard of her bed."

"Really?"

"Really," replied Holliday. "At least Charlotte will have a headstone."

They rode the rest of the way in silence, entered the little graveyard, and stopped the wagon by a recently dug grave where two men were standing, shovels in hand. Holliday tossed them each a gold coin, indicated the casket, and stood aside as they pulled it off the buckboard, carried it to the grave, and lowered it on ropes they'd left there.

Then they quickly filled in the grave, planted the headstone, and left on horseback.

"Maybe you should say a prayer over her, Doc," suggested Buntline.

"I don't know any," replied Holliday.

"Not one?" asked Edison.

Holliday shook his head. "Not one."

"I do," said a voice, and the three men turned to find themselves facing Geronimo.

"I thought we were even," said Holliday, frowning.

"We are," said Geronimo. "I pay tribute to a brave woman."

"I have no objection to that," said Holliday, stepping back and allowing the Apache to step closer to the grave.

"But *I* do," said another voice.

They all turned and saw Hook Nose standing some fifty yards away.

"Stand back, White Eyes," said Geronimo softly. "His battle is with me, not with you."

"My battle is with *all* of you!" said Hook Nose sternly. "But it is especially with *you*!" He pointed a finger at Geronimo and a lightning bolt shot out of it.

Geronimo held up his hand and deflected the bolt, then chanted something in his native language and a whirlwind instantly encompassed Hook Nose.

"Do you think to harm me with a mere wind, Goyathlay?" demanded Hook Nose, stepping forward through the whirlwind.

"What I harm you with is immaterial to me," answered Geronimo, making a mystic gesture. Instantly two hawks appeared thirty feet above Hook Nose and dove down, clearly aiming for his eyes. When they were halfway to him, he made a slapping gesture with his hand; the hawks screamed and vanished.

For another two minutes the two medicine men hurled mystical creatures and weapons at each other, while Edison and Buntline gathered up their luggage and began creeping away. Holliday, though fascinated by the battle, accompanied them.

"Not so fast, White Eyes!" yelled Hook Nose, conjuring up a dragon-like creature and sending it after them.

"They are under my protection!" said Geronimo, holding both hands up. The dragon stopped. Then he uttered a low command, and the dragon turned and began approaching Hook Nose. "Woo-Ka-Nay created him," said Geronimo, "Woo-Ka-Nay may have him."

Edison opened his suitcase and began rummaging through it. "Damn!" he muttered. "Wrong one!"

Holliday saw the device they had used to kill White Eagle, reached in, and pulled it out.

"We don't want that one, Doc," said Edison as Buntline opened the other case. "*This* is the ticket!" he said, and pulled out a smaller device.

"That's the thing that turned the Great Gray Owl into a fireball, right?" asked Holliday.

"Right," answered Edison.

"Put it away."

"What are you talking about, Doc?" demanded Edison. "It worked on the owl. It'll work on these two."

"I know."

"Then what—?"

"Geronimo's protecting us, Tom. You can't kill him."

"Then what do we do—just wait this thing out and hope he wins?"

"We lower the odds," said Holliday, holding up the device he'd taken from the first case.

Geronimo and Hook Nose had escalated their weaponry from conjured creatures to a rain of fire, huge boulders, tornado-like winds—and still each stood up to whatever the other hurled against him.

JSG

Holliday began moving forward, the device in his hand, trying to use Geronimo as a shield. Finally when he was just a few feet behind the Apache he took two steps to Geronimo's left, aimed the device, and fired it.

It didn't have the same deadly effect on Hook Nose that it had on White Eagle, but it clearly stunned him, and as he turned to concentrate on Holliday he lowered some part of his psychic guard, for Geronimo threw one last fireball at him. It exploded in his face, and an instant later Hook Nose's headless body fell to the ground.

Geronimo turned to Holliday.

"We seem to have made another trade, John Henry Holliday. What service can I do you in exchange for this?"

"I don't suppose you can make my consumption go away?"

Geronimo shook his head. "It will kill you. Even my magic cannot change that."

"I was afraid you'd say that," replied Holliday with a wry smile. "I have nothing else to ask of you. But I think my friend Tom has."

Geronimo shook his head. "He has done me no service. I will do none for him."

"That's not so," said Holliday. "He invented the device that I—" But suddenly he was speaking to empty air.

"What should we do about Hook Nose's body?" asked Buntline.

Holliday shrugged. "Do you feel like digging a grave?"

Buntline looked around. "They took the shovels with them."

"When we get to town I'll pay someone to come out and bury him," said Edison.

"*Do* Indians get buried?" asked Buntline.

"Unless someone claims him in the next couple of hours," said Edison, "this one will."

Holliday walked over to Charlotte's grave and looked at the headstone.

Charlotte Branson
?–1882
A true friend
Who might have been more

He stood there in silence for a minute, then walked to the buckboard.

"Ready to go back to town?" he asked.

Edison and Buntline nodded their assent, and ten minutes later he was packing his bags in the Grand Hotel, preparing to go back to Leadville, make his peace with Kate Elder, and face the slow, painful death that awaited him.

34.

EDISON AND BUNTLINE had gone to Tombstone to retrieve some devices they'd been working on, and Holliday sat alone in the stagecoach as it made its way north from Lincoln. He'd brought along a flat board, placed it on his lap, pulled his cards out of his coat pocket, and began playing solitaire. It helped him pass the time and ignore the myriad of bumps in the road, and finally, after three hours, the coach came to a stop.

"What's the matter?" Holliday called up to the driver.

"Changing horses," was the answer. "Stretch your legs, have a drink, visit the privy, whatever takes your fancy. We'll leave again in half an hour."

Holliday climbed down from the coach and went into the station. He walked up to the bar and ordered a beer, which was as close as he was willing to get to water to clear the dust out of his throat.

"Welcome back, Doc," said the bartender. "How'd things go for you down in Lincoln?"

"Pretty much as expected," answered Holliday noncommittally.

"And that lovely lady who was traveling with you?" continued the bartender. "I guess she's staying there?"

Holliday nodded his head. "She's staying there."

Holliday finished his beer, wiped his mouth with a sleeve, and went out back to visit the outhouse. As he was emerging a moment later, he became aware that he was no longer alone.

"I thought we were done with each other," he said.

"That was before I was aware of what your friend Edison had invented," said Geronimo. "You could have used it on me, but chose not to."

"I don't kill honorable men," replied Holliday. "At least, I try not to."

"You told me in the White Eyes' burial ground that you had nothing to ask of me."

"That's still true."

"But I have thought long and hard," said Geronimo, "and I have something to offer."

"What?"

"Exactly what your friend was sent here to wrest away from my people."

"Good!" said Holliday. "I'll tell you him said so."

Geronimo shook his head. "No."

Holliday frowned. "Then I don't understand."

"There is only one member of your race I will treat with."

"President Arthur?"

"No."

"Then who?"

"You do not know this man," said Geronimo. "But you will. He is a young man, younger than you, and he will not cross the Mississippi for another year. But he has greatness within him, and when he does cross the river, I will treat with him."

"If I don't know him, how can I set up a meeting?" asked Holliday.

"You and he have a mutual friend who will arrange the meeting when the time comes," said Geronimo. Suddenly he smiled. "The friend is he whom I turned into a bat last year."

"Bat Masterson?" said Holliday. "And what is the name of the man you want to meet?"

But there was no answer, for Geronimo had vanished upon the winds that swept across the prairie.

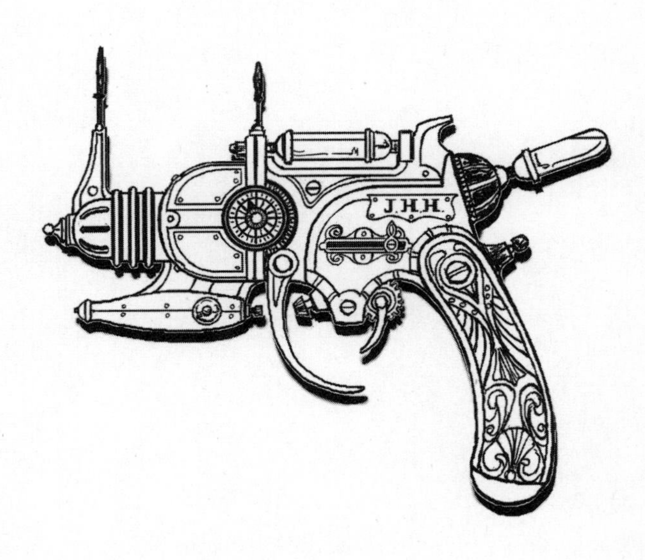

Appendix 1

There has been quite a lot written about Doc Holliday, Billy the Kid, Geronimo, Pat Garrett, and the so-called Wild West. Surprisingly, a large amount takes place in an alternate reality in which (hard as this is to believe) the United States did not stop at the Mississippi River, but crossed the continent from one ocean to the other.

For those of you who are interested in this "alternate history," here is a reference list of some of the more interesting books:

Alexander B. Adams, *Geronimo: A Biography*, Da Capo Press (1990)

Stephen Melvil Barrett and Frederick W. Turner, *Geronimo: His Own Story*, New York: Penguin (1996)

Bob Boze Bell, *The Illustrated Life and Times of Doc Holliday*, Tri Star-Boze (1995)

Glenn G. Boyer, *Who Was Big Nose Kate?* Glenn G. Boyer (1997)

William M. Breakenridge, *Helldorado: Bringing the Law to the Mesquite*, Houghton Mifflin (1928)

Walter Noble Burns, *The Saga of Billy the Kid*, New York: Konecky & Konecky Associates (1953)

E. Richard Churchill, *Doc Holliday, Bat Masterson, & Wyatt Earp: Their Colorado Carers*, Western Reflections (2001)

Pat F. Garrett, *The Authentic Life of Billy the Kid*, University of Oklahoma Press (1882)

Pat Jahns, *The Frontier World of Doc Holliday*, Hastings House (1957)

W. C. Jameson and Frederic Bean, *The Return of the Outlaw Billy the Kid*, Plano: Republic of Texas Press (1998)

Jim Johnson, *Billy the Kid: His Real Name Was . . .*, Outskirts Press (2006)

Sylvia D. Lynch, *Aristocracy's Outlaw: The Doc Holliday Story*, Iris Press (1994)

Paula Mitchell Marks, *And Die in the West: The Story of the O.K. Corral Gunfight*, William Morrow (1989)

John Myers Myers, *Doc Holliday*, Little, Brown (1955)

Frederick Nolan, *The West of Billy the Kid*, University of Oklahoma Press (1998)

———, *The Lincoln County War, Revised Edition*, Sunstone Press (2009)

Fred E. Pond, *Life and Adventures of Ned Buntline*, The Camdus Book Shop (1919)

Philip J. Rasch, *Trailing Billy the Kid*, Western Publications (1995).

Gary Roberts, *Doc Holliday: The Life and Legend*, John Wiley & Sons (2006)

Karen Holliday Tanner, *Doc Holliday: A Family Portrait*, University of Oklahoma Press (1998)

Paul Trachman, *The Old West: The Gunfighters*, Time-Life Books (1974)

Ben T. Traywick, *John Henry: The Doc Holliday Story*, Red Marie's (1996)

———, *Tomstone's Deadliest Gun: John Henry Holliday*, Red Marie's (1984)

John Tuska, *Billy the Kid, A Handbook*, University of Nebraska Press (1983)

Robert M. Utley, *High Noon In Lincoln*, University of New Mexico Press (1987)

———, *Billy the Kid: A Short and Violent Life*, University of Nebraska Press (1989)

Michael Wallis, *Billy the Kid: The Endless Ride*, W. W. Norton (2007)

Appendix 2

In that "alternate history" in which the United States extended all the way to the Pacific, there are also a number of films made about the principals in this book, and a number of very popular actors portrayed them. Here's a list of them:

Some Movie Doc Hollidays:

Victor Mature
Kirk Douglas
Jason Robards Jr.
Stacy Keach
Dennis Quaid
Val Kilmer
Randy Quaid

Some Movie Billy the Kids:

Johnny Mack Brown
Roy Rogers
Robert Taylor
Audie Murphy
Paul Newman
Michael J. Pollard
Kris Kristopherson
Val Kilmer
Emilio Estevez (twice)

Some Movie Thomas Alva Edisons:

Spencer Tracy
Mickey Rooney

Some Movie Ned Buntlines:

Lloyd Corrigan
Thomas Mitchell

Some Movie Geronimos:

Chuck Connors
Wes Studi
Jay Silverheels (four times)
Monte Blue

Some Movie Pat Garretts

Wallace Beery
Thomas Mitchell
Monte Hale
John Dehner
Rod Cameron (twice)
James Coburn
Patrick Wayne
William Petersen

Appendix 3

This is a "who's who" of the book's participants in that fictional alternate reality where the United States extended to the West Coast.

Doc Holliday

He was born John Henry Holliday in 1851, and grew up in Georgia. His mother died of tuberculosis when he was fourteen, and that is almost certainly where he contracted the disease. He was college-educated, with a minor in the classics, and became a licensed dentist. Because of his disease, he went out West to dryer climates. The disease cost him most of his clientele, so he supplemented his dental income by gambling, and he defended his winnings in the untamed cities of the West by becoming a gunslinger as well.

He saved Wyatt Earp when the latter was surrounded by gunmen in Dodge City, and the two became close friends. Somewhere along the way he met and had a stormy on-and-off relationship with Big-Nose Kate Elder. He was involved in the Gunfight at the O.K. Corral, and is generally considered to have delivered the fatal shots to both Tom and Frank McLaury. He rode with Wyatt Earp on the latter's vendetta against the Cowboys after the shootings of Virgil and Morgan Earp, then moved to Colorado. He died, in bed, of tuberculosis, in 1887. His last words were: "Well, I'll be damned—this is funny." No accurate records were kept in the case of most shootists; depending on which historians you believe, Doc killed anywhere from two to twenty-seven men.

Billy the Kid

He was born Henry McCarty in New York on November 23, 1859, became Henry Antrim when he took the surname of his stepfather when he moved to New Mexico, became William H. Bonney sometime during his teen years, and became known as Billy the Kid. He stood five feet eight inches tall, weighed about one hundred forty pounds, had brown hair and eyes, possessed buck teeth, and was said to be left-handed.

He killed his first man, "Windy" Cahill, on August 18, 1877, when Cahill was bullying him. He then joined a gang of rustlers and killers known as "The Boys."

By March 1, 1878, he had joined a group of pseudolawmen named "The Regulators." By March 9 he had killed two lawmen and a Regulator he believed was a turncoat. He and the Regulators shot themselves out of a number of ambushes in the spring and summer of 1878.

Eventually he was captured and made a deal with Governor Lew

Wallace: his testimony for a pardon. The deal didn't stop him from killing again, and finally Pat Garrett hunted him down and killed him on July 14, 1881.

Two different men later claimed that Garrett had killed the wrong man; each claimed that *he* was Billy the Kid, and each had a few experts believing it.

Pat Garrett

Pat Garrett was born in Alabama in 1850, grew up in Louisiana, and moved to Texas when he was nineteen. He was a cowboy and a buffalo hunter, then hired on as a "protector" when cattle rustling got too bad.

He moved to New Mexico just as the Lincoln County War was drawing to a close. While he was bartending at Beaver Smith's saloon he met and befriended Billy the Kid. They spent so much time together that they became known as "Big Casino" (Garrett) and "Little Casino" (the Kid).

He became the sheriff in Lincoln County in November of 1880, and captured the Kid on December 23 of that year. The Kid was sentenced to hang, but he broke out of jail, killing two deputies, and Garrett tracked him down again, killing him on July 14 of 1881.

That was the highlight of Garrett's career. He wrote a book about it, waited for Fame to find him, and waited, and waited. He lost his bid for reelection as sheriff in 1882; ran for the State Senate—and lost—in 1884; ran for sheriff of Chaves County—and lost—in 1890; and in 1901 he was appointed Customs Collector by President Theodore Roosevelt (who refused to reappoint him in 1905).

Garrett was shot to death in a financial dispute in 1908.

THOMAS ALVA EDISON

Born in Milan, Ohio, in 1847, Edison is considered the greatest inventor of his era. He is responsible for the electric light, the motion picture, the carbon telephone transmitter, the fluoroscope, and a host of other inventions. He died in 1931.

NED BUNTLINE

Buntline was born Edward Z. C. Judson in 1813, and gained fame as a publisher, editor, writer (especially of dime novels about the West), and for commissioning Colt's Manufacturing Company to create the Buntline Special. He tried to bring Wild Bill Hickok back East, failed, and then discovered Buffalo Bill Cody, who *did* come East and perform in a play that Buntline wrote.

KATE ELDER

Big-Nose Kate was born in Hungary in 1850. She came to America as a child, seems to have married a dentist in St. Louis at the age of sixteen, had a baby, and lost both her husband and her child to yellow fever. She got her start as a "sporting woman" by working for Bessie Earp, the wife of James Earp, eldest of the Earp brothers.

She met Wyatt Earp and Doc Holliday in 1876, hooked up with Doc shortly thereafter, and helped him escape from jail in Fort Griffin. She was partial to liquor, and at one point in 1881 Sheriff John Behan got her drunk and had her sign a false accusation that Holliday had robbed a stagecoach. She stayed with Holliday on and off until his death, then married a blacksmith, later divorced him, and lived to the ripe old age of ninety, dying in 1940.

Texas Jack Vermillion

A friend of both Holliday and Wyatt Earp, Texas Jack Vermillion (later known as Shoot-Your-Eye-Out Vermillion) participated in Wyatt Earp's Vendetta Ride, and was saved in at least one shoot-out by Holliday.

Oscar Wilde

Author of such classics as *The Picture of Dorian Grey* and *The Importance of Being Ernest*, Wilde was born in 1854, became the darling of the British intelligencia, was imprisoned for a lifestyle that would raise almost no eyebrows today, and died at the age of forty-six. He was in Leadville on a lecture tour in 1882.

Susan B. Anthony

Born in 1820, she became the leading force for women's rights and suffrage in the nineteenth century. She was lecturing in Leadville in 1882.

GERONIMO

Born Goyathlay in 1829, he was a Chiricahua Apache medicine man who fought against both the Americans and the Mexicans who tried to grab Apache territory. He was never a chief, but he *was* a military leader, and a very successful one. He finally surrendered in 1886, and was incarcerated—but by 1904 he had become such a celebrity that he actually appeared at the World's Fair, and in 1905 he rode in Theodore Roosevelt's inaugural parade. He died in 1909, at the age of eighty.

Appendix 4

Pat Garrett on Billy the Kid's Escape, Written in 1882:

On the evening of April 28, 1881, Olinger took all the other prisoners across the street to supper, leaving Bell in charge of the Kid in the guard room. We have but the Kid's tale, and the sparse information elicited from Mr. Geiss, a German employed about the building, to determine the facts in regard to events immediately following Olinger's departure. From circumstances, indications, information from Geiss, and the Kid's admissions, the popular conclusion is that:

At the Kid's request, Bell accompanied him down stairs and into the back corral. As they returned, Bell allowed the Kid to get considerably in advance. As the Kid turned on the landing of the stairs, he was hidden from Bell. He was light and active, and, with a few noiseless bounds, reached the head of the stairs, turned to the right, put his shoulder to the door of the room used as an armory (though locked, this door was well known to open by a firm push), entered, seized a six-shooter, returned to the head of the stairs just as Bell faced him on the landing of the stair-case, some twelve steps beneath, and fired. Bell turned, ran out into the corral and towards the little gate. He fell dead before reaching it. The Kid ran to the window at the south end of the hall, saw Bell fall, then slipped his handcuffs over his hands, threw them at the body, and said: "Here, d—n you, take these, too." He then ran to my office and got a double-barreled shot-gun. This gun was a very fine one, a breech-loader, and belonged to Olinger. He had loaded it that morning, in presence of the Kid, putting eighteen buckshot in each barrel, and remarked: "The man that gets one of those loads will feel it." The Kid then entered the guard room and stationed himself at the east window, opening on the yard.

Olinger heard the shot and started back across the street, accompanied by L. M. Clements. Olinger entered the gate leading into the yard, as Geiss appeared at the little corral gate and said, "Bob, the Kid has killed Bell." At the same instant the Kid's voice was heard above: "Hello, old boy," said he. "Yes, and he's killed me, too," exclaimed Olinger, and fell dead, with eighteen buckshot in his right shoulder and breast and side. The Kid went back through the guard-room, through my office, into the hall, and out on the balcony. From here he could see the body of Olinger, as it lay on the projecting corner of the yard, near the gate. He took deliberate aim and fired the other barrel, the charge taking effect in nearly the same place as the first; then breaking the gun across the railing of the balcony, he threw the pieces at Olinger, saying: "Take it, d—n you, you won't follow me any more with that gun." He then returned to the back room, armed himself with a Winchester and two revolvers. He was still encumbered with his shackles, but hailing old man Geiss, he commanded him to bring a file. Geiss did so, and threw it up to him in the window. The Kid then ordered the old man to go and saddle a horse that was in the stable, the property of Billy Burt, deputy clerk of probate, then went to a front window, commanding a view of the street, seated himself, and filed the shackles from one leg. Bob Brookshire came out on the street from the hotel opposite, and started down towards the plaza. The Kid brought his Winchester down on him and said: "Go back, young fellow, go back. I don't want to hurt you, but I am fighting for my life. I don't want to see anybody leave that house."

In the meantime, Geiss was having trouble with the horse, which broke loose and ran around the corral and yard awhile, but was at last brought to the front of the house. The Kid was all over the building, on the porch, and watching from the windows. He danced about the balcony, laughed, and shouted as though he had not a care on earth. He remained at the house for nearly an hour after the killing before he made a motion to leave. As he approached to mount, the horse again broke loose and ran towards the Rio Bonito. The Kid called to Andrew Nimley, a prisoner, who was standing by, to go and catch him. Nimley hesitated, but a quick, imperative motion by the Kid started him. He brought the horse back and the Kid remarked: "Old fellow, if you hadn't gone for this horse, I would have killed you." And now he mounted and said to those in hearing: "Tell Billy Burt I will send his horse back to him," then galloped away, the shackles still hanging to one leg. He was armed with a Winchester and two revolvers. He took the road west, leading to Fort Stanton, but turned north about four miles from town and rode in the direction of Las Tablas.

It is in order to again visit the scene of this tragedy. It was found that Bell was hit under the right arm, the ball passing through the body and coming out under the left arm. On examination it was evident that the Kid had made a very poor shot, for him, and his hitting Bell at all was a scratch. The ball had hit the wall on Bell's right, caromed, passed through his body, and buried itself in an adobe on his left. There was other proof besides the marks on the wall. The ball had surely been indented and creased before it entered the body, as these scars were filled with flesh. The Kid afterwards told Peter Maxwell that Bell shot at him twice and just missed him. There is no doubt but this statement was false. One other shot was heard before Olinger appeared on the scene, but it is believed to have been an accidental one by the Kid whilst prospecting with the arms. Olinger was shot in the right shoulder, breast, and side. He was literally riddled by thirty-six buckshot.

The inhabitants of the whole town of Lincoln appeared to be terror-stricken. The Kid, it is my firm belief, could have ridden up and down the plaza until dark without a shot having been fired at him, nor an attempt made to arrest him. A little sympathy might have actuated some of them, but most of the people were, doubtless, paralyzed with fear when it was whispered that the dreaded desperado, the Kid, was at liberty and had slain his guards.

This, to me, was a most distressing calamity, for which I do not hold myself guiltless. The Kid's escape, and the murder of his two guards, was the result of mismanagement and carelessness, to a great extent. I knew the desperate character of the man whom the authorities would look for at my hands on the 13th day of May—that he was daring and unscrupulous, and that he would sacrifice the lives of a hundred men who stood between him and liberty, when the gallows stared him in the face, with as little compunction as he would kill a coyote. And now realize how all inadequate my precautions were. Yet, in self-defense, and hazarding the charge of shirking the responsibility and laying it upon dead men's shoulders, I must say that my instructions as to caution and the routine of duty were not heeded and followed.

On the bloody 28th of April, I was at White Oaks. I left Lincoln on the day previous to meet engagements to receive taxes. Was at Las

Tablas on the 27th, and went from there to White Oaks. On the 29th, I received a letter from John C. Delaney, Esq., of Fort Stanton, merely stating the fact of the Kid's escape and the killing of the guard. The same day Billy Nickey arrived from Lincoln and gave me the particulars. I returned to Lincoln on the 30th, and went out with some volunteer scouts to try and find the Kid's trail, but was unsuccessful. A few days after, Billy Burt's horse came in dragging a rope. The Kid had either turned him loose, or sent him in by some friend, who had brought him into the vicinity of the town and headed him for home.

The next heard of the Kid, after his escapade at Lincoln, was that he had been at Las Tablas and had there stolen a horse from Andy Richardson. He rode this horse to a point a few miles of Fort Sumner, where he got away from him, and the Kid walked into the town. If he made his presence known to any one there, I have not heard of it. At Sumner he stole a horse from Montgomery Bell, who lives some fifty miles above, but was there on business. He rode this horse out of town bareback, going in a southerly direction. Bell supposed the horse had been stolen by some Mexican, and got Barney Mason and Mr. Curington to go with him and hunt him up. Bell left his companions and went down the Rio Pecos. Mason and Curington took another direction. Mason had a rifle and a six-shooter, whilst Curington was unarmed. They came to a Mexican sheep-camp, rode up close to it, and the Kid stepped out and hailed them. The Kid had designated Mason as an object of his direct vengeance. On the sudden and unexpected appearance of the Kid, Mason's business "laid rolling." He had no sight on his gun, but wore a new pair of spurs. In short, Mason left. Curington stopped and talked to the Kid, who told him that he had Bell's horse, and to tell Bell he was afoot, and must have something to ride out of the country, that, if he could make any other arrangements, he would send the horse to him; if not, he would pay him for it.

It is known that, subsequent to the Kid's interview with Curington, he stayed for some time with one of Pete Maxwell's sheep herders, about thirty-five miles east of Sumner. He spent his time at cow and sheep camps, was often at Canaditas Arenoso and Fort Sumner. He was almost constantly on the move. And thus, for about two and a half months, the Kid led a fugitive life, hovering, spite of danger, around the scenes of his past two years of lawless adventure. He had many friends who were true to him, harbored him, kept him supplied with territorial newspapers, and with valuable information concerning his safety. The end was not yet, but fast approaching.

Appendix 5

Bat Masterson on Doc Holliday, Written in 1907:

While he never did anything to entitle him to a statue in the Hall of Fame, Doc Holliday was nevertheless a most picturesque character on the western border in those days when the pistol instead of law courts determined issues. Holliday was a product of the state of Georgia, and a scion of a most respectable and prominent family. He graduated as a dentist from one of the medical colleges of his native state before he left it, but did not follow his profession very long after receiving his diploma. It was perhaps too respectable a calling for him.

Holliday had a mean disposition and an ungovernable temper, and under the influence of liquor was a most dangerous man. In this respect he was very much like the big Missourian who had put in the day at a cross-road groggery, and after getting pretty well filled up with the bug juice of the Moonshine brand, concluded that it was about time for him to say something that would make an impression on his hearers; so he straightened up, threw out his chest and declared in a loud tone of voice, that he was "a bad man when he was drinking, and managed to keep pretty full all the time." So it was with Holliday.

Physically, Doc Holliday was a weakling who could not have whipped a healthy fifteen-year-old boy in a go-as-you-please fist fight, and no one knew this better than himself, and the knowledge of this fact was perhaps why he was so ready to resort to a weapon of some kind whenever he got himself into difficulty. He was hot-headed and impetuous and very much given to both drinking and quarrelling, and, among men who did not fear him, was very much disliked.

He possessed none of the qualities of leadership such as those that distinguished such men as H. P. Myton, Wyatt Earp, Billy Tilghman, and other famous western characters.

If there was any one thing above another Holliday loved better than a session in a poker game, it was conflict, and, as Dallas was the home of conflict, the doctor was in his element. He brought up next at Jacksborro, a small, out-of-the way place just off the Fort Richardson Military Reservation, on the north-western border of the state, where civilization was only in a formative stage.

The doctor had by this time heard much about the man-killers who abode on the frontier, and regarded himself as well qualified to play a hand among the foremost of the guild. He was not long in Jacksborro before he was in another scrape. This time it was with a soldier who was stationed at the Fort, and who had been given permission to visit the town by his commanding officer. The trouble was over a card game in which the soldier claimed he had been given the worst of it by the man from Georgia. This of course, necessitated the fighting Georgian taking another trip on the road, for he knew it would never do to let the soldiers at the Fort capture him, which they would be sure to try to do as soon as word reached them about the killing of their comrade. He therefore lost no time in getting out of town, and, seated on the hurricane deck of a Texas cayuse, was well on his way to safety by the time the news of the homicide reached the Fort. It was a long and dangerous trip that he mapped out for himself on this occasion.

From Jacksborro to Denver, Colorado, was fully eight hundred miles, and, as much of the route to be traversed through was the Texas Panhandle and No-man's land, which was in those days alive with Indians none too friendly to the white man. And renegade Mexicans from New Mexico. The journey was a most perilous one to take; but the doughty doctor was equal to the task and in due time reached Denver without either having lost his scalp, or his desire for more conflict. This was in the summer of 1876 and while Denver was a much more important city than Dallas, its local government was conducted on very much the same principles. Like Dallas, everything went in Denver, and the doctor, after looking the situation over for a day or two, concluded that he had lost nothing by the change.

In all respects the Rocky Mountain town looked good to him, and as he had set out to build up a record for himself as a man-killer, he did not purpose lying idle very long. While Denver, in many respects in those days was a rough and ready town, it nevertheless enforced to the very letter the ordinance against the carrying of fire arms, and Holliday, for the once becoming prudent, put his canister aside, but straightway went and bought himself a murderous looking knife. Thus heeled, he did not long delay in getting into action, and in so doing, carved up the face and neck of one Bud Ryan, a quiet and gentlemanly looking sport, in a frightful manner. Bud Ryan still lives in Denver, and carries around with him the marks of his run-in with the fighting Holliday more than thirty years ago. It was again the doctor's turn to take the road and escape from the scene of his recent malefaction, and this time he headed for Dodge City, Kansas. It was there I first met him, although I had heard about his doings in Texas.

He went from Dodge to Trinidad, Colorado, where, within a week from the time he landed, he shot and seriously wounded a young sport by the name of Kid Colton, over a very trivial matter. He was again forced to hunt the tall timber and managed to make his escape to Las Vegas, New Mexico, which was then something of a boom town, on account of the Santa Fe Railroad having just reached there. Holliday remained around Las Vegas for some time, doing the best he could in a gambling saloon; then he had a quarrel with one of the town rounders by the name of Mike Gordon, whom he invited to step outside of the saloon in which they were quarrelling. No sooner had Gordon stepped from the door than Holliday shot him dead. From Las Vegas to Dodge City across country, without following the traveled road, was about five hundred miles and this was the trip Holliday was again compelled to make on horseback, in order to get away from the authorities who were hot on his trail. He reached Dodge City in safety and remained there until Wyatt Earp took him in his covered wagon to Arizona in the fall of 1880. Again he showed no disposition to quarrel or shoot while he lived in Dodge, and many thought that much of the trouble he had been having in other places had been forced upon him, but I am satisfied that it was pretty much all of his own seeking. His whole heart and soul were wrapped up in Wyatt Earp and he was always ready to stake his life in defense of any cause in which Wyatt was interested. He aided the Earp brothers in their street fight in Tombstone, against the Clanton and McLaury brothers, in which the latter two were killed, along with Billy Clanton.

It was Doc Holliday, who, along with Wyatt Earp, overtook and killed Frank Stillwell at the railroad station in Tucson for having participated in the murder of Morgan Earp in Tombstone. He was by

Wyatt's side when he killed Curly Bill at the Whetstone Springs outside of Tombstone. Damon did no more for Pythias than Holliday did for Wyatt Earp.

After Wyatt and his party had run down and killed nearly all their enemies in Arizona, Holliday returned to Denver, where he was arrested on an order from the Arizona authorities, charged with aiding in the killing of Frank Stillwell. This happened in the spring of 1882. I was in Denver at the time, and managed to secure an audience with Governor Pitkin who, after listening to my statement in the matter, refused to honor the Arizona requisition for Holliday. I then had a complaint sworn out against Holliday, charging him with having committed a highway robbery in Pueblo, Colorado, and had him taken from Denver to Pueblo, where he was put under a nominal bond and released from custody. The charge of highway robbery made against Holliday, at this time, was nothing more than a subterfuge on my part to prevent him from being taken out of the state by the Arizona authorities, after Governor Pitkin went out of office, but the Colorado authorities did not know it at the time. Holliday always managed to have his case put off whenever it would come up for trial, and, by furnishing a new bond, in every instance would be released again.

When he died at Glenwood Springs a few years afterwards, he was still under bond to answer to the charge of highway robbery I had caused a certain person to prefer against him. Doc Holliday, whose right name was John H. Holliday, lived during his stormy career in three states of the Union besides the one in which he was born, and in two territories; namely Texas, Colorado, and Kansas, and in the territories of New Mexico and Arizona. Besides the killing of the negroes in the river in his home town, he shot a man in Dallas, Texas, and killed another in Jacksborro. He stabbed Bud Ryan in a frightful manner in Denver, Colorado, and shot another in Trinidad in the same state. He killed a man in Las Vegas, New Mexico, and was directly connected with several killings in Arizona.

Kansas, it will be observed, was the only state in which he had lived in which he failed to either slay or bodily wound some person. The question as to the extent in which he was justified in doing as he did, is of course open to debate. I have always believed that much of Holliday's trouble was caused by drink and for that reason held him to blame in many instances. While I assisted him substantially on several occasions, it was not because I liked him any too well, but on account of my friendship for Wyatt Earp, who did.

About the Author

Mike Resnick is the winner of five Hugo Awards (and has been nominated a record thirty-five times). He is also a Nebula Award–winner, and has won other major awards in the United States, France, Japan, Poland, Croatia, and Spain, and has been short-listed for major awards in England, Australia, and Italy. He is, according to *Locus* magazine, the all-time leading award winner, living or dead, for short science fiction. He is the author of sixty-eight novels (nine of them for Pyr), more than 250 short stories, and two screen-plays, and has edited forty anthologies. He is the guest of honor at the 2012 World Science Fiction Convention, to be held in Chicago.